THE WAY OF THE ISLAND

To every girl with an orphan mindset, who needs to know she's a daughter of the King. There is no scarcity with Him.

Heads of Families

The Ten Families, each represented on Whitecroft Council:

General Hunter, leader
Xander Taylor, the Doctor
Francis Derby, head of Farming
Leon Crest, administration
Bryant Turner, industry
Daniel Stead, education
Alec Lane, water and sanitation
Chandler Swift, head of Fishing
Avery Mason, food production
David Hughes, head of Clothing, recently deceased

Year 53
The Day of Unity

ALICE

1

I wake up and the burning begins.

It starts as a dull, ever-present ache across my stomach. It rises to my chest in a vice grip on my heart. It chokes my throat and throbs from my temples, and by the time I remember it is the Day of Unity, my head is consumed with a raging fire.

Everything about today will remind me what I should have been, and what I am not.

'Alice?' Ada's voice calls from the other side of the door. 'Are you getting ready?'

'Yes,' I answer mechanically, but I stare at the ceiling.

I have come to like this room. It's just a guest room, but the wood smells fresh and it has a window. Ada makes sure the blankets are soft and that there are flowers on the sill. She says I can stay here as long as I want.

William helped to build this house with my brother Charles. I used to watch them working, carrying heavy logs around, and I would think: *Next year they will be building a house for me.* But it didn't happen that way.

'Breakfast is ready.'

I have to move now. I brace myself, one hand over my forehead, and sit up. I wait a moment for the pain to subside. I drink some water then slide my feet to the floor. My dress is hanging up, the colour of blood. I step into the rich fabric and feel the familiar sense of satisfaction at the snug fit of the tailoring. I look in the mirror. Even with my headache and lack of good sleep, I still look striking with my dark hair against the deep red shade. I arrange my hair around my face to hide the paleness and hopefully detract attention from the shadows under my eyes. I smooth my skirt and turn myself to examine every angle. I hope he notices me and regrets his decision.

I sit alone at the breakfast table while Ada rushes around, pinning her hair and dressing Frederick. As long as she doesn't give him to me to hold, I'll be fine. He's a good-looking baby, but I don't want to be stuck with him all the time.

Charles has already left. He will be helping to set everything up, and the Council members will all be there for the pledging. I don't know where our father will be. Since he was removed from the Council, he has been as still as a volcano. I'm waiting for the eruption.

Since I withdrew and refused to be pledged with Phillip Stead, I have been in disgrace. So it doesn't matter that he's in disgrace with the entire country, because all that matters is the way that I have failed him. He made an agreement with Phillip's father, but I ruined it.

'I think we should go now, to get a good spot.'

Ada puts her cloak on and looks at me anxiously.

'Are you feeling all right?'

No, I am not all right.

'Yes,' I reply, pushing back my chair and taking a final mouthful of bread. It might make the headache go away.

She holds Frederick, who looks at me blankly with his bright blue eyes. I take my cloak off the hook and we step outside.

2

The Harvest is over, and the air smells of leaves and fires. I walk through yellow and orange maple leaves, enjoying their scuffle and crunch. It helps to focus on the leaves, and not on the crowd that is gathering in the Square to watch William be pledged. All the Derbys will come from the Farmlands, in carts or on horseback. After the Pledge there will be dancing and probably further celebration at Pembridge. I'm not going to be there. I have no place in this picture.

I briefly consider whether I could leave Ada, take a path out to the sea or to the fields, and then I wouldn't have to stand there watching. Would anyone even notice my absence? But I know that I want to be there. Just in case.

I thought of so many ways to stop this from happening. I've spied, plotted, blackmailed and used every tool in my armoury, but it's all come to nothing. When my father lost his position, I lost my bartering power. I still have my place on the Council, at least. They'll probably find some way of taking that away, arguing that they only need Charles. Everyone loves Charles.

He's standing at the front of the Town Hall, next to Francis Derby. Francis, who gave me an inquisition about my feelings (or lack of them) for Phillip Stead, and encouraged me to withdraw.

'You don't have to do this,' he said, trying to be kind. 'It does not seem that there is any sense of affection on either side of this match.'

That didn't surprise me. The only thing Phillip loves is his books.

In the end, Ada and Charles made the decision for me.

'I'm going to Bryant,' Charles had said, striding out of the door while I was left, sobbing, with Ada.

I suppose he wants me to feel grateful for his intervention.

My eyes find William. I can't help it; it's been a habit for too long to break. He's standing towards the front and he's wearing his dark green jacket. His dark hair and tall figure are easy to find.

I've had so many imagined conversations with him. They grow more elaborate depending on my mood. The common theme is this: he notices me.

Ada holds Frederick tightly as she surveys the crowd. I know she's looking for her best friend. Even though I've been destroyed, she gets the preference, every time. She's portrayed as the victim and I am the villain. Ada tolerates me because I'm Charles' sister, and nothing more.

I see her before Ada does, walking with our grandfather. Her gown is nothing special and her hair is flying across her face with the wind. I watch William's warm brown eyes light up, in a way they never did for me. Elise scans the crowd, and I know she's looking for Ada. Her eyes rest on me for a moment, guilt behind her expression. I don't look away. She needs to know what she's done.

'There she is!' Ada finally notices her, and jigs the baby while trying to get a better view. I shift my weight and focus on the old, wooden posts. The fire is back, and it rages so hot it could consume this town in minutes.

'We are gathered together on this Day of Unity to celebrate the Pledge of William Derby and Elise Mason.' Francis Derby begins the ceremony.

All I can think about is how to make my sister suffer.

3

I found my father's books when I was twelve years old. I was looking for my mother's things, just to check if there was something I had missed. I don't even know what she looked like.

Instead, I found the books in a chest. I picked up the heaviest: *David Copperfield.*

When I couldn't sleep, I would take a candle and read, turning the pages carefully. They were yellowed and musty, and smelled of another world.

I think my father modelled Whitecroft on these books. The language, etiquette and social rules were long outdated when he and the first generation arrived. It was a chance to start again, and he preferred the world of Dickens to the one they had to leave behind them.

He never spoke of it.

I suppose they lived in a strange limbo while they were in an airship, waiting for Earth to become habitable once more. From ten families, we are now a town of a hundred people. But I've never felt like I fit in.

I'm not a Dora, and I'm not an Agnes; I can't be an accessory with no mind of my own, and I can't trust that sacrifice and selflessness will be rewarded here.

All my life, I've been taught to play the game. Be beautiful, stay aloof, and as the General's daughter, someone worthy would claim me at the Casting. I was determined that William Derby would choose me, but he chose Elise instead. As much as I'm glad that I'm not pledged to Phillip Stead, I now face re-entering the Casting next year. Now that my father has been suspended from his duties, I'll likely be blanked. No one will choose me.

If I was an Agnes, I would be content with sweeping the floor for the next twenty years, but I'm not. Even if Elise dies in childbirth, like her mother and my own, I wouldn't want to be William's second choice. I wouldn't want to be the mother for someone else's child. Not even if the child is my own niece or nephew, if Elise is the mother. She destroyed everything for me, and now everyone is celebrating her Pledge as if she's the centre of our community, rather than the illegitimate outcast she's always been.

I'm the one standing at the edge of the Square, while Elise and William are dancing in the middle, with Ada and Charles close by. Our grandfather is watching and smiling, no doubt relieved that she has someone to look after her when he's gone. I always knew that she was the favourite, but it was confirmed when I stayed there last winter and found the cloak he had made for her. I tried it on in front of the mirror, feeling the tears burn down my cheeks. No one ever gave me a gift like that.

He asked me if I would go there to stay with him, to help him adjust to Elise not being there anymore. Well, that's not how he put it, but that's what he meant. I suppose it will give Ada and Charles a break from me if I go. I hate feeling so helpless, and having nowhere to call my own.

I clench my fists at my sides. I imagine tying up a ribbon inside my stomach, and pulling it taut. No use getting upset; that won't achieve anything. What I need is a plan.

4

My father is not a likeable individual. He's controlling, stubborn and ridiculously old-fashioned. But the one thing I admire is his cool logic and his ability to think through any problem. Whitecroft isn't perfect, but we are a functioning community. Fifty years ago, there were just twenty people, struggling to build a town from scratch.

You don't achieve success without a cost. I know my father is mistrusted and despised; I see the way people look at him. It's how they look at me, too, as if I am an extension of him. If Francis had been in charge fifty years ago, no one would be left alive now. That's the brutal reality.

I tried to get Elise to leave, when I found out the Swifts were planning to take their fishing boat and never come back. Believe it or not, part of me thought that she would be better off leaving than staying. As much as I wished it was me taking a Pledge to William, everyone knows what happens next. She'll be carrying, on and off, for the next fifteen years. I need to focus on the fact that I am free from that burden. The thought of it curls my stomach.

But my freedom is limited by the borders of our small world.

Whitecroft is shaped by the sea on one side, and the forest on the other. We've cut the trees back to build our houses, and William's family live at the furthest edge of the woods, but it's hard to go beyond where there are no roads. Horses are limited, and I'm supposed to stay in the town as part of my Council position.

Part of me wishes that I'd gone on the boat instead.

How long will it take to build another boat?

If everyone in Whitecroft was ordered to help, it probably wouldn't take longer than a few months. The problem is the Freeze. At the moment, the leaves are rust coloured and the air has a soft mildness in the middle of the day. In just a few weeks, the sky will darken, and the snow will start to fall.

Usually, I'm in town for the Freeze, so I can still see people. William's family, the Derbys, are normally constricted to their own estate, Pembridge. On the Farmlands, there's Cressida and there's my grandfather. This will be his first Freeze living alone. My chest tightens.

Realistically, I'm not going to miss much in town if I stay with him over the Freeze. And it would probably get way too crowded in Charles' house with all of us tripping over one another.

A sudden silence falls, and my attention is drawn back to Francis Derby.

'On this day we celebrate the unity of all our families, living and working together. Something worthy of celebration. At one point, we hoped this unity would include more than just our families, but also another nation who live across the sea.'

My eyes widen in shock. He's actually telling everyone—the whole town—about the other nation. Something the Council kept hidden from the younger generations for years.

'We have received communication that the Swifts, along with Blake Hughes and Viola Taylor, have safely arrived at Cape. It is the ideal time for us to pursue the Unity which was originally intended between our two nations. We both survived a catastrophic disaster on Earth by living in two airships, while our planet was hit by a meteorite, and its shape and climate changed irreversibly. We landed in Year 0 and founded Whitecroft. The airship has become our Infirmary, and our centre of technology in this land.'

I grip on tightly to the wooden post next to me, holding up the Town Hall. I feel suddenly dizzy. They made it. They crossed the waters. No one has ever done that before.

It means it is possible to leave.

'We were meant to join with the people from the other airship, on the Day of Unity,' Francis continues. 'But we were too concerned with our own land, the farming and the cultivation of our crops. We were struggling to survive. We did not have a wide enough vision to include another nation.'

I look out at the crowd, who are beginning to turn to one another in an attempt to grasp the magnitude of this revelation. Walking away from the Square, I clearly see my father, with Xander the Doctor, and Leon Crest.

Without hesitation, I follow them.

5

I keep my distance and flatten myself into the shadows, my fingertips bracing lightly against splintered wooden surfaces. A fence post; a doorway; a wall. I know they're headed for the steel protection of the Infirmary. I won't follow them inside; no one goes in there unless they are dying and desperate. Perhaps I'll hear something useful. I can't change the habit of a lifetime now.

The three men walk purposefully, but not in any particular hurry. They can't really hide in Whitecroft, after all. Now that my father is out of favour, Xander and Leon are his only allies. I'm not sure friendship binds them, more like shared guilt.

My father invented the Casting system. Xander is held responsible for the high maternal mortality rates here—Elise claims that he let our mothers die, when he could have saved them. And Leon… Well, Leon's been known for a rather heavy-handed approach to Law and Order. Public whipping and other forms of torture and humiliation are his answer to any signs of dissension.

'You were right,' Xander says to my father, with a humourless grin.

'I'm always right,' my father mutters.

His face seems older in these past few weeks. I'd like to think that he missed me, but there's little evidence of that. He's not attempted to speak to me.

'Will this change everything, now that they know?' Xander asks.

'We'll have to be more careful,' my father says. 'But we knew that anyway.'

'What if they find it?' Leon asks, his voice deeper and harsher.

Xander and my father give him a sharp look.

'They won't,' my father says, in a warning tone, 'as long as we are discreet.'

Leon looks uncomfortable. They've reached the last houses, and the grey structure of the Infirmary curves around, an area of woodland on one side. Of course it was an airship; what other possible explanation could there be for this metal monstrosity, anachronistic in our primitive, barely surviving town?

My father made a rule never to speak of the past, but it wasn't one that he applied to himself. He often complained, in moments of frustration, of the hardships of living without infrastructure, without established industry.

'In the old world,' he would tell me, 'we had factories where everything was produced on a huge scale. We had electric power. The Infirmary's the only place that has that now. But when we set up the military school, we'll focus on physical power. The strength of an army. We will continue to build, and sow, and everything will be rock solid, because it is based on the foundation of blood, sweat and tears. Back then, everything was too easy, and we lost it all. I'm not going to let that happen again.'

It was usual for him to monologue, perhaps as a way of practising future speeches, and I noticed that he only did it in front of me, not Charles. I suppose that was because he was always busy with Charles, out visiting or running meetings. Whereas I was part of the background of our house, an integral part of the scenery but little more than a silent prop.

Not so integral anymore. And not so silent. I've enjoyed ruffling feathers at the Council meetings, surprising them when I actually have opinions and observations. Some of them expected me to be mute.

At this moment, though, I am succeeding in being completely still, while Leon stops and looks back in my direction. Satisfied, he challenges my father and Xander with a penetrating stare.

'We may all be discreet,' he says, 'but they're going to notice when we set sail.'

A thrill, like a butterfly's wing emerging from a chrysalis, flutters in my heart.

'The Swifts are gone now,' my father replies. 'Why would anyone be on the shore? By the time they realise, it'll be too late.'

He strides off, through the Infirmary's heavy door. Xander follows. Leon sighs, and then tramps after them.

I sink down onto the ground, the tall grass damp and overgrown around me. For once, I don't care about my dress. My heart is drumming a rhythm and I cover my face to focus on breathing.

Of course there was never just one boat.

6

I'm not sure how long I sit, considering possibilities, but I can hear music carrying from the Square. The dancing has begun.

I stare at the Infirmary. Only the Doctor's family, the Taylors, would know what was inside the vast structure. It would be easy enough to hide a boat in there. Maybe they brought it with them when they first arrived.

It's hard to grasp the depths of my father's patience. For over fifty years, he has watched Whitecroft build itself. Every house is painstakingly constructed over months; there are no shortcuts. I wonder what other modern secrets the Infirmary hides. Things which would make our lives easier.

It's easier to control people when they're struggling to survive.

My head throbs, the aching returning with a vengeance. I'm inwardly staggering under the weight of the suffering my father has caused this town, but also the fact that the others allowed him to do it. Where was my grandfather when all these decisions were made? Why did the Swifts wait for fifty years before leaving? It doesn't make sense.

But then again, I've sat in enough Council meetings to know how it goes. My father puts forward an idea, backed up with a mine of solid evidence. Barely anyone has the courage to object. While staying with Charles and Ada, I've found myself looking at Frederick and my stomach curls to think of him being marched around in a uniform from a tiny age. It means something different when you see the face of an innocent child, and you want to preserve that innocence for as long as possible.

Living with my father, I knew too much too soon, and I can't unlearn it.

I've grown up without the softness of a mother, an aunt, or a grandmother. I've always had to create my own comfort, through my own plans and schemes. I can no longer be cast to William, and there's no other boy remotely worth my time and energy.

I could immerse myself in Council work, and perhaps the others will learn to see me as an individual, separate from my father. I would still have the problem of where to live, and I would still feel the stigma of the breach of trust from him.

Or I could find a way to escape this small town, with its claustrophobic borders, and go with my father on the secret boat to the other nation. I have no idea how long it would take to get there, but I'm at the stage where anywhere is better than here. The thought of returning to the Square and having to congratulate William and Elise in their sickening happiness is enough to drive me away from Whitecroft forever.

What about my grandfather?

Yes, Elise is his favourite, but she won't be around after Pledging. I can spend some time with him, uninterrupted. I can do my duty and ensure he is ready for the Freeze. And then I can leave.

7

I drag my feet on my way back to the Square, although my stomach is churning with emptiness. I'll find some food, and I'll feel better. I studiously ignore the central group of dancers, as William and Elise will be in the middle, and head to the long table which holds drinks and breads.

'I recommend the twisted loaf. Cressida made it.'

Phillip Stead gestures towards the bread at the top end of the table, and gives me a nervous look, as if he's about to flinch. I should be pledged to him right now, but instead we're standing by the buffet, probably the same thought in our heads.

'I just wanted you to know... no hard feelings,' he says, gulping.

I blink at him. If my natural temperature is icy, I've now turned glacial on him.

'I'm glad to hear it,' I state, in a mocking tone.

He glances at my expression, then looks back towards the table. I hear him suck in a breath.

'My sister Willow...'

I stare at him, watching him blush as he trails off, then tries to gather his strength again.

'She wanted me to ask... but I never had the chance...'

His neck is flushed now, and I keep my eyes on him, enjoying his discomposure.

'Now that you're on the Council,' he looks up and catches my eye, 'she wondered if you could suggest more apprenticeships for girls. Blake Hughes was taken on by the Turners but the Taylors have never allowed any of the other families to work inside the Infirmary. She wants to become a doctor.'

I blink. It's flattering that he thinks I have influence, but I doubt Xander would let a Stead into that building in any other capacity than an injured party.

'I'll see what I can do,' I say noncommittally.

Taking some bread and a cup filled with water, I walk over to my grandfather.

'Phillip's not bothering you, is he?' he asks, looking back to the food table.

I'm surprised he noticed.

'No,' I shake my head, and bite into the roll. 'He's fine.'

We stand in silence. The dance finishes and people applaud.

'I thought I might come and stay with you,' I blurt out suddenly, before I lose my courage.

I focus on the bread in case he says no.

'Of course,' he says, and I can feel his eyes on my face, so I look up.

His voice is soft, and his eyes have an edge of puzzlement, searching my face, but there's no sign of a frown on his forehead. I called Elise a traitor in front of the whole town, because she knew about the Swifts leaving and helped them. I'm not going to apologise for that. But he doesn't seem to be holding it against me.

'Have you spoken to your father?' he asks.

My eyes sting with unwanted tears, and I blink fast to regain control.

'No,' I reply, in what I hope sounds like a tone with finality.

I want him to believe that I am no longer under my father's rules, that he can trust me to tell me all of the things he must have told Elise, if she knew about the Swifts leaving. I'm tired of finding the truth in a snatched, borrowed way. I want a full measure of honesty.

'I think they're getting ready to leave now.' He nods towards William and Elise, who are talking to the crowd of people around them, and the carriage, decorated with ribbons, is waiting.

I watch him walk over and, like some unique brand of torture, I can't drag my eyes away as he embraces Elise, holding her tightly. When she pulls back, there are tears on her face, but she is smiling too. He says something to her and she looks over at me unexpectedly. I immediately avert my gaze.

I start to walk towards Charles' house, feeling my eyes brim up. I use the back of my hand to wipe them and quicken my pace, until I finally push open the door and fall inside. Shutting it behind me, I lean against it and bend over, crushed by the weight of it all.

I allow myself to cry.

8

Hating my own weakness, I stumble into the guest room and start packing my clothes into a bag. I'm usually careful in neatly folding them, but I can't see properly because of the tears, so I stuff everything in hastily and try to ignore the stabbing pain in my chest.

When I stay with Grandfather, I will miss Charles, but I don't think he will miss me. He will be relieved that I'm gone.

It hurts that everyone is so dismissive of me.

After my mother died, I was sent to Abigail Turner. My aunt died, and Grandfather took Elise. It was a slap in the face when I became old enough to realise; she was chosen, and I was left behind.

Abigail was kind. She already had three children, and Charles was sent with me too. When he started school, he moved back in with our father. When I started school, father said I should stay with the Turners for another year. I felt the accusing stares of the Turner children, who wanted me gone, and I felt the absence of warmth from my only living parent. I was so keen to leave and be in what I thought was my own home, only to discover that it was much colder and barer than the one I had left. Charles redeemed it for me. He's always been a good brother.

It's for his benefit, really, that I need to go, and give him space with his new family. I can't stay in their spare room forever.

I smooth the blankets on the bed. I was comfortable here. I try to cling on to the happy memories of mealtimes, flowers on the table, freshly washed sheets and laughter. In this moment, it doesn't feel as though happiness belongs to me. Like I'll always be cheated out of it.

I take a grim pleasure in removing every trace of myself from the room. My life is reduced to this carpet bag, because I left most things in my father's house. I didn't think I would be gone for this long. In fact, as I evaluate my thin dresses, I consider that I'm going to need to pick up some of my winter garments, if I'm going to stay with Grandfather for the Freeze.

Sighing, I lug my bag to the front door, then step back outside. There's a raised volume of chatter carrying from the Square, so I don't think William and Elise have left yet. The street is empty. I look up and down to check, then hurry over to my father's house and slip inside.

It smells of stale darkness. Repressing a shudder, I tiptoe to my room, surveying it quickly. Everything is untouched, the way I left it. That day was a hard day. I remember packing my bag quickly, and turning up on Charles' doorstep. I won't forget his expression. Part of him was surprised that I'd actually left, but part of him expected it. We both knew that living with father was temporary; not something we would choose.

I find my suitcase and pack up a woollen cloak, winter hat and gloves, and a pair of boots. I add a few trinkets I missed before, and, on a whim, a notebook with thick pages. It was a birthday gift from Phillip, but I won't look a gift horse in the mouth.

Suddenly, I hear the door opening.

'If they've got the radio, how are we going to contact them?'

Leon Crest's voice sounds loud in the small hallway.

'Tobias will be able to fix us up with an alternative,' my father says, with his usual certainty.

'We need to ensure discretion.' That sounds like Xander Taylor.

'At least my daughter is out of the way now,' my father says, unaware that I can hear every word.

'How much does she know?' Leon asks.

'Enough,' he answers curtly.

'What about Charles?' Leon presses.

'He's been distracted with building his house and his family,' my father replies.

'Where is Alice now?' Xander asks. It would be funny if I wasn't petrified. 'Is she living with Charles?'

'Yes.'

'Will she tell him everything she knows?'

'I'm more concerned about the Derby boy. Out in the Farmlands, especially in the Freeze, we have no idea what they're planning.' Leon Crest is nothing if not suspicious.

'What would the Derbys be planning: to build another barn?' my father scoffs. 'They've got Pembridge. There's no way they'll jeopardise that, and none of them want to leave. Elise would have gone on that boat with the Swifts if it hadn't been for the boy.'

'Don't you think that the Swifts will make contact again with Avery? I don't trust him.'

'Maybe he would have gone if the girl had too.'

'We've always known that Avery and Chandler were dissenters,' my father says, dismissively. 'But they never had any power.'

'What about the girl? She seemed to come out of nowhere, shouting all your secrets to the whole town on the night the Swifts left.'

'She's just been pledged. You know what happens next.'

A chill settles in my stomach. Elise will probably be carrying in a few months. They must be determined to find a way to make sure that she doesn't survive.

Will William be able to protect her?

I tell myself that it isn't my problem, but my heart beats faster anyway.

'We need to see the Turners and the Steads tomorrow,' Xander says. 'Remind them of their loyalties.'

I hear the clink of glasses and start to panic. I can't stay here all night. I push open the window and shove my suitcase through it, hoping the dull thud is muffled enough to escape their notice. I clamber awkwardly onto the sill, then drop down to the grass below. I close the window over as best as I can, pick up my suitcase, and head for the Square. I need to find my grandfather.

9

Everyone is gathered to wave off Elise and William, who are sitting in their carriage about to leave. I stand at the back of the crowd. I refuse to smile and wave as though I'm happy for them. I tighten my grip on the suitcase.

Elise is about to throw her bouquet into the air. As I watch the bundle of flowers arc over their heads, I could be a thousand miles away. All of this seems so pointless. The bouquet lands on the ground, a foot away from me. I don't move. Someone snatches it hurriedly, and I laugh, then pretend to cough to mask it. Take the flowers, I want to shout. Dream your dreams. But don't expect someone to love you.

Finally, the carriage pulls away. I can hear cheers and whistles but muffled, as if underwater. I can feel some people eying me warily, and I'm sure the Turner girls are whispering about me, pointing at my suitcase. Sighing, I walk over to a chair and sit, resting the case on the ground. Hopefully Grandfather won't take too long saying his goodbyes.

'Where are you going with that case?' Cressida sinks down into a chair beside me. Her tone is wry but not sharp. I often had the brunt of her reproofs when I was sent to help her with dressmaking, which was hopelessly dull.

I look at her, unsure how to answer. She knows I'm not living with my father anymore. She's on the Council, so I see her at every meeting. She's the same age as my grandfather, and lives just across from his house. We'll probably end up walking back to the Farmlands together.

'I'm staying with Grandfather over the Freeze.'

She gives a small nod of approval.

'It will be good for you to have a break from… town.'

She's looking over to where the Steads are. I feel my cheeks grow warm.

'What do you think of the Council?' she asks, her no-nonsense tone demanding honesty.

I consider the meetings I've attended where my father was there, pushing forward his own agenda. In the meetings since he left, Francis has chaired, and Charles has struggled to sound like he knows what he's doing.

'You are allowed to give your opinions,' Cressida smiles wryly.

'That would require me to *have* opinions.'

'Everybody has opinions,' she argues. She pauses for a moment. 'You don't have to agree with your father.'

'Whatever I say, Leon will report back to him.'

'So what?' Cressida shrugs. 'He must be aware that you're old enough to have your own ideas about the world.'

I sigh.

'I thought I was going to be pledged today. All I've thought about is what I'm going to do next.'

'I would have thought the Council is the perfect distraction,' Cressida replies. 'Alice, you're young. Focus on what you can do to make Whitecroft better for the next generation.'

That sounds rather noble to me. It seems ridiculous to be looking after everyone else's future when my own hangs in the balance, but maybe Cressida has a point about distraction.

'You know, Phillip—' I begin, then break off, unsure of whether I should continue.

'Go on,' Cressida says.

'He said that Willow wants to be a doctor. He asked if I could suggest more apprenticeships for girls.'

'You should,' Cressida says firmly. 'It's about time we gave people more choice around here.'

She sees my skeptical expression.

'When we arrived here, it made sense to have very clearly delineated roles. Xander ran the Infirmary, your father governed, and Francis led the Farmlands. When you've only got ten couples, everyone has to have allocated jobs otherwise no one wants to grow food, and what do you do then? But now, there's a hundred people in Whitecroft. I think there's room for people to decide where they want to work.'

'What if Willow gets into the Infirmary, and doesn't like it?'

'Then she can transfer somewhere else. It's not the end of the world.'

My father would hate that. He would call it a waste of time and resources.

As if she can read my mind, Cressida leans forward.

'Remember that nothing is wasted,' she says. 'Everything you go through in life teaches you for the next step. The worst times in your life can actually pave the way for your greatest triumphs.'

Hmm. At this moment I can't imagine what triumph could possibly compensate for the past eighteen years, and what's scaring me the most is that I don't even know what I want anymore.

Maybe the best I can hope for is an end to this constant feeling of falling into an abyss.

'Are you ready to go?' my grandfather asks.

His eyes are red and watery. I didn't even notice him arrive.

'Yes,' I reply.

Then I remember I left my bag behind.

10

'What's wrong?' Grandfather asks when he sees my face.

'I went back to my father's house to get my case,' I lift it slightly to show him, 'but I left my bag behind. He doesn't know that I went there.'

'Do you need it?' Cressida asks.

I nod.

'It's got all my daily clothes in it. I just put my winter cloak and garments into the case for the Freeze.'

'We'll have to go and get it, then,' Grandfather says.

Grimly, he turns to walk towards my father's house. Cressida sets off too, and then beckons to me as my feet stay planted on the floor.

'Come on,' she says.

I trail behind them, lugging the case resentfully. I don't want to see my father, and I certainly don't want to see him with my grandfather and Cressida. He never trusted them, and always told me to be watchful whenever I went to visit, and report back to him when I returned. The most obvious thing I noticed was that Elise had everything I wanted: a warm home, and people around her who looked after her. It was ironic, because Elise was born outside a Pledge, and my father had practically exiled her out to the Farmlands. If it's really true that he's her father too, it makes sense.

I don't want to be a spy or a go-between anymore.

I'm worried that either my father will ignore me, which will hurt like a serrated knife edge on a wound that's been reopened many times, or that he will see my stay at the Farmlands as an opportunity to use me as a weapon against one of the only blood relatives I have left.

I hang back as Grandfather knocks the door. It takes several tense moments before Leon opens it. He sneers when he sees us.

'Well, look who it is.'

'Hello, Leon,' my grandfather says calmly.

'Preston!' he calls to my father.

When my father walks towards the doorway, my eyes are irresistibly drawn up to his face to look for something, some kind of reaction from him. He smiles grimly, and it doesn't meet his eyes.

'What do you want, Alice?' he speaks in an emotionless tone.

I open my mouth but my voice fails.

'She wants to collect some clothes,' my grandfather answers.

He says nothing, but steps aside and gestures for me to enter. Feeling sick to my stomach, I brush past him awkwardly and then hurry to my room. I pick up the bag I'd left behind and quickly scan around to check if there was anything I missed. The bedspread was made by Cressida, and Father gave it to me as a birthday present. I'm not taking it, out of principle. I don't want his gifts. I wonder, with an ache, if I'll ever sleep in this room again.

After months—no, years—of misery in this house, it seems anticlimactic to just pick up my bag and walk out. But it feels like life is full of churning emotions that ripple like the roll of the sea; when the wave breaks, you often expect a tsunami and you only get a handful of white foam.

Holding my breath to keep the tears inside, I walk out of the house and I don't look back.

11

The walk to the Farmlands feels longer because I'm carrying luggage. Grandfather took the case. It's still afternoon but the sun is cold and distant. There's a chill in the air, especially as we walk on a path shaded with overhanging tree branches.

Cressida makes a few light comments about the weather, but other than that, we're silent. They know I'm upset and I can't trust my voice, seeing as my eyes are constantly blurry. The hot churning inside me, though, is pure anger. I'm so angry that my father pretends he doesn't care. I believe he does, but he's too afraid to show it.

I said a quick farewell to Charles and Ada. They looked sympathetic, but I don't want to be a parasite, a bad smell they can't get rid of. Each step along the pathway is another step into exile, some type of banishment. Even worse, it's self inflicted.

The scent of the pines does help to calm me, and the sound of the birds. I can hear everything more clearly out here. As much as I hate being stuck out here, away from the conveniences of Whitecroft, life in the Farmlands does hold a certain charm. For one thing, the Crests are not prowling around out here, enforcing their version of Law and Order. The work is hard, in the fields, and I've never had the strength to do much whenever I stayed with Grandfather. Elise seemed to be able to do anything. She would cook, and then she would spend hours digging, planting or harvesting, and then she would come back and glow with energy as she talked to Grandfather. I've always felt useless next to her.

Even now, my hands are reddened from carrying the bag, and my arms are strained and tired. I feel like we should have arrived by now, but the path stretches on, like an endless tunnel in front of us. I remind myself that distance is good. I won't see my father out here, so I won't be daily reminded of his disapproval.

When Charles left, that was when things really became unbearable.

I don't even think Charles knows what our father is really like. He only ever sees his good side, his public front. Sure, he admits that he can be gruff and abrupt, but whenever I tried to tell him some of the things I'd seen, or heard, he struggled to believe me.

'Charles, did you know that Father keeps forbidden books in a chest in his room?'

'Everyone was allowed to choose personal items to bring with them when they went on the airship,' he told me. 'Those were his.'

'Why doesn't he allow them in the school then?'

'He's focusing the school on practical subjects. Reading some old books about a world we no longer live in won't help us to survive.'

I gave up after that. If he didn't see anything wrong with the books, then he probably wouldn't with the other things either.

When Elise publicly accused our father of manipulating and deceiving Joy Swift, and ordering forced sterilization on Joy and my aunt Loretta, I think Charles was definitely shaken. Typical that no one listens to me, but when Elise says something, everyone believes her. I had the feeling that Charles and Ada stopped talking about it in front of me, like I need to be shielded or protected from the truth. The irony, that I was trying to tell them about my father all along.

I don't mean to sound ungrateful. I mean, they let me stay with them. But I've had a growing realisation that I can't wait for someone—William, Phillip or Charles—to rescue me.

I need to face the horrifying, unflinching reality of being alone.

In some ways, even when I lived with Father and Charles, I was always alone with my thoughts. I wasn't being trained up to lead the country, like my brother. I was more or less a decoration.

After Charles made his Pledge to Ada, Father would be out of the house for long, endless hours. As if he was avoiding me. Each day, I invented reasons for myself to leave the house and find people to talk to. *We heard your child was sick. The General sent me with some medicine.* Mostly, I was met with a wall of suspicion. Sometimes I would set out to take some food to a family I knew were struggling—after all, we always had more than enough—but the hostility in their expression when they saw me approach would be enough for my courage to falter. I would have to find a way to leave it for them secretly. It became like a game. *Frown. Act haughty, like you're better than them. When they're not looking, hide a gift in their bag, or behind a vegetable box.*

I guess I'm a talented actress. No one seems to realise who I really am, not even my own father and brother.

Maybe I don't even know myself.

I managed to persuade my father to send me to Grandfather's with food to celebrate Elise's birthday. Not that she seemed very appreciative. There was another time, when I visited, and I hoped that the snow would prevent me from returning to Whitecroft. In a foolish fantasy, I imagined staying with Grandfather over the Freeze, cosy in his lodge, and out of the reach of my cold father. But everyone seemed determined that I should go home.

It's not my home anymore.

I'd only ever been allowed to stay with Grandfather during the summer, so even now, I'm oddly excited to be out in the Farmlands for the Freeze. Maybe I won't need to play my games anymore, because I'll have people to see and things to do. Perhaps if I made more effort, my sewing would improve. I just want to be useful, and not merely because I pass on information or goods, but because I, Alice Hunter, make a difference to the world.

Instead of just making everything worse.

12

Grandfather's house is built in a clearing, opposite Cressida's. The air is filled with birdsong and the sound of the river. It's a short walk to the fields, where the crops have just been harvested, and Pembridge is on the other side, along with the barns to store everything. I always enjoyed staying here as a child, with Elise being the only fly in the ointment. She's always set my teeth on edge. Knowing that she's just pledged and won't be around for at least a week gives me sweet relief.

I need time to think about the boat.

Cressida bustles off into her own house, and Grandfather and I take my luggage indoors. It always smells of bread and rosemary.

'Are you hungry?' Grandfather asks. 'Let me get you a drink.'

He fetches me a cup of cool water, and then starts lighting the fire. I sink down into a chair and pull a blanket over my lap, rubbing my hands to bring back circulation.

How long do we have before the first snow falls? Will my Father sail immediately, or wait until the Thaw? Is he going to go without the knowledge and authorisation of the Council? Would he be able to bring the Swifts back?

I don't even know how many people are out there, in this other nation.

I watch as Grandfather boils water and toasts bread. The Swifts were his closest friends, and even though they lived by the sea, he spent more time with Chandler and Aurelia than anyone else. His face is pensive, and he must be thinking about the tumultuous events of the past few weeks. He must be relieved that Elise is safe at Pembridge, although he's probably feeling her loss. All he's got is me as a consolation prize.

We sit and eat together, and the silence is safe and comfortable. Neither of us wants to disrupt it with difficult questions. Afterwards, we take my bags into my room. It used to be my mother's room, when she lived here. I unpack my things, and settle down for an early night. My stomach feels like it's been churned up repeatedly and now that this awful day is over, I can find some peace. I wasn't pledged, and I survived.

I sleep better than I have in a long time.

There's always fallow time after Harvest, so the morning is calm and still. I wake up with fresh energy, so I make some dough and leave it to rise, then walk out into the forest. On the way to the river, I pass trees where initials have been carved in: M for Millicent, my mother, and L for Loretta, my aunt. They were twins, growing up out here with my grandfather. My grandmother died in childbirth, like so many other women. I should be thankful that I wasn't pledged.

In my head, I thought I would spend an hour or two out here, alone in the quiet. In reality, I tire quickly and want to go back to the house. How can I be so exhausted from doing nothing? It's like my bones are made of lead, weighing me down.

There's something about this place, though, that heals and restores you. The days go by, quietly, inevitably, with a rhythm of baking, cooking, and I pick up a bit of sewing. Cressida comes over for a chat. She enlists my help in preserving berries and making jams, which is surprisingly enjoyable. Each night of sleep helps to still my inner turbulence, like pouring water over fire until there's nothing but smoke and embers.

Until the day when Elise visits.

13

Apparently, Elise was never meant to exist. Her mother, Loretta, was not pledged to anyone. She was blanked. My mother had been pledged to my father, and was receiving fertility treatment at the Infirmary. Elise claims that Gus Taylor was supposed to sterilize Loretta, but instead, he gave her my mother's treatment. Perhaps it was by mistake and Loretta deceived him—she and my mother were twins, after all. Seeing as both my aunt and my mother died in childbirth, and my birthday is so close to Elise's, Elise claims that we are sisters, and that our mothers were deliberately left to die when they could have been saved.

It doesn't change how we feel towards each other.

Quite simply, we've never liked each other, and that's never going to change.

I have a limited range of sympathy for Elise. Yes, she grew up with the stigma of being illegitimate, and without either of her parents (not even knowing who her father was), but she got to live out here on the Farmlands with Grandfather, while I was farmed out to another family. The fact is, everyone in Whitecroft has been through hardship. There's no one who hasn't lost someone in their family; no one who hasn't struggled. Things are certainly better for us than for our parents' generation. But still. Life's not easy, and it's not fair.

Elise has ended up being pledged to William Derby—who I had expected to be pledged to since I was old enough to work out we would be in the Casting together—and lauded as some sort of heroine by most of the town, so the 'pity me' act is somewhat diminished in light of these developments. She's now established in her own home with William at Pembridge, while I'm essentially homeless and my father is ignoring me, because I refused to allow him to use me like a bartering chip to pledge me to Phillip Stead.

Staying at Grandfather's, I had almost managed to forget the sting of my father's rejection, and the shame of remaining unpledged. I was getting up early and making bread, and I had formed a new habit of resting in the rocking chair by the fire in the later part of the morning once the chores were done. I'm lying peacefully, my eyes closed, when the door opens and Elise bursts inside.

'Oh!'

She can't contain her surprise when she sees me. My eyes fly open, and I scrabble to my feet defensively. She's looking around for Grandfather, but in the end, she can't avoid my eyes. We stare at each other. I can tell what she's thinking by the way her eyes narrow: *What are you doing here? Why are you sitting in my chair?* My hackles rise. I've a right to be here. I was invited. He's my grandfather too.

'Where's Grandfather?' she asks, finally.

'He went to the river. He'll be back shortly.'

There's a heavy silence. Elise's hair is still long, dark and unkempt as usual. She's wearing her usual plain dress, her cloak over the top. It's like she just popped out for a walk, and has come back to find everything different. Well, she can't expect everything to stay the same in her absence.

'How are you?' she struggles to get the words out.

I give a dry laugh.

'How do you think?' I snap.

'I'm sorry.'

She says it automatically, rather than genuinely meaning it. I give a scoffing laugh again.

'What are you even sorry for?' I challenge her.

She swallows.

'I'm sorry if… what I said at the Town Hall… has made things difficult for you.'

'You think my life was easy before that?'

Here we go, Elise's favourite narrative: that I'm the privileged daughter of the General, and she's the poor, unloved outcast. But I'm not buying it anymore.

'Whatever you said, or didn't say, at the Town Hall makes no difference to me,' I emphasise, hoping that stings.

Elise blinks, but rallies quickly.

'So the truth doesn't matter to you? What about what happened to Lily?'

I remember that night, when Lily was accused and sentenced to ten lashes and house arrest by Arnold Crest, her own match. Elise stopped him and Francis took his granddaughter, and her children, back to Pembridge. That's the first time a Pledge has been broken publicly.

'Look, it was all very noble of you to stand up for Lily,' I snarl, 'but have you ever considered that you're not the only one who cares? That you're not the only one who wants things to change in Whitecroft?'

'No one else seems to be doing anything about it.'

'That's where you're wrong,' I tell her. 'Remember, you're not on the Council.'

She rolls her eyes.

'You stopped Arnold because you were there. What happens when you're not there, Elise? If you want real and lasting change, it has to happen at a higher level than you becoming another administer of justice.' I pause before delivering my deadly blow. 'Because in nine months, we all know where you'll be.'

I look pointedly at Elise's (flat) stomach, and her hands instinctively grasp at it. Her face is pale.

'You chose this,' I remind her. 'You could have gone on the boat.'

The door opens, and as if on cue, my father steps into the room.

<h1 style="text-align: center;">14</h1>

I hold on to the back of a chair for support. My father, Arnold and Leon Crest, walk into the house like they own it. Although Leon and my father are the same age as Grandfather, he's no match for them. Too many Freezes out here on the Farmlands; too many hours of backbreaking labour. Arnold's not much older than Charles, but his body is hulking and thick. Charles is tall and athletic, whereas Arnold is heavy and driven through life by his fists. When he sees Elise, they immediately clench. He's probably been mapping out his revenge since Lily and his child left him.

'A touching family reunion,' my father sneers, looking from Elise to me.

'It seems we arrived at an appropriate time, given your conversation,' Leon adds.

Elise's eyes flick to mine, and I can see her fear. William is far away and she knows how much these people hate her. She came to see her grandfather, and instead she ended up with a room full of enemies. I could almost feel sorry for her.

'Leave now,' my father tells Elise, coldly.

'But—'

'Now!' he commands.

'What do you want with… Alice?' she says. I wonder if she was going to say 'my sister' but didn't dare.

I'm surprised that she's standing her ground. Why doesn't she just get out of here?

'Nothing that concerns you,' my father replies.

Elise looks at me, and our eyes hold. I don't know why my father wants to see me, but I don't want him to be prevented from speaking because of her presence. At the same time, Grandfather is not here and I don't want to be alone.

'All right,' she says quietly, and opens the door, stepping out. There's a soft thud as the door closes behind her.

'We're going to sail to the island,' Leon says, and I look at my father in shock at this honest admission. He nods curtly. 'We need you to accompany us.'

'What?' I exclaim. It's hard to believe. 'Why do you want me?'

'We need to negotiate, and taking a young person will make a better impression that we have peaceful intentions,' my father answers.

So it's nothing to do with him actually wanting me there. I swallow.

'Negotiate what?' I press.

'Get your things.' Father refuses to answer any more questions. His eyes are steely with determination.

I walk to my bedroom, feeling a sudden pang about leaving this place. I was ready to settle down for the Freeze. I unpacked everything. Looking around the room, I place a few items into a small bag: a comb, a spare set of clothes, and a handkerchief. Out of the window, I can see Elise a short distance away, and she is embracing Grandfather. He must be on his way back. I watch them for a moment, then tie my bag tight with a knot. He doesn't need me.

Hoping that we can leave without having a lengthy conversation with Grandfather, which might result in him getting into trouble, I stride back into the room and pick up my cloak from the hook. I sweep it around my shoulders and fasten it.

'Let's go,' I say.

I lead the way out of the front door, and deliberately avoid the direction where I know Grandfather and Elise are, around the back of the cabin. I pretend I can't hear Elise's voice and head for the path back to Whitecroft. Thankfully, they follow me without seeking out the others.

I tell myself that I'll be back. How long can a boat trip be, anyway? Elise will look after Grandfather. Charles and Ada will be fine. They will enjoy a break without me around.

I tell myself that I don't need to cry, as a few tears escape.

I tell myself that everything will be all right.

15

I'm left alone in my father's house while he makes further preparations with the Crests. Presumably, they are going to move the secret boat out of the Infirmary and down to the shore. They will probably wait until darkness falls. I lie on my bed and try to rest, but my mind is racing with what is about to happen. I could run back to Grandfather, and it would probably delay them too much to bother coming back for me, but then I would still have to face them when they returned.

What if they don't return?

I dismiss the notion immediately. My father has spent his life building Whitecroft; he's not going to just up and leave it behind.

Where is the boat going? I know about the island, but barely any details about where it is or who lives there. Is my father capable of sailing a boat? It wouldn't be the first time he had overestimated his own abilities. However, I don't think he would be foolish and risk his own life. He cares too much about his power and vision for Whitecroft for that.

The people of the island (Blake, Viola and the Swifts included) don't know that my father is no longer on the Council. The more I consider, the more I suspect that my father is undertaking this (unauthorised) mission regardless of the change in his circumstances here.

Perhaps this trip had been planned for a long time, and there was no way he was going to cancel it.

The question is, what does my father actually want?

If it all works, and they manage to get the boat to the shore, and they manage to sail to the island… I'd be going somewhere no one (apart from the Whitecroft absconders) knows me. I would finally get an adventure of my own, rather than watch everyone else do all the exciting things and leave me behind.

As much as I was enjoying my time with Grandfather, and the slower pace of life in the Farmlands, it isn't really much of a future for me. There's no one I want to be pledged to, so I will never have my own home like Charles and Elise. I can't face being pushed from pillar to post, darning socks to feel useful, for the rest of my life.

If only I didn't feel so alone.

I must have managed to sleep, because I wake up with a jolt, hearing heavy footsteps in the hallway.

'Are you ready?' my father calls from outside my door.

'Yes,' I lie.

I wrap my cloak around myself tightly and check my face in the mirror. I wish I didn't look as pathetic as I feel. I pinch my cheeks to redden them and rub my tired, red eyes. Taking a last look around my bedroom, I impulsively gather up the counterpane and roll it into a bundle, my hands wrapped inside it.

If I'm leaving, I need to leave my old life behind. It's time for a new beginning.

16

The air is sharp, and the night is black. My breath catches in my throat as I step outside and follow my father, who is striding ahead. I run to catch up with him, feeling clumsy with my bundle, and he turns down the street that leads to the coast path.

As my eyes adjust, I can see the tiny pinpricks of stars in the dark sky overhead. The sound of the ocean grows closer, a hush and roar repeated at varying intervals. I stumble along the dusty path, kicking stones. My father barely looks back; he can hear my noisy footsteps and that's enough for him.

We reach the crest of a hill, and as we look down, I can see the outline of the boat, silhouetted against the full moon. My steps falter as I stare at it, bobbing with the waves. It's so much bigger than I anticipated; it makes the Swifts' fishing boat seem little more than a canoe in comparison. Its mast is tall, and its sails are billowing in the wind. I can only tell where the water is by the inky blackness that is without starlight. I shiver and hurry to catch up with Father.

As we draw nearer, I hear the shouts of the Crests. There must be fifteen of them, and they must have pulled the boat down to the water using a large wheeled platform, which I can see on the beach. The tide is in, so there's only a thin strip of shingle. I can see a small dingy, ready to take us out to the boat.

My fists are clenched tightly to the counterpane. This is real now, not some glorious fantasy where I set off into the sunset. It's dark, cold and the unknown landscape of the sea is treacherous. My father doesn't seem to feel any fear, continuing his confident stride and shouting to the others. I'm definitely the odd one out here.

Why did Father want me to come?

I can't believe that it was any sentimental reason. He's coped well enough without me these past few months. But now that I'm here, I can't let him down either by showing my lack of courage and refusing to board the boat. Trying not to shiver, I continue to step closer to the white frothing tide.

The boat is still some distance away, but looks even larger as it looms over the horizon. I can't believe it's been kept hidden for fifty years. I know that the Swifts made their own boat, and it must have taken such a long time... Why didn't my father give them this one? It's another example of how he made things harder, deliberately. And how he made our world smaller.

It's easier to control ten square miles than fifty, a hundred, or more.

'First time?' Arnold jeers at me. 'Don't worry, you can be sick overboard. Just take care a wave doesn't carry you off too.'

He laughs at my expression. I hope Father meant for me to return from this trip. Looking across at him, his stern tones barking orders, I can't be certain.

Maybe Whitecroft is the only thing he really cares about.

'Arnold, get Alice in the dingy,' Father shouts over.

Arnold beckons to me and holds out his hand in a mocking fashion. I loosen one hand from my counterpane and reluctantly take it. I feel the water soaking my boots and the hem of my dress, and the seat inside the dingy is wet too. It feels like stepping onto nothingness, as there's no firm support in the base of the small boat. I gather my skirts up and huddle myself into the bundle. My father sits next to Arnold and they use an oar each to row out to the boat. More than once, I consider hopping out and running through the shallows, but there's an army of Crests waiting for me. Plus, I have no idea of the depth. As we draw out further into the water, the shore looks increasingly unreachable.

From the deck of the main boat, Leon Crest calls out instructions. He throws down a rope ladder and I hurriedly start tying the counterpane around me like an extra cape, realising I will need both hands to climb. I just about manage to secure it, messily, and Father lifts me by the waist so that I can grab onto the ladder. It seems terrifyingly flimsy, and my hands shake as they reach up for the next rung. Just focus on the next step. My skirts are wet and heavy around my ankles, and the counterpane weighs down at my back. Gusts of wind blow icy air into my face, and salty foam from the waves. Finally, Leon grabs my arm and hauls me upwards, lifting my body over and onto the deck. I scramble to get to my feet, hoping that I don't look as helpless as I feel, as Arnold follows after me.

'Secure the dingy,' Arnold shouts, handing a rope to his grandfather.

'Clear,' Leon calls down to my father.

Father climbs up and they pull the dingy up by the rope. It fits neatly into the side of the boat, showing how large the deck area is.

'Hoist up the anchor!' my father commands.

We're about to set sail.

17

I don't think I've ever felt fear like this before. I've had a few accidents with horses – a few times where I was thrown to the ground – but that's nothing compared with the lurching of this boat as it's tossed and turned upon the waves of a black, deadly sea.

I sit with my knees drawn up to my chest, the counterpane wrapped tightly around me like a shroud, and clasp my hands together, thinking over and over that it will be all right and we'll make it to the other side.

My father shouts orders to Leon and Arnold, but it's clear that setting any kind of course is difficult in these conditions. Initially, they seemed satisfied that we were going in the right direction. Now, judging from the gestures and facial expressions, they seem to be arguing.

No one speaks to me.

A terrible nausea grips my stomach and I try closing my eyes, imagining that we're actually on a calm lake with barely a ripple in the cool waters. But it's hard, given that I'm sliding up and down the deck with each pendulum swing of the vessel. Sprays of seawater regularly shower my face. The counterpane becomes useful to try to dry my eyes. I must be crying as well but I barely notice; there's just a stream of salty water on my face. I look up at the sky. Where it had been clear, now a blanket of cloud has descended. Occasionally small patches of sky are visible. On top of the spray, there's also a drizzling rain in the air.

Arnold is steering the boat, but he's clearly struggling to keep control of it. My father and Leon are pointing up at the sky, arguing about the right direction. They stagger when the lurching is particularly heavy, and I just wish that they could agree and get us off this water.

Time drags slowly on.

The rain gets worse. The drizzle has become more defined raindrops, falling with pelting force, and the wind is blasting my face so hard that I can barely open my eyes. Despite the darkness, I can see the cresting waves around the boat, rolling high around us. My father is carrying something bright and orange which he puts around Arnold's neck. He has one over his jacket, and he gives one to Leon too. It's hard to see, and I can't hear anything except the roar of the storm, but it looks like he is attaching the orange things to a long rope.

Leon looks towards me and points, and my father nods. Just then, the boat gives a terrible lurch, and a wave crashes onto the deck. My father and Leon scramble around, and I'm paralysed with terror. My mouth is open in a silent scream, and only the taste of seawater makes me aware of it.

All I can think is, *Someone help me.*

My eye is drawn to a wooden chest at the foot of the mast, in the middle of the boat. Not really knowing why or what I'm doing, I hold on tightly to my counterpane and run to it. I just about have time to haul up the lid and snatch at something orange inside, before the boat lurches again. The lid falls heavily on my hands, and I have to force myself through the pain to lift it up again, to pull them out. I put the orange material over my head, and find a large clip at one end. Bracing myself, I lift up the lid once more, and root around inside until I find a piece of rope. I pull out a section of it, leaving the rest inside the chest, and pull the lid down tight on it. I try to fasten the clip onto the rope, but it's too wet and dark and my fingers are clumsy and painful after the lid fell on them. I pull the rope around my waist and knot it as best I can. Then I huddle on the floor by the box, and wait for the dawn.

18

When we see land, a fluttering hope grows in my heart, but the anxiety still weighs me down like a heavy slab of rock. Father, Arnold and Leon seem to have recovered from the storm, and shout to one another as they steer the boat towards the tiny strip of sand.

As we move closer, we can see two other boats, anchored by the island. One of them is the Swifts'. I can just about discern two figures, standing on the shore.

My heart drops at the sudden thought: what if they're not friendly towards us? What if they kill us? I have never heard anything about the people of Cape.

'Drop the anchor,' my father commands.

They lower the dinghy into the water and Arnold climbs down first. My father looks round impatiently at me.

'Come on,' he says.

My fists clenching tightly in the bundle of counterpane, I try to stand, and then remember that I'm knotted to a rope. My fingers are bruised and clumsy as I try to untie myself.

With an angry snarl, Father strides over and loosens the knot.

'What did you do that for?' he asks, ushering me to the edge of the deck.

To save myself from drowning. Because you wouldn't.

Instead of answering out loud, I focus on the task before me of climbing down the rope ladder. It's considerably more daunting than climbing up. The sea, while calmer than in the night, is rolling the dingy around, and I haven't been able to shake the gnawing nausea as the boat moves up and down.

'Hurry up,' my father gestures towards the ladder.

He seems to be gripped with some kind of mania. He's usually so calm. I can see he's desperate to get onto the island, to meet the men waiting for us, and there's no time for fear in his mind.

Reluctantly, I hold on to the side and swing my leg over. One. I pause to inhale a deep breath before swinging the other over too. Two. I'm clinging tightly to the rungs of the ladder, but my hands are still sore from my injury with the chest, and I don't feel my grip is as solid as it was yesterday. I shakily start to descend, counting each step as I go. I have to bring my feet together on each rung before descending to the next one, and I can hear my father's impatient expressions above, but I block him out and focus on the next step. There can't be many more.

'I think my grandmother would be faster than you,' Arnold calls up from the dingy.

I make the mistake of looking over my shoulder down at him, and my hand slips. Grasping at thin air, I lose my balance and fall backwards off the rope ladder with a cry of helplessness. It's only a short distance and Arnold roughly catches me, but I'm shivering uncontrollably as I crouch down to sit in the dingy, pulling my counterpane cape more tightly around me.

It doesn't take long for Father and Leon to climb down, and then we're rowing to shore, but somehow every minute stretches into eternity. Even though the beach looks close, it still takes a surprising amount of time to reach it. The two figures come into closer view. There is a boy, about my age, and then a man who could be his father. Their skin is a warm shade of brown compared to our paleness, and their smiles are dazzlingly white. The beach is otherwise deserted.

As the dingy pulls towards the shore, they stride out into the water to meet us. Leon and my father jump out, and the water is up to their knees. Arnold quickly follows and pulls the rope of the dingy, while Father greets the two men. The younger one gestures to Arnold and takes the rope from him, then holds out a hand to me. His eyes are rich with kindness. Trembling, I put my cold and bruised hand into his warm grasp, and tentatively stand. I lift one foot over, but my leg gives way as I try to stand in the water. The next moment, the boy has scooped me up into his arms and is carrying me to the shore, ignoring the shouts of my father about the dingy, which he leaves behind. He lays me gently on the sand.

'Are you all right?' he asks.

All I can do in reply is sob.

19

The floodgates have opened and all I can do is cry, feeling the warm sand and solid ground beneath me once more, and with all the pain of my hand, feeling cold and shivery, and the fact that no one on the boat cared enough to save me in the storm. This total stranger has been kinder to me than my own people.

He looks at me now with some alarm, calling the other man over and speaking in hushed tones with him. My father is standing a few feet away with the others, looking embarrassed at my display of emotion. Arnold has retrieved the dingy and crossly deposits it on the sand.

'She is not well?' the older man asks my father.

'She is fine,' he replies grimly.

'She will be all right to sail to the island?' he presses.

The island? I wipe my nose and look up in confusion.

'But we're already on the island,' I say.

The younger one looks at me with sympathy.

'This is just the meeting point. Cape is still another journey away.'

I can't restrain my fresh sobs at hearing this revelation. Did my father already know this? Why did no one tell me anything about this terrible, never-ending voyage?

'Here.' The younger man hands me a flask to drink from, and I take a gulp between sobs.

'You need to eat something.'

He passes me a sweet biscuit, and I eat it gratefully. The nausea is finally subsiding.

'Rough sea?' he asks, knowingly. 'No sleep? You rest before we leave.'

'We have no time to rest,' my father cuts in. 'We have no provisions. We must leave for your island immediately.'

The two islanders exchange worried glances.

'If that is what you want,' the older man says, after a short pause. 'We can leave your vessels moored here, and all go together in our boat.'

'I don't want to be a prisoner on your island,' my father says sharply.

'We will bring you back any time you want,' the older man promises, laying a warning hand on the younger man's shoulder. He seemed about to respond angrily to Father's accusation.

'It will save us having to sail,' Leon says to my father. 'We're all exhausted, Preston.'

'Fine,' my father says, tight-lipped. 'Let's go.'

I watch as the older islander takes my father on board their vessel. It looks similar to the one we sailed, with a mast of the same height. Theirs has a cabin—perhaps it was originally the same design, and they modified it over the years. Theirs certainly looks more weather beaten.

The younger islander sits down beside me, offering me another biscuit.

'My name is Palmiro,' he says.

'Alice,' I say, taking the biscuit gratefully. 'Thank you.'

'He is your father?' Palmiro gestures towards the boat.

'Yes,' I nod. 'And is that your father?'

Palmiro grins.

'I heard you had a brother.'

'Sorry to disappoint you.'

Typical: even the islanders want Charles instead of me.

'I am not disappointed,' Palmiro says, still grinning. 'Do you want to shake hands?'

He holds out his hand, but with the palm facing upwards, so that I have to place my hand into his. He runs a finger lightly over the bruising over my knuckles.

'What happened to your hand?'

I try to ignore the sensation of his warm touch, but I feel my face flare up.

'I was trying to get… something… in the storm. The lid of the chest fell on my hands.'

I'm struggling for any coherence now; his eyes are so deep I could drown in them.

'This is your first time on the water?' he asks.

'Is it that obvious?'

He grins again. He seems to have a radiant joy about him, like sunshine. I want to stay stuck to his side, and when we are called, I flush with pleasure when he offers me his hand to help me up.

'This will be a simple journey,' he promises.

I think I would believe anything he tells me.

20

It makes such a difference to sail in the daylight, and the sea is undoubtedly calmer, but I also notice how skilful Palmiro and his father are in controlling the boat. They make it look effortless and easy. My father, Leon and Arnold sit together on the deck, talking in low voices. Palmiro shows me the different parts of the boat, talking me through what he's doing. He tells me things as if he expects me to understand, rather than treating me like I'm stupid or useless. The more he teaches me, the less I fear being on the water once more. He even allows me to steer, standing behind me to guide me, and I resist the strong urge to lean backwards into him.

I can't stifle my yawns, though, and Palmiro's father, whose name is Cayman, takes over the wheel.

'You need to rest,' Palmiro says, beckoning me to follow him.

He takes me to the cabin and opens the door. It's a small space with a bed.

'Sleep,' he says, simply.

I smile and step into the cabin. Palmiro gives me a cheeky wave and closes the door. I breathe out. The boat still moves with the waves, but it's nowhere near as violent as in the night. I climb onto the bed and spread out my counterpane – still damp and soggy, but a lifeline to anchor me in this strange new place. As I lie down and close my eyes, the strangest thought pops into my head.

I feel like I've come home.

'Alice?'

At first I don't recognise the voice calling my name. I open my eyes and my vision is blurry, but I can't stop a smile spreading across my face when I see him.

'Palmiro.'

He's standing in the doorway, his frame lean and tall, with his arms folded. I can't help but notice the shape of his muscles.

'We are about to moor up,' he says, returning my grin. Perhaps he saw the way I was looking at him.

I sit up hurriedly, bundling up my precious counterpane, and run a hand over my dishevelled hair. I follow him and step out of the cabin, shielding my eyes from the dazzling sun.

The heat is immediate. We have some warm days in Whitecroft, but we never get heat like this. It takes my breath away.

The sky is a rich, beautiful blue, and the water shimmers in the sunlight. We've anchored the boat next to a wooden pier, and Cayman is already lowering a thick plank so that we can walk easily off the deck. I follow the pier as it cuts through the water, and leads up to a beach with golden sands, framed with tall trees with large, green spikes for leaves. The shore is crowded with people, carrying baskets, pushing small canoes in and out of the water, calling to one another. Many are pointing towards our boat, and I feel suddenly self-conscious as I wait my turn to step onto the plank.

As if sensing my emotion, Palmiro holds out his hand to help me onto the boat with a reassuring grin.

'Welcome to Cape, Alice,' he says.

21

At least I'm not the only one who feels over-awed. Arnold's mouth hangs open as he stares at these new surroundings, and Leon looks unsettled and twitchy. My father bounds forward eagerly, just on Cayman's heels, and the mania in his eyes is back as he assesses this idyllic paradise. I have no idea what he's thinking, but I push it out of mind. I want to focus on walking without stumbling, and I can only take brief glances at the unfamiliar faces waiting for us.

Most seem curious; some look grim. They are all dressed in much looser clothing. The women wear sleeveless dresses in brightly coloured material, and the men wear looser shirts with shorter trousers, sometimes just down to their knees. The women have long, dark hair, braided with beads and some tied with scarves. I must look a complete mess to them. My dress is damp with a heavy hem, and hangs stiffly.

Palmiro smiles at me encouragingly, and helps me onto the sand, gesturing for me to stand with him. Leon and Arnold are a few feet away, and Father stands with Cayman in front of the crowd. Cayman raises a hand for quiet.

'We are happy to welcome, from Whitecroft, the General.'

Father nods, and surveys the rather stony-faced crowd without fear.

'His daughter, Alice,' Cayman points towards me, 'and Leon and Arnold Crest.'

At that moment, my eyes fall on the familiar faces from Whitecroft of the runaways: the Swifts, Viola Taylor and Blake Hughes. They left around a month ago, and they stare in disbelief at my father. They weren't expecting him to follow them. Joy is wearing a brightly coloured scarf in her hair, but her expression is the most horrified. My heart sinks. I'm guilty by association and they're not going to see me any differently.

'Let us prepare food for them and give them a place to rest,' Cayman commands.

As the crowd disperses in a hubbub of noise, the Swifts disappear from view. I tense and stay rooted to the spot, even though my father and the Crests are being ushered away.

'Alice?' Palmiro's voice draws my attention from them.

I turn to him, looking at me questioningly.

'I don't want to go with them,' I say.

His mouth twitches upwards.

'You want a tour of the island?'

≡

I'm hungry, tired, and longing to get rid of my dress, but somehow I forget all of that when I'm with Palmiro. Everything feels new and exciting. He shows me their beach shelters, then leads me through more of the tall trees, where sand dunes turn more into a dirt track. When the trees clear, their whole village is spread out on a flat plain, with the river running alongside it down to the sea. They've easily got double the population of Whitecroft, looking at the number of houses. A lone mountain rises up, some distance from the edge of the village, and it's covered in scorched grass and scrub.

'What's up there?' I ask.

'Not much,' Palmiro replies.

'What about the other side?'

'There's grasslands. Cattle, buffalo. But the Drought was bad last year. We need better irrigation and we need to start building more permanent communities out there. Trouble is, no one wants to leave the village.'

'What about you?' I ask, fascinated.

He shrugs.

'I love my family, but I want to make Cape stronger for the future.'

After walking around the different parts of the village, Palmiro leads me to a hut and knocks on the door. My smile fades as Viola opens it.

'I wondered if Alice could stay with you,' Palmiro says.

Unable to directly refuse, Viola gives me a suspicious look.

'She had a rough voyage,' he adds, sensing her reluctance.

Viola sighs and swings the door open a little wider, stepping back.

'You'd better come in.'

<h1 style="text-align:center">22</h1>

Palmiro leaves, promising to return soon, and I stand awkwardly in the room.

'You need dry clothes,' Viola observes. 'Follow me.'

She leads me into the bedroom, and lays out some garments for me on the bed. She's a similar height and build to me, though her ginger hair is a striking contrast to my blondness.

'I'll help you out of your dress,' she says, helping me to pull it over my head.

'Why are you here?' she asks suddenly.

'My father asked me to come.'

My voice is croaky and small.

'Why is he here?' she presses.

'I don't know.'

She clearly doesn't believe me.

'Tell him from me,' she says, 'that we are not going back.'

That would require me having a conversation with him. I can't promise anything, so I keep quiet.

'Once you're dressed, come and have something to eat.'

She closes the door, leaving me to pull on a loose blouse and a skirt that just touches the floor. The fabric is lighter and softer than my usual clothes. I look at myself in the mirror. I don't resemble the starched, awkward girl I was in Whitecroft. The clothes make me appear softer and brighter, like someone new. On a sudden impulse, I start removing the pins from my hair, which kept it carefully scraped back in a bun. As it falls down messily, knotted and kinked, I scrunch it as best I can with my hands and comb through it with my fingers.

I tentatively push open the door and hover, until Viola notices me. A hint of surprise passes through her expression when she sees me, but it's quickly suppressed. She knows me as the General's daughter and nothing's going to change that.

'Take a seat.'

She speaks without looking at me, and gestures to the kitchen table, where she has set out a plate with bread and fruit.

'Thank you,' I say, my cheeks burning as I sit down.

It's humiliating that I'm dependent on someone else to feed and provide for me, although I should be used to it by now. It feels different when it's not your own family. When I was living with Abigail, Viola's aunt, I saw Viola frequently at their family gatherings. They never felt like *my* family.

Viola moves around the room, cleaning surfaces and sweeping the floor.

'Is this your house?' I ask.

She turns to look at me, and nods, wiping her brow.

'Do you like it here?'

She stares at me for a moment.

'It's very different to Whitecroft,' she finally answers.

'You can say what you think,' I reply, hoping that she will be more open.

'Overall, I like it better,' she says. 'There's more freedom here.'

What kind of freedom? I long to ask more questions, but I think I've already annoyed her. What kind of leader is Cayman? How do they run Cape? And Palmiro... I have so many questions about him, but she'd surely laugh at my pathetic crush if I voiced them. He's warm and friendly—that's his personality—so it probably signifies nothing that he's been so kind to me.

It feels like he's the first person who's really noticed me. And that isn't a good enough reason to lose my head over him.

After eating, I lie on Viola's bed to rest. Even though the storm was terrifying, and my father didn't seem to care whether I drowned, I'm here on Cape. I'm alive, and I'm safe. Something new burns in my chest, a tiny, flickering but unmistakeable flame. Hope.

23

I wake to the sound of raised voices.

'You said it would take them months to build another boat!'

It's Viola, and she's upset.

'They had it hidden away. They knew all about our plan to leave. They let us go.'

I recognise Blake's voice. He sounds frustrated.

'But they always said it was forbidden. Why would they have just let us sail away?'

'This is all exactly as he wanted. He planned this, Viola. All of it.'

My head is muddled with sleep and I sit up, trying to make sense of what I'm hearing.

My father knew that a group from Whitecroft were leaving, and he allowed them to go, because it was all part of his plan?

This makes no sense. For my entire life, Whitecroft has only had one boat and it was only to be used for fishing. Barely anyone apart from the Swifts knew how to sail. We were brought up singing the Whitecroft anthem about our duty to the town, knowing that its success—or more soberly, its survival—depended on all of us staying and playing our part. We were never allowed to leave. We hiked into the forest for hunting, sometimes staying out overnight, but that was it.

Why would my father *want* people to leave?

'What does he want?' Viola's question echoes my thoughts.

'War,' Blake answers grimly.

I clap my hand over my mouth in shock. War? Surely not! We've barely succeeded in building Whitecroft to a functional level; we couldn't possibly send out an army without our farmland becoming a wilderness and our harvest failing.

'This is a game of chess,' Blake continues. 'This is just one move and the General has many others planned. First group sails away; he can come to the island with a legitimate grievance.'

'He can't attack Cape because we left!' Viola cries.

'He won't attack,' Blake says, 'but he will execute a counter-move.'

'Like what?'

There's a moment of silence.

'Do you think she knows?' Viola asks.

'No,' he replies.

I have a horrible feeling they're talking about me.

I throw the blankets off and spring to my feet, smoothing my hair with my hands, before opening the door and confronting them.

'Know what?' I demand.

Blake looks startled, not least because I'm dressed in Cape clothing. He wears the same lighter, looser garments as Palmiro, but he's still kept the cowboy hat he always wore in Whitecroft. It suits him. He's always had a certain wildness about him. Our eyes meet.

'Your father has brought you here as a bargaining chip,' Blake tells me bluntly. 'He's going to act all annoyed and hard-done-by because we left with the main boat, but actually, he needed an excuse to come here.'

'How is he going to bargain with me?' I ask, confused.

'He'll probably want some sort of exchange,' Blake says, matter-of-factly. 'He's lost his sailors, so he'll want someone experienced to come to Whitecroft.'

'And he's going to leave me behind?'

I don't quite know how to respond to this idea. I feel insulted that Father says so little to me, and never explains his actions, and expects to use me as an asset of sorts. Equally, the idea of staying here, exploring the whole island with Palmiro… It's appealing. Probably for all the wrong reasons.

'Has he told you anything?' Viola eyes me suspiciously.

'No!' I insist. 'I haven't been living with him for months. He barely speaks to me.'

Blake and Viola exchange a look. He has the kind of face that is very expressive, whereas she is cooler and more measured.

'If she stays, where will she live?' Viola asks.

Blake gestures with his hand in the air. Here.

They lock stares in silent negotiation.

I'd love to cut in and tell them it's all unnecessary, because I can sort myself out, but I have no clue where else I'd go.

'I need to think about this,' Viola says, finally.

Couldn't agree more.

There's a knock at the door. It's Palmiro.

24

I spring forward to open the door, even though it isn't my house, because (I tell myself) I want to escape being third wheel as Viola and Blake argue their way through the predicament of my presence. My main motive is definitely not a) seeing Palmiro or b) surprising Palmiro with my new improved Cape style.

'Hello,' I say breathlessly.

I'm grinning and definitely not hiding my feelings, but Palmiro looks me up and down and then smiles wide enough for all his white teeth to be visible. Utterly dazzling.

'Alice,' he says, and I love the way he says my name, 'you look beautiful.'

I didn't expect him to actually say it out loud. My cheeks flare up and he rescues me from embarrassment by suggesting that we go for a walk before meeting Cayman and the others. Calling a hurried goodbye to Viola and Blake, who are probably still thrashing things out, I follow Palmiro through the dense undergrowth and shaded path, until we reach the open plains. He gestures for me to sit next to him on a rock. We can see the mountain ahead, and the long yellowy grass. I bask, my face up to the hot sun, while there are only a few white clouds in the sky. What a difference from Whitecroft.

'Do you like it here?' Palmiro asks.

'What's not to like?' I respond, opening my eyes just enough to squint at him.

'So, you wouldn't mind staying for a little while?' he continues.

I sit up straighter and open my eyes fully.

'Have you been talking to my father? Blake said something about him wanting to leave me here?'

He winces slightly. His eyes have that odd mix of warmth towards me, not wanting to cause me pain, but also the hardness of knowing painful truth.

'I overheard him talking with my father,' he says.

'Does he want to leave me here, and then take someone else back to Whitecroft?'

Palmiro pulls a handful of dry grass, avoiding my gaze.

'Tell me,' I insist, laying my hand on his arm. His skin feels warm and smooth.

'He wants to take me,' Palmiro finally answers.

My breath catches in my throat. I know I've barely met him, but the idea of being left here at Cape without him is unthinkable. Plus, I have no idea what my father has in mind for this 'visitor'. I don't trust him, and there's no way I want Palmiro to be in the firing line.

'Don't go,' I blurt out.

'It is not really my decision,' he says. 'But I don't think my father will allow it, if he knows that I wish to remain here.'

'Is that... what you want?' I ask, tentatively. Perhaps I have poured cold water on something he was desperate to do.

He hesitates.

'I always wanted to explore the world,' he says. 'I have sailed since I was a boy, and gone to the meeting point island. It would be untruthful to say I have never wanted to see Whitecroft for myself.'

'Perhaps you should go, then,' I say quietly.

'But you don't want me to?' he says, like it's a probing question.

'I don't want to be left here alone,' I tell him. 'Viola and Blake don't trust me. I've only just met you but you're the closest thing to a friend that I have right now.'

'I *am* your friend,' he says.

He gives me his characteristic, gleaming white grin, and I can't help but return it.

'My friend might be willing to go instead of me,' he says, looking more sober, 'but I have to vow to help him return safely. If he gets in trouble, I will have to go to help him.'

He's staring into my eyes, and his face seems closer to me than it was before.

'Do you think your father intends for him to return safely?' he asks me.

I consider lying, but I feel like his eyes can read my soul.

'I don't know,' I reply honestly, 'but I don't trust my father.'

It hurts to say the words out loud, but I also find a sort of relief in admitting the truth. I would never have said that in Whitecroft. Something about being here on the island has lifted the invisible barriers I've lived with all my life. Here, I don't have to be the General's perfect daughter anymore.

Palmiro says nothing, but turns his hand towards me, palm outstretched.

'Do you trust me?' he asks.

I place my hand in his.

'Yes,' I whisper.

He closes his fingers around my hand and squeezes it.

'I promise you that if I have to leave, I will come back for you,' he says.

Yesterday he'd never met me, and now he's making me promises. Serious promises. My head is screaming that I shouldn't believe it; he doesn't know me. If he knew the Alice from Whitecroft, he wouldn't be holding my hand like this now.

He wouldn't be standing so close to me, leaning in so that I can almost feel the heat radiating from his tall, lean frame, close enough for me to breathe him in. I wonder if he tastes like the sea.

'Alice, I have to ask you something,' he says.

My heart soars—maybe he'll confess his feelings for me?

'Can you try to find out what your father is planning?'

Oh. I stumble backwards, pulling my hand out of his grasp.

'How am I supposed to do that?' I snap, then regret it when I see his hurt expression.

'I don't know,' Palmiro shrugs. 'You might overhear him talking with the others.'

'Is that why you're being nice to me? So that I can spy on my father?'

I take another step back, shaking my head. At least I didn't do anything too stupid… yet. I'm terrified at how weak my resolve is. I'm so pathetic, I'm an easy target for any boy who's willing to offer me help.

'You said yourself that you don't trust him,' he points out. 'If he wants to leave you on this island, then you have a right to know why. It's your future.'

Hearing him say those words gives me an instant pang in my heart. My future has never belonged to me; it was always dependent on my father's wishes. The idea of having control makes me giddy, but also feel like I'm falling with nothing to hold onto.

'And if you think I'm being nice to you just because of your father, then you clearly don't trust me,' he continues.

'I'm sorry,' I say. 'There's just… a lot of things I'm trying to understand. And I don't.'

'You don't trust me?' Palmiro's voice is full of disappointment.

'No, I meant that I don't understand,' I hastily explain.

'There are many things I don't understand,' Palmiro says. 'I don't understand why no one from Whitecroft ever came to visit us, why we always had to meet in secret at the meeting point, and why our two nations have been kept apart for fifty years. But I feel like finally, we might be closer to getting some answers to these questions. If we don't work together, then things may go back to how they were before. Is that what you want?'

'Of course not,' I reply. Already it's unthinkable to go back to Whitecroft and forget that he exists. To return to who I was before.

***

When I get back, Viola's rearranged the furniture to make a camp bed for me in the corner of the main room.

'I'm sorry you won't get much privacy,' she says. 'You can dress in our room if you want.'

'It's all right, I'll manage,' I say, feeling guilty that I'm intruding on them just like with Charles and Ada. But what else am I supposed to do?

'I leave early in the mornings to radio my parents,' she says. 'I should be back by the time you get up.'

But the next day, I wake up when someone moves a chair at the table. I sit up with a start, checking my hair isn't sticking up on end, and stand up to see Blake sitting there.

'Sorry if I woke you,' he says. 'Go back to sleep if you want. You looked like you needed it.'

'Thanks,' I retort sarcastically, and then remember that he's allowing me to stay in his home. 'Sorry, I didn't mean—'

He laughs and shakes his head.

'You hungry?' he asks, holding out a bread roll.

I step forward and take it, then slide into a seat next to him at the table.

'I can bake, you know,' I say, keen for him to see that I don't wish to be a burden. 'I don't want to get in your way, but I can help. With anything.'

'Is that so?' Blake looks amused. 'I didn't think Whitecroft's princess would have to do many chores herself.'

I look up sharply from my roll, but he's teasing me again.

'I'm not a princess,' I protest. 'I bet I can even chop wood, if you teach me.'

'For all those fires we need in this raging heat,' he says wryly.

My face falls, and he laughs heartily.

'Only joking, Princess,' he says, nudging my arm with his elbow. His skin feels warm against mine. 'We do need fuel for the stove, and water from the well. Most folk are up early to fish around here.'

'Do you fish?' I ask. Back in Whitecroft, only the Swifts would do that.

'Yes,' he says. 'Or I go wherever I'm needed.'

I look out of the window. It's morning, but the sun is long since risen.

'I should get up earlier,' I say. 'Sorry, I guess I was tired.'

'Sailing is no picnic,' Blake says. He clears his throat. 'I'm sorry that you had a frosty welcome from us yesterday. We were just surprised—'

'I know,' I say. 'A week ago I had no idea I was going to be in Cape.'

'What's new in Whitecroft?' he asks, pouring a drink into a cup and handing it to me.

I taste it and it's hot, and bitter.

'Elise announced that she's my sister,' I say, watching his expression to see if he knew about that.

'What?' He slams his cup down and stares at me in shock.

'I know,' I say.

'How..?' he trails off.

'Her mother Loretta received the fertility treatment meant for my mother,' I explain. 'Elise and I were born within a week of each other.'

'Come to think of it, you do resemble each other,' he says, scrutinising my face.

I make a face, and he laughs.

'How did your father react?' he asks.

I meet his eyes, then shake my head and look away.

'That bad?' Blake asks.

I take another sip of the drink. It doesn't taste so bad the second time.

'I bet you weren't running towards her with your arms open wide either,' Blake continues.

'Why should I?' I ask. 'I forgot you were in Elise's fan club.'

He laughs loudly at this.

'You sore because she got cast to William? Did they get pledged?'

I nod, focusing on my cup.

'Did you get pledged?' he asks, his voice quieter this time.

'I wouldn't be here if I had,' I say, setting my cup back on the table.

'Good,' he says, raising his cup to his lips with a smile. 'You're too good-looking to be wasted on Phillip Stead.'

I can't help smiling at this.

'Is Viola radioing her parents?' I ask.

Blake's smile fades.

'She goes every morning,' he says.

I raise my eyebrows. Maybe Viola's adamant words about not leaving were masking homesickness.

'Is she happy here?' I ask.

Blake looks at me, then sighs.

'I don't think she's happy anywhere,' he says.

He stands up, brushing down his light-coloured trousers.

'I'd better go to work,' he says.

'Can I come?' I stand too.

He lifts an eyebrow in surprise.

'Sure, Princess. Your wish is my command.'

I shove his shoulder this time as payback, then skip nimbly out of the door before he can get me back.

═══

'Every day, I turn up at the beach and find someone to tag along with,' Blake says, pointing towards the stretching, golden sand. 'Mostly, we fish. But I have helped with other things like crops and building.'

'What does Viola do?' I ask.

His jaw twitches.

'Uh… various things,' he says vaguely.

I raise an eyebrow.

'She's still finding her feet.'

'Are the people nice?' I ask, watching them on the beach, throwing baskets to each other and laughing.

'You mean, are they all as nice as Palmiro?'

Now it's Blake's turn to raise an eyebrow. I feel my cheeks turn pink.

'Yes, everybody's nice and welcoming,' Blake says, with a grin. 'It's so different to Whitecroft.'

'Do you miss Whitecroft?' I ask, curious.

Blake hesitates.

'I miss certain things.'

'Like Elise?' I tease. It's payback for the Palmiro comment.

'She's just my friend,' Blake frowns.

'A friend you flirt with.'

'Doesn't everyone have one of those?'

He gives me a cheeky grin and my heart skips a beat. What, am I flirting with *Blake* now? I just crossed an ocean and I'm going boy-crazy.

He seems to realise it's inappropriate at the same moment, as we both look away at the sea. It looks so calm and inviting in the sunshine. The water laps the shore and it's peaceful—such a contrast to my storm experience.

'I miss my family,' Blake says, breaking the silence. 'Especially my sisters. Having to leave suddenly without saying goodbye… it's weighed on me.'

I nod, and resist the urge to lay my hand on his arm.

'For me, being here… It's like a weight has been lifted,' I tell him. 'I can't even explain it.'

'You can be anyone you want to be here,' Blake says, and I nod excitedly. 'Perhaps for you, you can finally be who you really are.'

I look at him in surprise. He's perceptive.

'I know you always had to be little Miss Perfect in Whitecroft,' he says. 'It's good to see you smile and enjoy yourself.'

That's exactly how I felt yesterday, when I was talking with Palmiro. I don't know how, but Blake has *seen* me, the real me. Back in Whitecroft, I barely gave him a second glance.

He looks back to the fishing group.

'I should go over there. You coming?'

'Will they be all right with that?'

He laughs.

'It's not like Whitecroft, where I was given an official transfer to work at the Forge over the Freeze. Anyone can join in. It's the way of the island.'

His words give me a shiver of delight. Already, I feel like a new person. The island has worked its magic, and now it feels like my island, too.

ELISE

25

Each day we're one step closer to the Freeze, but time burns slowly, like the agonising smoulder of a fire that never really catches aflame.

I know I should be thankful, and I am, but a cold fear grips me whenever I think about the General. Whether he believes I'm his daughter or not, I know he hates me. While out in the Farmlands, I'm far away from the Infirmary and all the General's friends, but I also feel an increasing isolation. I take walks, listening to the birds, and watching the leaves fall and carpet the ground in rich shades of red and gold. I shiver from the sharpness in the air.

Will is obsessed with building a canoe. George left him detailed instructions, and he's been working on it for hours each day, sanding and shaping and chiselling it.

I see Grandfather every day. We share soup together for lunch, and freshly baked bread. He's subdued since Alice left so suddenly. We both know that things aren't right between Alice and her father... my father, too... but what can we do? I don't want him walking all the way to Whitecroft at this stage in the year.

I've been waiting and hoping each day for Ada and Charles to visit. They promised they would come, in their carriage, to see us in our new home before the Freeze. I know Charles must be busy with his position on the Council, now that his father is no longer

on it, but I hope that Ada is longing to see me as much I long to
see her.

She must be kept busy with Frederick. I still remember the
day he was born, when Eden Taylor helped to deliver him, and I
understood for the first time some of the wild euphoria of
bearing a child. It still terrifies me. Alice made a comment about
me carrying before too long, and the thought keeps coming back.
How long will it take? Will I be sick, like Ada? Will I die, like my
mother?

I still re-read her letters and keep them by my bed. It's
devastating that the people who knew her best, George and Joy
Swift, have left Whitecroft forever. I wished I had asked them
more questions, spent more time with them.

I'm pleased with my new home. Will and Charles worked so
hard to build it, and furnish it. I can while away a couple of hours
each day cleaning and arranging things, and cooking batches of
stew. This is what I always wanted, and never thought I'd have. I
thought I'd be blanked just like my mother.

But there's a deep, aching loneliness I can't get rid of.

Will doesn't seem to understand. He's happy with everything,
and there's nothing else he wants. His family are nearby, and he's
essentially carrying on with his duties as normal. Apart from
being pledged to me, his life is unchanged.

I feel I've been turned upside down.

I wrap my warm travelling cloak around me, and take some
warm stew to the barn where Will is building the canoe. His face
brightens into a smile when he sees me, and he takes the stew
from me, sets it down, then gives me a long, lingering kiss.

'How was your morning?' he asks.

'Fine,' I reply.

Boring and mediocre doesn't have quite the same ring to it.

We sit together on some old tree stumps that Will uses as chopping blocks. I love the smell here of pine needles, fresh wood shavings, and bonfires.

'You should go and see Cressida, ask if she wants you to help with tailoring.'

'Sure,' I say dully. Sewing is not my strong point.

I look around the barn. I'm impressed at the progress he's made with the boat, and he shrugs modestly when I voice this.

'It's getting there,' he says. 'I just hope the Crests don't come visiting.'

'I think I'll visit Lily tomorrow,' I say, thinking of Arnold's broken match. She's been through such a difficult time. It'll be good for me to remember how lucky I am.

'Make sure you see Jemima. She'll be very disappointed otherwise,' Will grins.

His sister is very sweet—at times a little bouncy for my temperament—but it will be refreshing to spend time with others. I could call in on Ruby in the stables, too, maybe go for a ride…

'You know, you don't have to stay around here all day,' Will says, as if reading my thoughts. 'I'm not expecting you to always be in the house.'

'I know,' I sigh. 'I just… need to find my way around, now that everything's changed.'

'Nothing has to change,' he reminds me.

But it already has.

26

In the end, I don't get past the stables. Ruby is in the courtyard as I walk through, and enthusiastically beckons me over.

'Elise! How are you? Foxtrot's missed you.'

I grin. Ruby taught me to ride and it made such a difference, to be able to get to Whitecroft and back in half the time it takes to walk. Something Will arranged for me in an unexpected kindness.

'I was just about to take Chestnut out,' she says. 'Fancy a ride?'

'Definitely.'

Once we're cantering in the paddock, I instantly feel the heaviness lift. Even though the sky is grey, the air tastes crisp and fresh. The trees burn brightly, colouring the landscape with vivid shades, and the world feels bigger and wider than it did a few hours ago. It's all about perspective.

'It's been ages since I've caught up with you,' Ruby says, as we slow to a walk. 'So much has happened.'

'How's Lily?' I ask, guilty that I've been easily sidetracked from visiting her.

'She's better,' Ruby says, though her face shows concern. 'There's been no sign of Arnold… so far.'

'Do you think he will try to take her back?'

'Who knows?' she sighs. 'My grandfather moved into Will's room so that she could have his house. My mum's over the moon because she sees Stephanie every day. I don't think they could go back to how it was before.'

Lily was isolated and alone in Whitecroft, while her match was running Law and Order. I shudder, remembering how she was nearly flogged in front of the whole town, for a crime she didn't commit.

'I never got a chance to thank you, for what you did for Lily,' Ruby says.

I blush and concentrate on the harness, knowing how poor and insignificant my actions were.

'It was nothing,' I say. 'I'm just glad she's back with her family.'

It makes me wonder how many others are suffering, though—behind closed doors. At the time, I felt hopeful because the General and the Doctor were taken off the Council. Now, I just feel overwhelmed that so much needs to change in Whitecroft.

'Do you think the Pact will meet again?'

It feels like a distant memory, when we all sat in the barns with Francis Derby leading the meeting. Everyone voted to resist the General. Ruby had only just joined. Now that Francis is leading Whitecroft, perhaps there will no longer be a need for the Pact. I'd love to know if Francis was open to visiting the other nation, and building stronger connections with them, rather than just meeting on a random island to exchange information once a year.

'I don't know,' I reply. 'You're one of the first people I've seen for a while. I feel like I've missed everything.'

'You know what it's like after the Day of Unity,' Ruby says. 'Everything starts to shut down, ready for the Freeze. My mother's been making tons of jams and preserves. I was glad to escape, there was so much steam in the kitchen.'

Maybe that's what I need to keep myself busy: mountains of blackberries and glass jars. We have a shortage of sugar so it would have to be on the tart side.

'How's Will?' Ruby asks.

'He's good,' I smile. 'He's building a boat.'

'What?' Ruby's eyes pop wider in surprise.

'George left him instructions.'

'Wow,' Ruby breathes out. 'So, will it replace the boat the Swifts took?'

'I think it's more like a canoe,' I say. 'Nowhere near as big as the Swifts' boat.'

'Imagine if every family had one,' Ruby says, her eyes staring dreamily off into the distance.

I follow her gaze. You can't see the sea from here, but it certainly enlarges the boundaries of our world if the ocean is no longer something that traps us.

'I love your spirit of adventure,' I tell her, grinning.

Ada, for example, would be quite happy staying in Whitecroft forever. It's refreshing to be with someone who feels the same way I do.

'Do you think Will would let me go on the boat when it's ready?'

'I'm sure that would be fine.'

We finish our circuit and join the road from Whitecroft, heading back to Pembridge. I can see a figure in the distance, riding towards us.

'Who do you think that is?' Ruby asks.

'Possibly Charles?'

I strain my eyes. It's been an adjustment, going from seeing Charles as my cousin, to my brother. I feel I know him better now than ever before, and I understand why Will trusts him as his closest friend. He really is nothing like his—*our*—father.

The rider notices us, and gives a shout and a wave. It's not long before Charles gallops towards us, then grinds to a halt.

'Charles!' I greet him, excited to see a friendly face.

'Elise, Ruby,' Charles says, and his expression is serious, 'I have to find Will and Francis. Gus Taylor just came to me, with a radio message from Viola. My father has sailed to Cape.'

27

I'm stunned.

Literally, my whole life, I was taught that loyalty to Whitecroft meant never wanting to leave. There was only one boat, which was strictly to be used for fishing and nothing else, so when I ended up going on a secret trip to the meeting point, and discovered there was a whole other nation of people I knew nothing about, I struggled to find footholds in this strange new world. A world where there were other possibilities. In the end, I didn't leave with the Swifts. I chose Will.

Now the General has sailed to the other island. How?

'Where did he get the boat?' I ask immediately, thinking of Will's canoe.

He surely couldn't have made a new one that quickly.

'I have no idea,' Charles says.

He looks flustered, and hurt that his father has gone without telling him. Personally, I'm glad that Charles is seeing more of his—*our*—father's true colours.

'Once I've told Francis, I need to see Alice,' Charles says. 'Maybe she'll know more about it.'

'Alice?' I repeat, in instant confusion.

'Yes, she may have picked up on something.'

Charles is impatient to leave, and starts to stir his horse to move on.

'I thought Alice was staying with you,' I say.

Charles pulls on his reins sharply.

'What?'

'Alice left with the Crests and your father… several days ago now.'

Charles looks genuinely horrified.

'But I thought she was staying with Grandfather for the Freeze?'

'That's what we thought, too, but the General came for her. Is she not in Whitecroft?'

'She's not in my father's house, and she's not with us,' Charles shakes his head.

'Is it possible that she's gone with him?' Ruby speaks up.

I stare at Charles. My stomach is churning up with guilt and fear. When they arrived to collect her, I left them to it. I didn't question it. If she's gone to the other land, and I never see her again, I can't help but feel some sense of gnawing regret that there was so much hatred between us. That things were never put right.

'We need to find out exactly who's missing,' Charles raises his hand to his forehead, overwhelmed.

'Let me take your message to my grandfather,' Ruby suggests. 'Elise, you find Will. Charles, go to your Grandfather. You'll need to take him and Cressida to Whitecroft in a carriage if you want to hold a Council meeting.'

'Yes…' Charles murmurs distractedly. 'Elise, you and Will should ride to town too. You can use the Swifts' cottage.'

'What will the Council do?' I ask, feeling a growing sense of dread.

'We'll need to decide if we should go after them,' Charles says, his tone sombre. 'We need to find out why they've gone there.'

'I don't think they've gone to sight-see,' Ruby says.

'Maybe Father wants to get the boat back,' Charles suggests.

I can't help feeling that it's more than that. A lot more.

<h1 style="text-align:center">28</h1>

It's the first Whitecroft Council meeting I've ever attended, and it's only because everything is in such chaos that no one's really noticed me.

The Council is made up of the Head of each family in Whitecroft, with Charles as his father's successor, and I don't really know why Alice was added (she probably bargained her way on somehow). It's quickly discovered that the General, Alice, Leon and Arnold Crest are missing. Felix Turner has replaced his father, the Doctor, but his brother, Gus is here for questioning. Gus got the radio message from his daughter, Viola. Henry Crest is standing in for his missing father, so there are nine Council members present. We only started with ten families, and now one of them has left. It strikes me how small and few in number we are. This is our nation. These are the ones who have to decide what we do next.

Francis, Will's grandfather, chairs the meeting. First, Gus recounts the details of the message he received. It wasn't entirely clear, but he heard that the General was there on the other land. It is confirmed that no one has seen any of the missing people for several days.

'How did they leave?' Francis asks the room. 'Where could they have sourced a boat from?'

No one volunteers any information. I look at Grandfather. He's been very quiet since finding out about Alice. He looks worried.

I knew that Alice was going through a difficult time since she withdrew from being pledged to Phillip Stead, and that she'd been living with Charles and Ada, but I think it would take a lot to break her loyalty to our father and the system that's given her so much privilege her entire life. I grew up out on the Farmlands, working every hour of daylight in the fields, while she fussed around with getting Cressida to make her new dresses. I don't have much sympathy for her predicament.

'Is this linked to the Swifts?' Alec Lane asks. 'Did they have another boat?'

'No,' Will clears his throat. He's not on the Council either, but he holds up the papers which George gave him. 'George gave me instructions to build another boat, and told me they would leave their boat at the meeting point island for us to collect. I've been working on this, and it's nearly ready.'

The thought of Will travelling over the turbulent sea in what looks like a fairly flimsy canoe makes my heart sink. I knew he was making it, I just didn't really think about him using it so immediately.

'If we get the Swifts' boat back, then we can fish again,' Charles says.

'We could use the canoe to fish,' Bryant Turner points out.

'If George has left instructions,' Francis says, breaking into a hubbub of discussion authoritatively, 'then we can do both. Bryant, Edmund can make two more canoes. In the meantime, we can send a group over to collect the Swifts' boat.'

'Who's going to go?' Felix asks, looking anxious.

'I will,' Will says. 'I made the canoe, and George taught me to sail.'

'I'm going with him,' Charles says immediately.

'How many can fit in the canoe?' Francis asks.

'Only one more,' Will says.

'Take me,' I speak suddenly.

Everyone's eyes stare at me. No one had even noticed me before.

'I had sailing lessons too,' I say, clearing my throat to sound less croaky.

I focus my gaze on Will, but he looks back at me and shakes his head slightly. He looks at Charles.

'I think we should ask Edward,' Charles says. 'He came out with us before.'

Edward is Will's cousin, eight years older.

I look at Grandfather, but he says nothing. I don't want to be left behind, and a rising panic fills my heart.

'Edward has a family,' I argue. 'Who knows how long you'll be gone?'

'We're going to the meeting point island, getting the boat, and coming back,' Charles says, making it sound much simpler than it will be, in practice.

'What about the General?' Felix asks. 'What is he doing over there?'

'If we regain the Swifts' boat,' Francis says, 'then we stand in a better position to travel to the meeting point, or even to the other nation, if we need to.'

'Surely it makes more sense to travel from the meeting point to the other nation, while they're there?' Alec points out.

'But then they'll be gone for weeks!' I protest.

I'll be alone, in the Freeze.

'We can't keep losing groups of people to the other island,' Daniel Stead complains. 'It's hard enough running Whitecroft as it is. It may be the Freeze, but there's still work to be done.'

'I agree,' Francis says decisively. 'The main objective is to recover the boat. Any exploration will have to wait until we understand more what is happening.'

'I still think I should go instead of Edward,' I say, mainly to Will.

'It's too dangerous,' he says.

I know he's only trying to protect me, but it stings. Is this how it's going to be, now we're pledged? I just have to sit at home and wait while he has all the adventures?

'What about Alice?' Grandfather finally speaks up.

An awkward silence falls.

'What about her?' Cressida asks. 'She's chosen to go with her father. Goodness knows what they're up to over there. Probably want to cause mischief with the Swifts. Preston just couldn't let them leave without a fight.'

'What if she didn't choose to go?' Grandfather says.

'They would hardly have dragged her on a boat kicking and screaming,' Cressida scoffs. 'That girl knows how to make a fuss when someone asks her to do something she doesn't want to do. Trust me, I've tried to get her to sew.'

'Perhaps the General is trying to bring the Swifts back,' Felix says.

'Maybe Viola will come back,' Gus says hopefully.

I doubt that.

'If the General had access to another boat, he should not have concealed it from everyone,' Bryant says. 'It just shows that he's acting on his own agenda, regardless of what this Council decides.'

'He's not even on the Council anymore,' Francis points out. 'Henry, can you give us any information about why your father and son left with the General?'

'I don't know anything about it,' Henry answers, with a surly expression.

'Gus, we need to try to radio a message back to Viola,' Francis says. 'We can see what she can find out for us. Will, Charles and

Edward will sail to recover the Swifts' boat. In the meantime, preparations for the Freeze must continue.'

The meeting is adjourned.

29

'I'm trying to protect you,' Will says.

We've been arguing since we arrived home and closed the door, finally alone.

'That doesn't mean you make decisions *for* me.'

A hot, raging anger has seized me, and I'm not going to let this go.

'Elise, there's a very real chance that the waves will be too powerful for my tiny little boat, and Charles and I might find ourselves swimming for our lives. That's not a situation I want to put you in.'

Will opens his arms, as if to draw me close, but I step away out of reach.

'So I just have to stay at home and wait? Don't you realise how hard that is, too?'

His arms fall to his sides.

'The General and two of the Crests are out there. Who knows if we might meet them on their return journey? We have no idea what they're doing, but it's not going to be promoting peaceful unity or they would have kept to their agreement years ago to join with the other nation.'

'Why did George give me sailing lessons – just to humour me?'

'I'm glad you learned,' Will says earnestly. 'If Edmund makes more boats, you can help with fishing trips.'

'Canoes don't have sails,' I point out bitterly.

'I don't understand why you're so angry,' Will shakes his head. 'I would much rather stay here, and keep safe, and be with you. But it's my duty to go and recover that boat, and I promised George I would.'

'Of course you don't understand!' I can't help raising my voice now. 'You've never known what it's like to be on the receiving end of a token gesture. *Sure, Elise, you can learn to sail.* Only no one ever intended for me to actually sail, in a situation where my skills were needed. *Whitecroft is changing,* you keep telling me. Well, things look pretty similar to how they've always looked, from where I'm standing. The General was taken off the Council, and he still managed to find a boat and sail away without anyone knowing or anyone giving him permission. If I did that, I would be excommunicated. But I bet when he comes back, he'll find a way to frame it all to make himself a hero and things will all go back to exactly how they were before.'

'You don't know that,' Will points out, reaching out to hold my arm.

This time, I let him. I allow myself to sink against him, to be held, because it's the only thing to help stave off the total misery that threatens to engulf me. I don't even have any tears.

'Listen,' he says, after a few minutes. 'I'm really glad you learned to sail, and I will absolutely support you in using those skills. But there's another reason I didn't want you to go. If there's a chance...'

He trails off, and I pull back to look at him.

'A chance of what?'

'You know,' he says, reddening slightly.

'That I might be carrying?'

There it is again: that sick feeling of dread.

'We only just took our Pledge.'

'It is possible, though,' he says.

What he means is that he hopes it's true.

'I just think we should make decisions on the basis that you might be,' he says.

He tips my face upwards by gently pressing his thumb under my chin, and kisses me. I kiss him back, and allow myself to be distracted by his warm proximity. I have to make the most of it while he's here.

But later, when he's asleep, I lie restlessly. Every thought of him being gone stabs my heart, and yet, I also can't shake the bitter disappointment of the inevitability of it all. However loving and supportive Will is, his default is to revert to the traditional roles that Whitecroft has promoted through every generation. He must be dutiful, and embrace situations that require courage and bravery. For me, though, duty involves staying put, and accepting my lot.

My hands press against my stomach, as if I would be able to feel if anything was different. Will another heart start beating there soon? Will doesn't seem to realise how terrifying it all is, because his body is going to carry on as normal, and I will be the one who's changed forever.

When I dream, I plunge through an ocean of darkness, hear the roar of the swell, the crashing waves, and the hammering of my own, petrified heart.

30

The day when he leaves is overcast, with a weak sun barely filtering through the thick layer of cloud.

We've been staying in the Swifts' cottage for a short reprieve, while Will and Charles try the boat out and gain confidence navigating through the waves, and I finally have the joy of seeing Ada and Frederick again. This helps to soften the blow, especially as Ada shows so much more strength and resilience than me. She's got more reason than I to protest, yet she speaks positively about the mens' courage, and reassures me that they will return in no time. I'm not convinced, but it won't do any good to share my gloomy predictions. I try to focus on one day at a time, enjoying the beach, throwing stones into the sea, and watching the waves. At night, Will and I are cosy in the little cottage, hearing the murmuring ocean outside, and warm with the stove burning and heating the whole house.

But it has to end, and I knew it would.

Each day they check the clouds, temperatures and sailing conditions. They want to make sure, as best they can, that they pick the right time to go. But the clock is ticking. The Freeze is on the way, and the longer they wait, the more likely the conditions will be more perilous. It feels like we only just settled when Will breaks the news that they are going.

He hugs me tightly, his strong arms crushing me against his chest, and he gives me a lingering kiss, but then he's running off, pushing the boat out. He jumps in, with Charles and Edward each holding a paddle, and we watch them as they move further and further away from the shore. It feels like a frighteningly brief time before they are small dots on the horizon. We stand, still watching, with the waves lapping at our feet. Every time the wind whips up our hair, we're thinking of how little their boat is, and how large the waves might be.

'Come on,' Ada says, taking my hand. 'Let's go and bake some bread.'

She keeps me busy all day, helping with Frederick, and doing chores. I stay the night in her spare room, just because I can't face going to the Swifts' cottage alone. It's hard to sleep, with thoughts of boats and islands and shipwrecks filling my mind. The good news is, it didn't rain, so conditions were hopefully as favourable as they were likely to be at this time of year.

Gus managed to get a few more details from Viola: how many days ago the General arrived, where Alice is (staying with her and Blake), and what seems to be happening. The General has asked for George to return, but he has refused. Cayman is trying to find a skilled sailor who's willing to come to Whitecroft to train others. This seems odd, given that George had already trained a few of us, but perhaps the General was unaware of this. Gus told Viola the General has been removed from the Council, but not to make this publicly known unless necessary.

It fills me with a grim foreboding, that the General sailed across to the other island, with a boat he managed to conceal, and make demands with authority even when he's been deposed from leadership.

It also makes me reconsider what happened when the Swifts left. It was all too easy—the only real obstacle was Alice's threats, which turned out to be fairly empty. Whilst I don't think the General wanted the Swifts to go, and I certainly don't think he expected the sudden revelations about being my father, he seems to have quietly faded into the background a little too willingly. In the background, where he can't be noticed as easily, and where he's unlikely to be questioned…

The positive outlook I had when I took my Pledge to Will has now been gradually overshadowed by the realisation that peace in Whitecroft is more brittle than thin ice on a pond. It will only take a small stone to shatter it.

And as I think of Will, Charles and Edward in their canoe, heading for the meeting point island, I wonder if they're sailing right into a trap.

ALICE

<h1 style="text-align:center">31</h1>

One of the first things I learn about Cape is that no one is in a rush here. Time doesn't seem to be measured with the same strictness as in Whitecroft, and this is probably one of the reasons that Cayman isn't quick to send Father away, along with some kind of sailing agreement. I gather that the discussions are ongoing, but in the meantime there's so much for me to discover.

The day starts early, but I love that the sun sets the rhythm of life here. It sends glittering brightness over the rippling water, and the expansive blue of the ocean and sky, along with the warmth of the white sand, become the staples of my new world. I can smell the sea everywhere, even from Blake and Viola's cabin. When she goes to radio her parents in the morning, Blake and I sit together at the table. He taught me how to make the hot, bitter drink, so sometimes I make it for both of us if I get there first.

We walk to the beach, and I listen to the tinkling sound of shells being swished around by the shallow, lapping waves. There are so many beautiful conches; I've started my own collection. Blake laughs at me every time I add another one.

'Pretty soon our house is going to be buried by shells,' he jokes, but I don't think he really minds.

Where the beach ends, tropical forest begins. There is lush, rich greenery at every level: giant leaves forming a canopy, and large stems from the ground open out like outstretched hands. Exotic birds call to one another, and there's the humming of insects forming a background noise over the layer of the sea soundtrack. And the flowers… there's a luxurious variety of scents and colours, and I reverently touch the velvet petals, watching the bees travel from one to the next.

'Which is your favourite?' Blake asks.

'These white lilies,' I say, admiring their delicate shape.

'Why don't you pick one to wear? It would stand out against how dark your hair is.'

'They're not supposed—'

Blake ignores my protest and picks one, then hands it to me. I tuck it behind my ear.

'Do you just break rules for fun now?' I tease.

'It's one of the best ways to have fun,' he grins. 'You should try it sometime.'

From what I've seen, he just loves to act like the bad boy, because as soon as he joins the islanders, he rolls up his sleeves and works like a trooper, following all their instructions to a tee. I tag along for fishing, although I'm not much help to anyone, and find that I'm most useful with cleaning. With a scrubbing brush and a bucket, I clean my way through the boats, and it seems to be appreciated.

I usually stay on shore and pick a boat that's not being used for fishing, and it's easy to get lost in the rhythm of the task: swilling the brush in the bucket and scrubbing away the dirt. It's so satisfying, watching the grime recede and running my fingertips over the worn, grained wood.

In a strange way, I feel like I'm washing my old self away. Here in Cape, I'm a newer, better version of Alice. A version I actually like.

You can't erase the past though, however much you try.

I'm scrubbing a boat one day, the sun high in the sky, when a shadow falls over me.

'What are you doing?'

My father's sneering tone gives me a shock. I fumble with the brush, and try to clear my hair away from my face. He's standing over the boat, looking down at me, and I'm sure I look red-faced, flustered and dirty.

'Just cleaning,' I say, trying to sound cheery.

'We are guests here, not servants,' he snaps.

'No one's treating me like a servant,' I say.

'Why don't you show a little more… decorum?'

'Because I want to be useful,' I say, going back to the business in hand.

I rub into his shadow, until he tuts and moves away.

Why does he always want me to be someone else?

'You missed a spot.'

I'm so lost in the overwhelming pull of the whirlpool of thoughts about my father, I don't notice Blake approach. I jump, startled again, the brush flying out of my hand and landing with a thud. He laughs, but the familiar rise of anger overpowers me.

'It's not funny!' I say sharply, turning away from him to retrieve the brush.

'No harm in constructive criticism.'

'Yes, well, I don't need it from *you*, Blake Hughes.'

This is Old Alice. Like a tight shoe I don't want to wear anymore. Suddenly I want to cry.

'Where's this come from, then?' he says, in a softer voice this time, climbing into the boat to sit next to me. I don't answer. 'Alice?'

'Sorry,' I say finally, not meeting his eyes. 'I was just… angry about something.'

'Right,' he says slowly, drawing out the sound. 'Come on, then.'

He gets to his feet and gestures for me to stand.

'You just need to hit something really hard,' he says. 'Here.'

He holds up the palm of his right hand.

'Try hitting my hand.'

I raise my eyebrow questioningly, and when he doesn't lower his hand, I clench my fist and throw a punch at it. It smacks against his hand, but he looks at me in a pitying way.

'Is that really the best you can do?' he asks.

'I have weak arms,' I huff.

'Well, if you ever get into a fight,' he says, 'you'll need to grab a weapon. Because your fists are like kitten paws.'

I frown at him, my eyes squinting in a scowl, but in the next moment, we both burst out laughing.

On the way home, I pick a lily and tuck it onto his cowboy hat.

'To say sorry for hitting you.'

'I think the sea breeze did more damage than you.'

'I'm a pacifist,' I reply, holding my head high in the air. Until he gives me a playful nudge on the shoulder.

'Only until I do this,' he says, dodging to avoid my return blow.

'I'll get you,' I threaten. 'Next time.'

The next part of life here that is instantly noticeable is music. In Whitecroft, we have dancing at various celebrations, and we sing our anthem, but in Cape, music is a constant accompaniment to everyday life. It's as regular as breathing. There's always someone beating a rhythm, and the singing is filled with joy and life.

Palmiro takes me to collect water from the well when he sees that I'm cleaning the boats.

'It's cleaner than seawater,' he points out. 'No salt.'

There are probably three other families there at the same time. A woman starts singing, and they all join in, with a sound richer than I've ever heard before. I listen, wishing I could sing like that.

'I'm sorry I have been busy,' he says. 'Do you want to walk to the hilltop later?'

I'm quite happy to go anywhere with him, and instead of finding it a tedious drudge to tramp up the hill, it's liberating. From the top, we look down over the sea, the boats, the huts and the forest. The sun is going down, and the air is cooler, the wind sweeping my hair from my face.

Palmiro sits on the ground and pats the spot next to him. He takes off his bag and pulls out some fruit.

'It will be a beautiful sunset,' he says. 'Each time it's a surprise that never gets old.'

In Cape, the past is a well-trodden ground, a heritage that is passed on through stories and conversations, whereas in Whitecroft, it's an abyss, a shapeless void. We are not allowed to speak of it. At first, I flinch when Palmiro starts talking about it. Gradually, my fascination overtakes my scruples.

'The first story we learn,' Palmiro tells me, 'is how we began.'

'You mean, when the spaceships landed?' I ask, keen to discover more.

'That is a different story,' Palmiro says. 'I mean, before the spaceships. When the world was young.'

In Whitecroft we never discussed philosophical questions. My father always said we had to focus on what we could see with our own eyes, and not waste time on speculation. Palmiro seems to thrive on the uncertainty of Before: before the spaceships, before the meteor, before there were people.

'We are all here for a purpose, you know,' he says. 'By the will of the Creator.'

'Who is the Creator?' I ask, confused.

'Don't you have the Book?' Palmiro asks.

'Which one?'

He reaches into his bag, then holds up a battered looking, black leather-bound volume, with yellowed pages.

'There is only one!' he exclaims. 'We are people of the Book.'

'What does that make us in Whitecroft?' I ask.

'You are people of the snow,' Palmiro grins. 'George told us a story of the snow once, and we passed it on so that the whole island would know it.'

'What is it?' I ask, aware that I'm sidetracking, but I have to hear this.

'I'll tell you,' he grins.

PALMIRO

George and the wolves in the snow

32

It was during what you call the Freeze. It was colder than it had ever been before in Whitecroft. The snow was deep, up to the windows of every house. If you tried to walk, every step was a struggle. Some days the wind blasted against you, so it was virtually impossible to move forwards. Daylight hours were short, and some days, no one wanted to get out of bed.

The most pressing need was for fuel. Each day some would brave the terrible conditions to gather wood, and it took three times longer than usual to find anything suitable. George would look for driftwood on the beach, and the snow was much lighter along the shore. George was worried about his friends who were much further away.

One day, George found a large piece of driftwood, and decided to build a sledge. He sanded and shaped it indoors, and the work helped to keep him warm. Then he bundled up a load of firewood, and bound it tightly onto the sledge.

George put on every layer of clothing he owned, wrapped his face up in a scarf, and drew a thick hat down over his forehead. He made loops in some pieces of rope and used them to pull the sledge. He went through the town, and then took the path out to the Farmlands.

Many times he wanted to stop, wanted to give up, but he couldn't shake the feeling that his friends needed him. He pressed on, by sheer will and determination. The path looked endless, but finally, he saw the shape of houses in the distance.

George staggered the last stretch of the journey, and called out to his friends. Soon faces started appearing at the windows. There was Avery, the best friend of George's father, and his granddaughter Elise, who was only about two years old.

George went into their house and warmed up by their fire. Avery gave him hot soup and Elise was excited to see someone new, after so long indoors. It was growing dark, and Avery encouraged George to stay the night.

As usual, darkness fell quickly. George was used to hearing the sound of the sea, and the forest was quiet in contrast. But in the middle of the night, George woke to hear the bloodcurdling howl of a wolf.

They were all sleeping in the main part of the house, where the fire was, and George stood up to creep over to the window. What he saw utterly astonished him.

A pack of wolves were sitting, encircling the small wooden cottage. They were large, with white streaks through their fur, and yellow eyes glowing in the darkness.

'George?' Avery whispered.

George beckoned to him, and he gave a low whistle when he looked through the window.

'They must have tracked your scent,' Avery said.

The wolves did not try to scratch at the cottage walls. They simply sat, in the silvery moonlight, and howled their strange song. George stayed awake long after Avery went back to bed. Elise slept through it all.

The next day, George unloaded the wood from his sledge and prepared to return. He felt an eerie sense of unease, but if he stayed any longer, he would become a burden to his friends. Avery was particularly grateful for the fuel, because chopping wood felt a lot more dangerous now there was a pack of wolves in the forest.

Waving goodbye to Avery and little Elise, George embarked on his journey. He was much faster without the load of wood, and some of the path was sloped downhill enough for him to push the sledge and jump on to ride it.

Just as he boarded the moving sledge, the wolves ran out from the trees on either side of him. Absolute terror gripped his heart. He used his feet to help increase the speed of the sledge, and was surrounded by these giant animals, running and keeping pace with him.

However, after a few minutes, with his pulse hammering like a woodpecker, George realised they were not trying to attack him. They were running and forming their pack around him, making him part of their group.

George did not slow down. Whistling along the track, far quicker than when he had journeyed along it yesterday, he could see the streets of Whitecroft ahead. Suddenly, the pack leader veered off to the side, and the whole group disappeared back into the forest.

Panting for breath, George dragged the sledge through the town and out to his cottage by the sea, where his family were glad to see him. They too were amazed at his story.

'Perhaps the wolves had already eaten,' his sister, Joy, suggested.

George told me he still, to this day, does not understand why the wolves did not attack him. But here we say that he was being protected. He had a special mission, and the wolves were sent to help him complete it.

ALICE

33

'Who sent the wolves?' I ask, confused.

Palmiro grins, brandishing his black Book.

'The Creator, of course!' he says. 'The One who made all things.'

I have so many questions, but the sun is setting and Palmiro wants us to walk up to a better vantage point to see it. He seems to sense that my thoughts are weighing heavily upon me, and doesn't talk much, allowing me to mull over and over again what he's told me.

George's story is incredible. I can't believe that I'm only hearing it for the first time now, and from someone who has never set foot in Whitecroft. The rule about never speaking about the past has robbed us of so many treasures. I feel a strange bereftness, mourning all the stories I never knew.

I can't get out of my head the image of Grandfather and Elise, stuck inside their cottage in the coldest Freeze, with snow piled high all around them. I had always felt that Elise had a much more idyllic childhood, but now I'm realising that things must have been much harder out there, away from the rest of the population. Much more isolated. I can't remember this Freeze as I would have been a similar age to Elise, but I never had to struggle for firewood. Whether I was with the Turners or my father, we always had the best of everything.

It doesn't seem plausible that the wolves didn't attack. But then, George isn't the type to exaggerate. He would have no reason to lie to Palmiro.

'Did you see your father today?' Palmiro asks.

I nod, looking down at my clasped hands.

'What did he say?'

'Nothing consequential,' I say. 'He told me not to clean the boats.'

'Well, that's easy to fix,' he says. 'I can take you to the food tent tomorrow.'

'I like cleaning,' I say.

'Sure, but I don't want to make your father angry,' he says. 'Come on, let's go and sit on that rock.'

Palmiro takes my hand to help me onto a flat, level rock, where we can sit and gaze at the sky's palette of red, orange and pink. I feel like the sunsets are more vivid here.

'Isn't it beautiful?' he says. 'You see why we believe in a Creator now?'

'I was never taught about that,' I tell him. 'We have no religion in Whitecroft.'

'Religion?' Palmiro makes a face. 'That sounds like a form of disease. We are people of Faith, not religion.'

'What's the difference?' I ask. For each statement he makes, I must ask him fifty more questions.

'Faith is trusting what you do not see. What you do not know. What you do not understand.'

'Like the wolves?'

'Like the wolves.' He grins, shining his white teeth at me. 'Come on, Alice. You can't tell me that you've never experienced something incredible, or out of the ordinary. You may not have been surrounded by wolves, but has there been a time when you were in danger, and you were kept safe? Where you cried out for help, and the Creator answered you?'

I look at him with wide eyes, remembering the boat. That moment when I was so terrified that I was going to drown, when my spirit cried out *Someone help me*. And I can't really explain how I knew how to get the rope, or how I managed to tie it as the boat was tipping so precariously. It was inexplicable.

Palmiro reads the answer in my expression.

'You see?' he says. 'Have faith.'

We stay there, until the red sky turns blue, and the first stars begin to shine. The coolness of evening weaves around us like a magic spell, and the birds make their last flights and songs before returning to their nests.

I think I'm beginning to understand.

34

The next day, I come through the door singing one of the island songs, and then falter when I see Viola crying at the table.

'What's wrong?' I ask, taking a step closer.

She shakes her head and wipes her nose with a handkerchief.

'Is it something I can help with?'

She shakes her head again, sniffing and wiping her eyes. I look around. There's a pot on the stove, bubbling with water, and some vegetables are set aside, ready for chopping. I pick up the knife and start slicing them, although I'm clumsy and nowhere near as efficient as the group I was working with today. I was supposed to help them, but they quickly realised how limited my experience was of cooking. Palmiro demonstrated how to prepare the food, standing closely behind me and intervening every time I made a mistake. Which was very often.

'What are you so happy about?' Viola asks. Still hasn't lost the sharp edge to her voice. 'I didn't know you could cook. Didn't you have your meals brought to you in Whitecroft?'

I blush.

'I've been learning.'

'Let me guess: with Palmiro.'

My face heats up even more. Viola scoffs and shakes her head at me.

'I suppose you think this is some kind of paradise.'

Using her hands, she gestures towards the view out of the window, where blue sky and sunshine are visible.

'Don't you think so?' I ask her.

After all, she was the one who decided to move to live here, not me.

Losing some of her angry energy, Viola looks out of the window and sighs.

'When I arrived, I was just like you,' she says. 'Everything was so wonderful. The sun, the heat, the food, the music… Whitecroft felt a million miles away.'

She turns back to me, and there are tears in her eyes.

'Now, everything's just… hard. I miss the rain. I miss my family. Whitecroft feels so far away, that I can never get it back again.'

'If you really want, you could go back,' I say, although secretly I doubt that my father would be very happy about that.

Even if Viola did return, what punishment might await her in Whitecroft for daring to leave?

'I just need to adjust,' she replies firmly. 'I can't go back.'

I say nothing, and tip the vegetables into the pot. I spoon out some spice from a jar, just like Palmiro did today. The strong fragrance starts to spread throughout the room.

'I told my family about you being here,' Viola says.

I'm amazed the radio actually works across the distance.

'What did they say?'

We look at each other, and suspicion hangs in the air between us. My stomach sinks at the thought of being blacklisted further, now that I've left with my father without the Council's permission. But Viola's not overly confident in her own position, as a rebel and an outlaw, either. Whatever we say could be repeated to others, and we'd rather they remained in the dark.

'I won't tell my father.' I break the silence.

'He doesn't seem too concerned with you these days, does he?' Viola remarks.

I blink. She looks a little repentant to have been so harsh.

'Sorry,' she adds.

'It's true,' I shrug.

'I wonder what he thinks about your little romance.'

'It's not a romance,' I deny, blushing.

Clearly it is.

Viola raises an eyebrow at me and then sighs.

'Alice, sit down a minute.'

I give the pot one last stir, and then sit next to her. She rubs her hands over her eyes, bridging her fingers over her nose and then drawing them down over her face.

'Have you ever considered that your relationship with Palmiro might be a little unwise?'

'That's a bit rich coming from the girl who ran away with Blake Hughes.'

'Your father is the General,' Viola raises her voice. 'He's Cayman's son. Do you not see a conflict of interests there?'

'As you said, my father isn't interested in what I do,' I say.

'If he knows you care for Palmiro, he could use it against you… against both of you.'

It's not as though I've never thought about this. Viola is right to consider what someone like my father can do with something that's meant to be pure, something that's actually mine. Something that brings me happiness.

'What am I supposed to do, pretend to hate him?'

I always come back to the same dilemma. It may be hasty, and it may be unorthodox, but what else am I meant to do?

'You could be a little more discreet,' Viola says. 'Blake and I kept our feelings hidden from everyone for months.'

'By lying to your family?' I ask.

She winces, but she's been dealing out hard truths to me.

'I didn't have a choice,' she says defensively. 'It was either stay in the Infirmary and face being cast with someone I didn't love, or leave and have a future.'

'You're not the only one who feels that way,' I say.

It's funny, I would never have admitted that back in Whitecroft. It took months before I was willing to admit that I didn't want to be cast with Phillip.

'You've got more chance of having the future you want if you're careful,' Viola advises. 'The whole island's going to be talking about you if you're not more guarded.'

I nod and go back to the broth, stirring it again. Viola starts preparing the table for dinner, and above the clattering of plates, I can hear a group singing not far from the window. Perhaps they are the field workers coming home. I wonder where Palmiro is now, and whether he's talking to his father about me.

The fact is, I've spent my life being guarded, and now it finally feels like the right time to let the walls down.

Maybe love is an act of faith.

35

Blake returns in time for dinner, and I don't miss the way he and Viola look at each other. It's tense. They must have argued, or something. The three of us sit at the table with bowls of stew, our spoons making the only sound.

'This is good,' Blake says, looking at Viola. 'Nice kick to it, a bit of island spice.'

'Alice made it,' she says flatly, rebuffing the compliment.

I wince. Blake clears his throat.

'A bunch of folks are going swimming later, down at the beach. You want to come?'

Viola pierces him with a fierce stare, like cold fire.

'No,' she says. 'I don't.'

They stare at each other, and I wish I could disappear. Suddenly, Viola stands, scraping her chair back from the table.

'I'm tired,' she says. 'I'm going to bed.'

I watch her leave, and Blake stares off into the distance, the food forgotten.

'Hey,' I say softly, holding my palm up. 'You want to hit something?'

He starts out of his trance, looks at my hand, and chuckles. He swipes my hand down with his own, and perhaps it was just meant to be a quick gesture, but his hand lingers on mine and suddenly my chest tightens.

'I would never hit you, Alice,' he says.

I can't breathe.

'That's too bad,' I breathe. 'I was looking forward to beating you up.'

He laughs, and we both focus on clearing up, although I can't help blushing every time he stands close to me or brushes my arm. I've just had a great day with Palmiro, and last night I watched the sunset with him, so why am I feeling giddy now? Blake belongs to Viola. He's a flirt, but it doesn't mean anything.

The next morning, Palmiro knocks on the door early, while Viola and Blake are still in bed. While part of me feels disappointed to break my usual routine of breakfast with Blake, maybe that's not such a bad thing. I need to spend less time around him before I do something stupid. Viola's caution about Palmiro pops up in my brain for about two seconds, and then he grins at me and I have to go with him; there's no other choice for me.

'I want you to meet my friend Riel,' he says, leading me through the shadow of the trees until we're in the exposed area of the shore. The sky has the milky hue of morning, the sun just risen and glowing on the water.

Like Palmiro, Riel is lean and muscular, with bronzed skin, but his eyes have a sharpness. He looks at me doubtfully, despite Palmiro's enthusiastic introduction, and then speaks mainly to Palmiro.

'Boat's ready.'

'Perfect,' Palmiro grins again.

Riel leads us down the wooden pier, and a small boat is tied up at the end of it. There are other people on the shore, sorting baskets of fish—they must have just returned.

I can already feel the warmth of the sun, and the water is a beautiful shade of aquamarine, but I peer nervously at the boat and look at Palmiro.

'You want me to go on this boat?'

'It's the best way to show you the island,' Palmiro says.

'Are you scared?' Riel asks.

'They were in a bad storm when they came over,' Palmiro tells him, then turns to me and gestures to the still horizon. 'No storms today!'

Riel jumps into the boat, and holds out his hand to me like a challenge. Trying not to shake, I take hold of it and step down into the small vessel.

Because it's so much smaller than the boat we sailed on from Whitecroft, it tips and wobbles much more as I stand in it, trying to regain my balance. Palmiro joins us, and guides me to sit on the wooden bench seat, as he grabs the oars to paddle while Riel steers the rudder and opens out the small sail.

'Don't worry,' Palmiro reassures me. 'We will stay close to the shore. No big waves.'

My heart hammering in my chest, I sit on my hands and try to breathe.

'In Cape,' Palmiro continues, 'we are all in boats from a very young age. We all swim and go fishing. It's our way of life.'

I think of what Blake said about going swimming tonight, and hope that I can go too. Then I feel guilty for thinking about him.

'Is it true that only George sailed in Whitecroft?' Riel asks me.

'His family were our fishers,' I explain, grateful for the distraction.

'You only had one boat?'

I wonder what rumours have spread over Cape, and what George himself has been saying.

'Yes,' I reply. 'Except… my father had another one. We sailed on that one to the smaller island.'

'I don't understand why more people in Whitecroft don't sail or have boats,' Riel says, more to Palmiro than to me.

'After my experience sailing here, I do,' I say, with a touch of impatience. 'Remember, where we are, it's cold. The water is icy and deadly. People don't swim. We focus on farming the land for our crops and the fishing helped, but it's not our main diet. If everyone left the fields to make boats and fish, then there wouldn't be enough bread.'

'My father told me that each family has their own trade in Whitecroft,' Palmiro says, in a soft tone, evidently trying to smooth my ruffled feathers.

'Yes,' I nod. 'Ten families, each with their own area of expertise. That's how it works.'

'So when George and his family left, you have no sailors,' Riel says.

'He did give some lessons to Leon and Arnold,' I say. 'Otherwise, we wouldn't have been able to get here.'

Although I personally wasn't signing up for another voyage with the Crests at the helm.

Riel looks at Palmiro.

'So it's true then: they need George back.'

'Or someone else who can train others to sail,' Palmiro says, pointedly.

'The General wants you,' Riel says. 'But that may be for more than just sailing. Your father is our leader.'

'That's why I need you to volunteer,' Palmiro says.

For once, his characteristic grin is absent. He looks at Riel seriously. Riel holds his stare.

'I need to know more,' he says.

'Here is the perfect opportunity.' Palmiro holds out his hand, pointing towards me. 'We are on the water now where no one can hear us. Ask her what you want to know.'

I had begun to relax, as the movement of the boat was clearly nothing like the jolting seesaw it had been in the storm, but now

I'm on edge again. Palmiro clearly wants Riel to go instead of him, and I selfishly want that too, but I can't be dishonest and paint Whitecroft differently to what it is. If Riel knows the truth, will he still want to go?

'Your father,' Riel begins. He's very direct. 'What's he really like?'

If we were in Whitecroft, I would smile and give the mild answer expected of me. I might even gush with praise. But I look into Riel's hardened eyes, and I know that's not going to wash. I take a deep breath, and I tell the truth.

'My father is obsessed with power. He runs—or he used to run—Whitecroft with tight control, and many rules.'

'What do you mean, "used to run"?' Riel picks up on my phrase immediately.

'Recently, some things came to light that had been hidden.' I can feel myself blushing. 'My father was removed from the Council.'

'So he's not your leader anymore?' Riel asks, and Palmiro looks equally shocked.

'When did this happen?' Palmiro asks.

'Just after the Swifts left,' I tell them.

'He never told you anything?' Riel checks with Palmiro, who shakes his head. 'This makes things interesting.'

'What do you think it means?' Palmiro asks.

Riel looks out to the horizon, and then replies,

'He came here as soon as he could, before we find out the truth.'

'I think he planned this a long time ago,' I say, and both turn to look at me. 'I know my father. He plans everything in minute detail. He doesn't mind waiting for fifty years.'

'What do you mean?' Riel asks.

'When George and the others left, they planned it all in secret,' I tell them. 'I found out about it.'

I blush as I remember giving Elise an ultimatum to go on the boat. It didn't work as I had anticipated.

'But my father said that he knew about it all along. He didn't stop them because he wanted them to leave, so he could travel here and then…'

'Take Palmiro back with him,' Riel finished.

Palmiro looks at me with concern.

'Why does your father want me?'

'Leverage,' Riel answers, before I can open my mouth.

'So this isn't just about sailing,' Palmiro says.

'Exactly. Which is why if I volunteer…'

'It puts him in an impossible position. He won't be able to refuse you because you would meet his demand for a trained sailor,' Palmiro says, excitedly.

Riel doesn't look impressed.

'No, it just means he won't take me.'

'He'll have to,' Palmiro insists.

'I don't want to go blind into a strange land where a deposed leader wants to use me to start a war!' Riel raises his voice.

Instinctively I look around, but of course, there's no one. Just the waves, coolly lapping, in contrast to this fraught conversation.

'He may not want war,' I say, although I don't have much confidence this is true. 'He may see it as an opportunity to earn his way back onto the Council, if he replaces the sailors we lost.'

'No offence, but I don't care enough about Whitecroft to risk my life training your people to sail,' Riel says bluntly. 'Your whole system should have protections in place so that if you lose one family, your whole trade doesn't collapse. Cape has got enough problems—'

'Riel,' Palmiro says, in a sharper tone than I've heard him use before. Riel stops abruptly.

'Problems?' I echo. 'What problems?'

Riel looks at Palmiro for permission to speak. After a long pause, Palmiro sighs and explains,

'The climate here is very difficult for farming. We have the sea, but the other side of the mountain turns into desert. As our people grow, we are running out of space.'

'What did your father tell you about us?' Riel asks me.

Palmiro has stopped rowing, and we're drifting along with a gentle breeze. I look at them and think how I didn't even know they existed a year ago.

'Nothing,' I admit.

'Nothing?' Riel repeats. His fists clench and his face reddens.

'Calm down,' Palmiro tells him. 'Remember George used to sail to meet us. He was part of a Pact of people in Whitecroft who did know about Cape.'

'How many people live in Whitecroft?' Riel asks me.

'About a hundred,' I answer.

'How many are in the Pact?'

I look at Palmiro, who shrugs.

'Ten? Fifteen?' he suggests.

'Well, six of them are now living here,' Riel points out.

'I met two new members, at the last meeting,' Palmiro says, then gives me a grin. 'You know Elise, from George's story?'

I can't return his smile.

'But your elders, they must all know about us?' Riel returns to his interrogation.

'They were forbidden to speak of you,' I say. 'And the past. No one speaks of the past in Whitecroft.'

'They do not have the Book, and they do not have the Stories,' Palmiro says to Riel.

'They don't know the Story of the Nations?' Riel looks appalled.

'Could you tell it to me?' I ask, and try a tentative smile. 'Please?'

Palmiro grins and leans back against the side of the boat.

'You'll enjoy this one,' he says.

RIEL

The Story of the Nations

36

Once, when the world was wide and full of people, disaster came. A meteor was going to strike the planet. Some said it was the judgement of the Creator for the evil of mankind. Others said it was a sign that the End was near.

Two airships were built, and launched, from different parts of the world. They were both funded from the same source, and built to the same specification. A selection of people were chosen to go on board, representing different fields of expertise. One requirement was that they all had to speak the same language, across the two airships, for communication.

It was a dark time. Those on board had said goodbye to the world and people they loved, and had to travel a safe distance from the impending disaster. Afterwards, they voyaged above the Earth and were shocked at the impact. The shape of the planet had changed, and with this, its climate. Ice now spread across vast regions, and desert. They did not believe it was habitable.

On board the airships, people started families. Life continued, but the provisions on board were soon running dangerously low. It became inevitable that the ships had to land. Of all the planets, Earth was still the only viable option for life. The ships voyaged closer to the surface, this time searching more carefully for the ideal place to land and rebuild society.

One ship favoured a northern region, where close to the sea, the snow was not there all year round. The other ship favoured an island in a warmer climate.

Each group tried to persuade the other to choose their preferred destination. In the end, the two ships landed separately, with the agreement that on the Day of Unity, the two nations would meet together.

When the Day arrived, the people of Cape waited eagerly, but the people of Whitecroft never came. The radio equipment from the airships never received any communication.

Those early years were hard. The land was inhospitable. It was a struggle for survival. If the two ships had landed together, they would have been able to help each other and thrive sooner. As it was, both nations struggled on apart.

Finally, a group from Whitecroft made contact, and sailed to a meeting point island in secret to meet with the leaders of Cape. Over the years, friendships were built, and information was shared. Each nation developed their own way of life in this strange new world. But when nations come together, the world can be wider, bigger and stronger, and more joyful than anyone could imagine.

ALICE

37

'That's the end of the story?' I ask, appreciating the profound note, but unsatisfied at the lack of resolution.

Palmiro laughs.

'*You* are the end of the story. For whatever motives your father has, Whitecroft has finally come to Cape. Which means that even if he does not want unity, it is still possible with those who believe in it.'

'I envy your optimism,' Riel says darkly, picking up the oars and starting to row.

I look back towards the changing landscape of Cape behind us. As we move around it, there are some steep cliffs, and gulls fly back and forth over our heads, diving to the water's surface. The visible land seems covered in shrub. I realise I've never seen Whitecroft properly from the water, or travelled north from it either.

'You like this boat ride?' Palmiro asks with a smile.

'It's definitely much smoother than the last one,' I smile back. 'I was just thinking I'd like to do a boat trip like this around Whitecroft. It would look so different from this angle.'

'Didn't you see it when you left to come here?' Riel asks.

'We left at night,' I reply. 'And to be honest, I was too terrified to look at the scenery.'

'I don't understand why you don't all travel around in boats more,' Riel says.

'There's only one boat, and it's only used by the fishermen.'

'Tell us more,' Palmiro invites me. 'Tell us everything about Whitecroft.'

And so I begin. I describe the Square, with the Town Hall, the School and our simple houses. I picture the sky with its heavy greyness at this time of year, contrasting with the bright colours of the leaves falling from the trees. With a smile at Palmiro, remembering George's story, I tell them about the Freeze, when the snow lasts for months, until finally the Thaw breaks through.

'Out in the Farmlands, where my grandfather lives…' I break off suddenly, feeling an unexpected clogging in my throat. 'We sow the fields and then bring in the Harvest. There's a river, and you can hear all the different bird calls in the woods.'

There's a literal ache in my chest as I speak of it, and I realise that I miss being there, with my grandfather, hidden away from the rest of the world. But then I remember my father walking into his cottage, casting a shadow over the pleasant memory. As long as my father is around, he will cast an iron-grey shadow over my life.

'I want to hear more about Cape,' I say, brushing dark thoughts aside.

We spend an hour exchanging stories about our different lands and customs, and everything I learn about Cape only whets my appetite more to fully explore it, and discover it all for myself.

'We will have our weekly celebration tonight,' Palmiro tells me. 'Would you like to join in?'

Is this linked to the swimming? Why do I care so much about seeing Blake? Palmiro's the one I should focus on.

'Sure,' I agree.

The celebration takes place on the beach. In the last golden hour of sunshine, everyone swims and plays in the ocean. I watch longingly until Palmiro takes my hand and leads me into the water. It feels warm, and the pull of the tide is a strange sensation.

'Try jumping the waves,' he says.

Soon I get used to the regular crashing of the white foam, and jump and splash with Palmiro. I keep my dress on, but he removes his shirt, and I watch the water glisten on his skin. He's just... beautiful. No other word for it.

Gradually, we move further out into the water, until it reaches my waist.

'Now try kicking off the bottom,' he says, 'and use your hands to paddle.'

It feels so alien to me, to stretch out in the water, and as soon as I dip my head under, I hurry to right my feet on the sand and come up spluttering.

'It's all right,' Palmiro laughs. 'You can breathe out underwater, then come up for air.'

He shows me, and makes me practise.

'I'm so scared of drowning,' I tell him, wiping my face.

'Learning to swim is the best way not to drown,' he points out.

He tells me to stretch out again, and supports me, telling me to kick my legs. I splash water all over him, and by the time I stand up again, we're both shrieking and laughing.

'Now you have to practise being still,' he says. 'This time, stretch out your arms and legs, like a starfish. See how long you can float.'

His hands on my back to support me, he helps me to get into the right position, and then takes his hands away. I manage a few seconds before I'm going under, and I splutter and stand up.

'We need to get back to shore,' he says.

Everyone else is getting out of the water, and as I wade back to the beach, feeling my dress clinging to me, and my hair dripping down my shoulders, I spot Blake. He's at the edge of the water, his shirt off like the other men, his hair wet. I feel the strangest urge to run my fingers through it.

Suddenly, he looks straight at me, like he knew I was there all along. His eyes travel down my body, then back up to my eyes again. We must be fifty feet apart, but an unmistakable heat burns between us.

'Alice, this way,' Palmiro says, taking my hand.

I allow him to lead me to the shore, and I avoid looking at Blake. I allow my heartbeat to settle back to normal.

It's sunset, and everyone gathers around a large fire, passing around food. Then Cayman calls for our attention.

'It is time to give thanks to our Creator for the blessings we have enjoyed this week.'

Cayman lifts his hands, and everyone copies him. Then all at once, everyone starts speaking at the same time. Startled, I look round and tune in to Palmiro's voice.

'Thank You for the sunset. Thank You for Alice.'

He looks at me and smiles as he says it, and I feel my cheeks turning red, but I smile back at him.

The noise of everyone's voices continues for a few minutes longer, until Cayman begins singing. Then, everyone joins in. It's an upbeat, joyful song of gratitude. The song seems to go through all the things to be thankful for. There are many verses and it seems endless, so much longer than our songs in Whitecroft. But everyone is clapping, and smiling, and so I join in too, as much as I can without really knowing the words. At one point, I catch Blake's eye. He seems to be watching rather than joining in, but he smiles at me.

Finally, when the song is over, Cayman calls up a woman to read from the Book. Although she looks nothing like her, she reminds me of Cressida. The sort of woman who speaks with authority and looks after everyone.

It's a story about two sisters who love the same man. He loves one of them, but not the other. One of them is chosen and special, the other is rejected. It's funny, because I know it's just a coincidence, but it feels a lot like Elise and me. William chose her. I clearly didn't feel anything that strong for William, apart from wanting him to want me, because I never felt as happy in William's company as I do with Palmiro, or even Blake.

I need to stop thinking about Blake.

Then Salomon, an older man, talks to everyone about the story. He speaks of the Creator's love, and how none of us have to be unloved and rejected. I get confused when he talks about another story, this time about a Son who is chosen and special, but I don't really understand the connection. Maybe I should ask Palmiro later to explain.

Anyway, there is more singing, then bread and wine are passed around, and by this point the sky is dark and stars are visible. The fire burns bright, along with other smaller blazes around the shore. The music starts up again, and people start dancing. Our dances in Whitecroft are taught to us in School. There's an exact number of steps and we all do the same thing at the same time. Here, the dancing is much freer. It doesn't look prepared, and everyone is smiling and laughing and clapping along.

'You have dancing like this in Whitecroft?' Palmiro asks, handing me another drink.

'Not like this.' I shake my head. 'This is brilliant.'

'You want me to teach you?'

He stands up and offers me his hand.

My face redder than the fire, I take it and follow him into the edge of the circle.

'Now you just move in time to the music,' Palmiro says, dipping his shoulders and bending his knees.

I copy him awkwardly, but my legs feel wooden and stiff.

'Loosen your hands so they aren't just at your side,' Palmiro instructs.

I try to swing my hands more, but I can feel how ungraceful and out of sync my movements are. Palmiro winces.

'Drop your shoulders. Lean with your right, then with your left.'

He places his hands on my shoulders and moves me in time to the music. I try to continue the movement.

'Now stop frowning and smile!' he says. 'This is supposed to be fun.'

I stop moving and raise an eyebrow at him.

'You're forgetting this is my first time. You make it look easy.'

'It is easy!' he says, moving from side to side with poise and rhythm. I long to move as smoothly and naturally as he does.

'You're over thinking it,' Palmiro says. 'Just let go!'

I laugh as he over exaggerates his movements, trying to get me to copy. I do, half-heartedly. He valiantly continues, even though I know I'm rubbish, and manages to make me smile. Then his expression changes, and he stops moving. I turn to look over my shoulder, and I see my father walking towards us with a face like thunder.

38

'What do you think you are doing?' my father says, his tone clipped and cold.

'Palmiro was teaching me the dance,' I answer, trying not to blush and failing.

Father casts a disdainful look at him.

'You call this dancing?' he sneers. 'Get over here now. I need to speak with you.'

I'm too embarrassed to meet Palmiro's eyes. My head down, I follow my father out, beyond the lanterns, to a deserted section of the sand. The wind is sharper here and makes me shiver.

'Have you lost your mind?' Father explodes. 'We've only been here a few days and you are eating with them, dressing like them, and I hear you even attended their worship.'

'I thought that's why we were here?' I ask in confusion. 'To find out more about their culture?'

'Culture!' my father gives a caustic laugh. 'You call this culture? Have I taught you nothing? All the books they could have saved, and they save that one. Don't believe a word of what they tell you. They are ignorant, delusional, and everything I've learned in the past few days has confirmed that this island is on the brink of disaster because of poor management and leadership.'

'No,' I say, before I realise what I'm doing.

My father gapes at me in shock.

'What did you say?'

'You're wrong,' I say, flushing and terrified but I have to speak. 'These people are kind and welcoming. If there's going to be a disaster, it's because we betrayed them. And yet, they've not held that against us. They could have left us on the meeting point island, but they chose to help us. We owe them our lives.'

'Don't be ridiculous,' Father snorts. 'How dare you suggest that we *betrayed* them! You know *nothing* of the past fifty years.'

'Because you won't let us speak of the past!'

'I will not be interrupted by you.' He glares at me. 'I would have thought my own daughter would trust me. Where is your loyalty to me? To Whitecroft? To your own people?'

I think my blush has now been drained out of my cheeks, to leave me a deathly shade of pale.

'I have always been loyal to you, Father,' I say, tears starting in my eyes. 'And I love Whitecroft.'

He assesses me with his hard stare before responding.

'Don't forget it,' he says sharply. 'You're a naïve, young girl, Alice. You don't understand what is at stake here. By all means be polite and courteous to these people, but do not make the mistake of trusting them. They may seem honest and gentle, but they have their own weapons.'

'What do you mean?' I ask.

'Have you seen how many boats they have here?' He gestures to the dock. 'It's a fleet. Enough for them all to abandon this desert island and appear on our shores, demanding that we feed them and look after them because they could not manage to care for themselves.'

'They don't want to leave Cape,' I argue, but the seed of doubt is planted in my mind. After all, Palmiro had said that he really wanted to see Whitecroft. Father was right, there *were* a lot of boats.

'If they do, we'll be ready for them.' My father spoke more to himself than to me, looking out over the black sea. The waves crashed and I shivered again. The moon was a more diminished crescent tonight, so it felt like everywhere was shrouded in shadows.

'I want you to persuade your little friend Palmiro to come back to Whitecroft with us,' Father says.

Us? So I'm not staying on the island?

'Palmiro?' I echo, stupidly.

'Yes. He's a talented sailor,' Father says. 'We need someone skilled who can train our people to take the boat out like George used to, before he betrayed us.'

My thoughts rage as I debate internally whether to clarify if I am definitely accompanying them home to Whitecroft, because as far as my father is concerned, I never knew anything different. But this has a crucial impact on whether I talk to Palmiro about going to Whitecroft. If I persuade him to go, and then Father leaves me behind, I will have lost my only friend, and more importantly, potentially led him straight into a trap. Father could hold him hostage and make demands of Cayman. What would the Council be able to do to stop him?

If I don't persuade Palmiro, Father probably won't trust me enough to leave me here on Cape without his watchful presence. Father will be convinced of my disloyalty to Whitecroft, and haul me away. Whitecroft without Palmiro is a miserable prospect for me.

Yet again, my father has manoeuvred the chess board so I'm in a lose-lose position. Checkmate.

39

Father doesn't let me go back to Palmiro; instead, he orders Arnold to accompany me back to Viola's. Annoyed, Arnold strides ahead of me, turning around to glare at me and check I'm still following at every corner. I scowl back. I've got no reason to show deference to Arnold.

Still, it would be good to try to goad him into giving me some information.

'Have you been around the island?' I ask. 'Or stuck on the beach?'

He gives me a suspicious look.

'I've seen enough,' he says.

'Enough of what?'

'An island's an island.'

He shrugs and walks on. I try to match his pace.

'Have you been sailing?'

He doesn't answer.

'I suppose you wouldn't want to, after being so scared in the storm.'

'I wasn't scared,' he snaps. 'They said I was very competent. I've got some advanced training tomorrow. From your friend *Palmiro.*'

He sneers over his name, and I try to keep my expression neutral.

'Great, perhaps you'll be better equipped to deal with the next storm, then.'

'Shut your mouth.' He whirls around, and for a moment I think he's going to hit me. I try not to flinch and simply blink. 'It would have been good if a big enough wave had come along and swept you away so you weren't weighing us down.'

Perhaps that's what my father wanted.

We're outside Viola and Blake's house now, and their voices carry through the thin walls. Blake must have left when the dancing began.

'What are we supposed to do if he leaves her here? She can't live with us forever.'

Viola. My heart sinks.

'She's been no trouble,' Blake says.

'She may be persuaded to join the Pact.'

Is that George?

'Just because she has a crush on Palmiro doesn't mean she's suddenly on our side.'

Ouch. Viola doesn't pull her punches.

'You should listen to yourself sometimes,' Blake says, angrily.

Arnold rolls his eyes.

'It must be sad for you to hear how no one wants you.'

He knocks loudly at the door, grins savagely at my burning shame, and then walks away. I angrily blink back tears and throw all my weight into opening the door, but someone opens it at the same time, so I stumble through it and into the house. Just before I fall on my face, strong arms catch me and pull me upright. I look up into Blake's eyes, my breath catching in my throat, and he reads my expression, his grip tightening around me. I still can't breathe, not when he's holding me and I'm hypnotised by his proximity, and now the fierceness in his eyes has changed to something darker, more primal… Desire.

I jump back from his hold, breaking the spell, and become aware of how the conversation has stopped abruptly. Viola is at the table with George and Joy Swift. I straighten up, brushing down my skirt.

'Looks like I arrived just in time to hear you talk about me behind my back,' I say, hoping my voice stays steady.

I look mainly at Viola, until she sighs and throws up her hands.

'Yes, we were talking about you,' she admits. 'I'm sorry if you feel it's behind your back. We're just trying to work out what to do. We never expected this all to happen.'

'A year ago, if you'd told me a group of people were going to leave Whitecroft for ever, I wouldn't have believed it either,' I say pointedly.

George clears his throat. He's in his forties, with short grey hair, but a strong, muscular frame. He's missing his left forearm—I never knew why. His eyes, a sparkling blue, assess me, although not in an unkind way.

'Is that how you view us, Alice: as rebels who deserve punishment?'

I look away.

'Why are you here, Alice?' George asks.

His question sounds genuine. Viola and Blake are staring at me with guarded expressions, flavoured with dislike. Joy, striking with her long, red hair, examines me too, but looks less hostile.

I waver. What do I tell them? The truth? Would they even believe me?

'Why don't you sit down?'

Joy indicates to an empty chair, next to her at the table. It makes me feel surprisingly emotional. Not many people invite me to sit at their table with them, and I've been in a lot of houses. I take the seat.

'I went to stay with my grandfather for the Freeze,' I begin. 'I don't know if you know, but I haven't been living with my father… for a while now. He came to the house with Leon and Arnold, and told me I had to come with them to this island. He wanted me to be there so it looked as though he was coming peacefully, to help negotiations.'

'Why didn't you refuse?' Viola asks, skeptically.

I fix my gaze on her.

'My father doesn't take no for an answer.'

There's a long pause.

'What's your father trying to negotiate?' Joy asks.

'He wants Palmiro to come back to Whitecroft with him to teach others to sail. But I think he may want to use him as leverage because he's Cayman's son.'

'You must be happy if Palmiro goes home with you,' Viola comments, raising her eyebrows.

'Not if my father leaves me behind,' I shoot back.

'An exchange,' George exhales.

'You don't have to look so horrified,' I direct at Viola. 'I'm sure I can find somewhere else to live so that I'm not in your way.'

Feeling tears spill out onto my cheeks, I stand hurriedly to leave, but Joy lays her hand on my arm.

'Alice, don't go,' she says kindly.

I stand there, my chest heaving with a sob.

'I don't want to stay where I'm not wanted,' I cry. 'Only, that's everywhere.'

Joy stands and wraps her arms around me, drawing me against her while I continue to sob. There's no stopping these tears now.

'I'll make some drinks,' Blake says.

I can hear the clattering of cups behind me, and try to control my ragged breathing.

'Why don't you sit down again?' Joy says.

I sink back into the chair, sniffing. She passes me a handkerchief.

'Does Palmiro know what the General wants?' George asks me.

I nod, wiping my wet face.

'He wants his friend Riel to go instead. We were going to try to persuade my father, but now I think my father will punish me if Palmiro doesn't go.'

'Here you go.'

Blake places a warm drink in front of me. I sip it gratefully.

'I'm going to attend a meeting tomorrow with your father and Cayman,' George says. 'They won't let you attend, but we could find a place for you to hide and listen in.'

'At the caves?' Blake asks.

George nods.

'I can take you there, but it'll have to be early,' Blake tells me. 'It'll be a long time, waiting on your own.'

'I'll go too,' Viola says.

Joy smiles at her. I look at her in surprise.

'That is, if you want me to,' she adds, with a shrug.

I nod, thankful that I won't be alone. I'm not sure I'm going to hear anything good.

40

It's warm even when it's early here. Blake leads Viola and me to some shadowy caves, around the corner from the main beach, where apparently this important meeting will happen later this morning. As Viola and I settle into the dark and dank viewpoint, I'm grateful for the coolness. The short walk has made me sweat.

I'm nervous about all this time with Viola. She fusses about and spreads out a blanket to sit on. I hope she's not going to hold this long wait against me.

'Alice,' she says, breaking the silence. 'Are you sure about Palmiro?'

'What do you mean?' I ask defensively.

'Well, you haven't known him very long.'

'And?'

She sighs.

'Never mind.'

'I took what you said on board about being careful,' I say, 'but this is my first chance to actually find someone who feels the same way about me as I do about them.'

'That's what worries me,' Viola replies. 'I'm sure Palmiro's not going to be the only one who could ever love you. Wouldn't it be easier to find someone back in Whitecroft?'

'Like who? I've been cast once already and that didn't work.'

'If you stay with Palmiro,' she says, 'will you stay on the island?'

'I don't know,' I answer, 'but I do prefer it out here. I feel... different.'

'It's nice to know that you can do what you want without your whole family arguing and lecturing you about your duty,' Viola says.

'They wanted you to stay in Whitecroft,' I say. I remember Viola's parents sobbing in the Square when they realised she had gone.

'I wouldn't mind Whitecroft so much if it wasn't for how restricted everything was,' Viola says. 'I mean, I like it as a place. I like the people. I love my family. But the family trade is so inflexible, and the casting system… I just had to leave.'

'The family trade is slowly starting to change,' I say. 'Blake was apprenticed to Edmund Turner. Phillip Stead's sister wants to go into the Infirmary.'

'Really?' Viola looks surprised. 'Well, that makes me feel less bad for abandoning them.'

'I can't see the casting system changing, though,' I confess. 'There seem to be so many happy couples.'

'But they could still be happy without the casting,' Viola argues. 'Elise and William, for example.'

I pull a face. The less I can think about them, the better.

'Did you like William?' Viola asks, noticing my expression.

I shrug.

'He was better than anyone else,' I reply. 'But he wasn't interested in me.'

Viola is quiet for a moment.

'I think he's a bit too serious for you,' she says. 'He wouldn't make you light up.'

I smile, but it feels slightly hollow. I don't even know why.

Viola tells me more about what she's seen in Cape, and what the people are like, until we hear the noise of people approaching. We shrink back and hide as Cayman, my father, George and a few other islanders sit together on some rocks, not far from the cave entrance.

'I came here because we lost our sailors,' my father says. 'If George will not return, we need experienced men who can train our people to sail and to fish.'

'Riel, one of our best sailors, is willing to go to Whitecroft,' Cayman says.

'I am willing to leave my daughter, Alice, here, as a sign of trust and pledge to you that I mean no harm,' my father continues. 'But seeing as she is my only daughter, why don't you send Palmiro, your son? It seems a more proper exchange.'

'Palmiro expressed reservations about going,' Cayman replies carefully. 'One of which is that he is enjoying his friendship with your daughter. Are you trying to separate them?'

'Not at all,' my father says smoothly. 'If they are keen to be reunited, it means he will teach us in the most efficient way, so that he can return swiftly. A good motivation, I feel.'

'A union between our children would be the perfect way to promote wider unity,' Cayman says, and I blush. I can feel Viola staring at me for my reaction.

'Exactly,' my father lies.

I am certain that he would not permit it.

'Why don't we allow Palmiro to stay here and continue to court your daughter?' Cayman suggests. 'When Riel has completed his task, you can come back here with him, and they can be—how do you say it?—*pledged* to one another.'

I can't see my father's face, but I can imagine he isn't hiding his feelings very skilfully. The idea of that probably fills him with revulsion.

'I must admit the journey was very challenging,' Father says. 'I do not think I shall attempt it again. You would have to send

Palmiro to Whitecroft with Alice—after all, we have ceremonies and customs that need to be completed for pledging.'

He's happy to use me as an excuse to lure Palmiro to Whitecroft. I feel sick at the thought of Palmiro suffering there because of me.

'That seems reasonable,' Cayman says, in a level tone. 'However, I must insist upon regular communication. You have the radio devices from the airship?'

'Yes,' Father says. He's lying again. Gus Taylor has one of the radios, and Viola brought the other one over to Cape. I did hear him mention that Tobias Stead could make another one, and given that he'd hidden a spare boat in the Infirmary, I wouldn't be too surprised if he had other sources. Still. Cayman must know that he's lying, but he doesn't openly challenge him.

'Perhaps we could send some test messages over,' Cayman says mildly.

'As you wish,' Father says, rather gruffly. 'Of course, I won't know if they've been received until I return…'

'Well, if they are in working order, we should be able to receive the responses,' Cayman points out.

'If they are in working order.'

Suddenly George's voice breaks into the conversation. His meaning is clear: he doesn't believe my father either.

'I think I have a better knowledge of what is working in Whitecroft than you do,' my father replies, in an acidic tone.

'Is that all you have to say to me?' George raises his voice. 'Did you not think to question why a group of six people risked their lives to leave Whitecroft, rather than stay there while you were in charge?'

'Some people always want to question everything,' Father replies. 'They can never be happy to just play their part and be satisfied. They want more. In your case, you wanted to use your boat for more than just the fishing it was intended for.'

'The people of Cape live on an island. They all have boats. It's accepted here.'

'And what happens if all those boats arrive at Whitecroft one day? If everyone in Cape decides they'd like to try living in a cooler climate with better farmland?'

'I think it highly unlikely that our people will want to move to Whitecroft,' Cayman says.

'At first, it will just be Riel and Palmiro,' my father continues, 'but it won't be long before another group arrive, and then another.'

'You were the one who wanted Palmiro to come to Whitecroft,' Cayman points out. 'Anyway, we are losing track here. Why don't we send Riel, Palmiro and a few other sailors back to Whitecroft with you, and Alice? You can run the ceremonies as is your custom. Then they can sail back here to visit us.'

'Is Palmiro willing to come?' my father asks, skeptically. 'And is he willing to take vows and pledge to Alice when he's only known her for such a short time?'

'I will talk to him,' Cayman says. 'We will give you an answer by sunset.'

I feel my heart sink. My entire future depends on his decision.

ELISE

41

It's another cloudy day when I walk back to the Farmlands.

I haven't seen blue sky for at least a week. I've cleaned up the Swifts' cottage and packed my things into a small bag, and I've said goodbye to Ada. The next time I see her will be when they return, and I hope it won't be much longer. But I couldn't stay away from Grandfather any longer, especially when the first snow is due.

I've driven myself mad with considering all the different possibilities of what's happened to Will. Now, I'm just trying to focus on what's immediately in front of me. The familiar, dusty path with crows cawing overhead. The trees, looking barer than when I travelled down this road with Will. That wasn't even a full fortnight ago, yet it feels like forever. The season is on the brink of changing, and I can feel the sting of cold in the air. The Freeze is coming.

Weighed down with the heaviness of the unknown, I can't face going to our little cottage in Pembridge. It's just too raw that Will isn't there with me. I turn towards Grandfather's house, and although it feels like a regression to be going there now I've left, the thought of his presence overcomes that scruple. I remember the first time I walked inside after being pledged, and Alice was there. Even now, my stomach curls to recall how it felt to see her cloak on the hook, bread that she baked on the table, and the way she stood in my kitchen. Replaced.

I know it's wrong to begrudge it to her, because I'm pledged now and she isn't, but I can't control my immediate responses. It's just... instinct.

I wonder if Alice and my father will sail back to the meeting point island, and arrive there to find Will, Charles and Edward. Surely they wouldn't have a problem with them recovering George's boat? If they all sailed back together, then we'd have two boats in Whitecroft.

The uncomfortable truth is that they should have returned by now.

Will and I once went to the meeting point island, sailing in the night, stayed there for a few hours, and then were back by lunchtime the next day. Admittedly, George and Joy were sailing, and they're experienced sailors. And I suppose I need to factor in that Will and Charles were going there in his canoe. They had tested it out in short stints, but never that kind of distance before...

But even if it took them twice as long to arrive on the island, and to return, they should still be back by now. Unless something happened to them...

No. I have to stop thinking about this.

The uncertainty is like a fizzing in my veins; it's infected my whole bloodstream. I feel constantly on edge. My stomach churns with every 'what if'.

By the time I arrive at Grandfather's cottage, my cheeks have flared up with exertion and cold air, and my eyes must be wild, let alone my hair. I push open the door and step into the quiet, and Grandfather turns from building the fire. For a moment's pause, we stare at one another. His eyes are blank for an alarming time before recognition kicks in. In that split second before, I'm shocked at how old he looks. He's somehow greyer and paler, like the colour has drained out of him. He shuffles towards me.

I'm there, breathing all the chaos and turbulence of my life, and he looks on the verge of death.

We hug, and I hold him more tightly than usual. His thin frame feels more fragile.

'Are you well?' I ask him anxiously.

'Don't worry about me,' he says.

He doesn't ask about Will. At first, I assume that's because he's being sensitive and doesn't want to upset me. But as we fall back into our old routines, I start to wonder if he's forgotten that I'm pledged now and that I don't live here anymore. Well, it's preferable staying with him to going back to my cold house. And the way he looks, I don't want to leave him.

I keep busy. After all, there's wood to be chopped and broth to be cooked, and life doesn't allow you to stand still and mope. The fizzing anxiety froths into a ball of panic that rises in my throat like bile with each day that passes. I'm actually sick once or twice, that's how strong my fear is.

Grandfather is definitely ill. One day, he just doesn't get out of bed. The next morning, I feel awful too, and I'm worried that I've caught it, but we need fuel for the fire so I force myself to get up. I stagger outside and barely manage to chop a few pieces of wood. Cressida sees me and marches over.

'What's the matter?' she asks, her eyes assessing me keenly.

'Grandfather's sick,' I tell her. 'I'm just a bit tired.'

'You look pale,' she says, frowning. 'Go back inside. I've got a big basket of wood I'll bring over for you, along with some stew. I'm going to Whitecroft to see if there's any news about Blake.'

Cressida fusses over us, sorting out the fire and giving us some food. She takes Grandfather a bowl into his bedroom and comes to see me afterwards.

'He's not looking too good,' she admits.

'Is there anything I can do?'

She shakes her head.

'He's been through a lot out here,' she says. 'Now that you've got Will to look after you, his body might be ready to let go. He's done a lot of fighting and maybe he wants to rest now.'

'I don't want him to die,' I blink, my eyes filling with tears. 'And Will's not even come back yet.'

'Don't worry about Will,' Cressida says. 'I have no doubt they'll be back. The sea's tricky. If it looks dicey, they won't risk it, because they're not experienced sailors. Just be patient. You need to look after yourself.'

I feel better for seeing her, but when I check on Grandfather, he seems to be sleeping throughout the whole day. That afternoon, I stand outside, drinking in the fresh air and staring at the clouds overhead. They are beautifully textured in powdery pockets of grey, but with a looming, dark, purple-coloured mass on the horizon. I'm not standing there long, but I feel the first drops of rain, and the thundery cloud has already taken over more of the sky. There's a storm coming.

42

When it hits, the rain is like a monsoon.

I station myself by the fire, adding more logs when needed, but I feel so ill when I sit up that I mostly lie on the rug with a blanket. I drift in and out of sleep, the round of the rain hammering on the roof providing a constant soundtrack. Maybe this storm is the reason why Will isn't back yet. Maybe they've had to stay on the meeting point island.

Grandfather takes a few sips of water, but that's it. He can't manage any stew. I can eat a little with some slightly stale bread, but I don't have the energy to bake anything fresh.

I lose all sense of time. The daytime is dark and dingy, and the night is black and wet. The sound of the rain changes, though. Out of the window, I can see that it's more like sleet.

The next morning, there's an unearthly silence. Outside, the world is covered in snow.

Given that the ground was so wet, I'm surprised that it didn't all melt away. But the flakes are still falling, thick and fast, from the sky, and the white carpet is going to turn into snowdrifts before long. I stagger to the door, wrap my cloak around my shoulders, and step outside, shutting the door behind me to keep in the meagre heat from the fire.

The air is cold, but fresh, and I take a few deep breaths while bracing myself against the doorpost.

Grandfather keeps a broom just outside the door, so I grab it and manage to push some of the snow back. I don't want to be trapped when it gets deeper. I feel stupidly weak. Why is the broom so heavy? I clear a decent pathway, but start coughing and heaving. There's nothing there to come up.

I stumble back inside, and collapse back onto the rug. It takes a while for the dizzy sick feeling to subside. I close my eyes and imagine white sails, filled with a gentle breeze, on a boat smoothly crossing the ocean.

ALICE

43

Viola and I have not long been back when Palmiro comes to call for me.

'Tonight is a special celebration,' he tells me, with his eyes shining. 'You must learn the dance, so we are going to see my friend Amita.'

I try to stop my heart from cartwheeling out of my chest. He doesn't know that I know. But hopefully tonight we will announce to everyone that we want to be pledged to one another. Viola raises her eyebrows at me, and I wave goodbye.

Palmiro leads me to a nearby hut, and Amita steps outside to join us. She is tall, long legged, with dark hair cascading down her back. Her eyes are the colour of hazelnuts, but flecked with gold. She gives me a cold, haughty stare, and I shrink back.

'Amita,' Palmiro grins with his usual warmth, 'I want you to meet Alice.'

She gives me a cursory nod, then looks at him, eyes flashing with anger.

'So this is the reason for your recent disappearance,' she snaps.

Ouch. Palmiro seems unfazed.

'Don't be like that,' he says, still smiling. 'I need you to teach Alice the dance for tonight.'

Amita gives a dry laugh.

'The dance is hours away. Is she any good?'

'Of course she is,' Palmiro says.

I watch the exchange nervously. Palmiro and Amita are staring at each other, having a wordless conversation. Finally, Amita relents.

'Okay, but not here.'

'Where do you want to go?'

'The river.'

Taking huge strides, Amita heads off, with Palmiro in her wake. I stumble behind them. We cut a jagged path through the trees, and I have to dodge all the thorns. I'm still not used to this landscape, and the heat makes me breathless. I can hear Amita laughing ahead, and wonder how she has enough oxygen in her lungs.

Finally, we arrive at a clearing, with the river gushing behind us.

'First, we will demonstrate,' Amita says, holding out her hand imperiously to Palmiro.

There's a glint in her eye. I step backwards awkwardly, while Palmiro takes her hand and holds it high. Their eyes lock.

Moving to an invisible rhythm, they step in the same direction, both facing the same way. Then they spin and walk the other way, and Palmiro twists their hands up while Amita turns on the spot, then catches her low, his face inches from hers. Then they're moving again, this time facing each other. Their hands raise up above their heads and then slowly arc downwards.

They've done this before.

As they repeat the sequence, they add flourishes. Palmiro lifts Amita as if she weighs nothing. They shout cues to each other and they're moving so quickly, I can't make out the steps. As Amita gazes possessively at Palmiro with her fiery eyes, I know that she's in love with him. I scrutinize his face but I can't tell if he has feelings for her or not.

I still don't know him well enough to read him, and there's a lot about him I don't know.

He's told me stories about everything except himself. His past is an unchartered landscape, and I feel ridiculous standing here now, with the evidence before me that Palmiro has loved others before me.

Why am I surprised?

With a final spin, Amita gracefully takes a finishing position. She makes it look easy, and she knows it, because there's triumph in her expression.

'That was amazing,' I say, unenthusiastically. 'You look well suited as partners.'

Palmiro pulls a face.

'It's just a dance,' he says. 'We'll teach you.'

I shake my head and back away.

'I really don't think I'm going to be able to learn that before tonight.'

'Alice.' Palmiro leaves Amita behind and walks up to me. 'Please, give it a try? For me?'

'I won't be good enough.'

'Hey,' he says, gently tipping my chin up so I'm forced to meet his gaze. 'You are good enough, however well you dance.'

I look over his shoulder to see Amita scowling in the background.

'And Amita is the best dancer I know, so she is the best person to teach you,' he says, turning to appeal to her.

She rolls her eyes, then snaps her fingers.

'Come on, we're wasting time.'

44

It's slow and awkward, but after an hour, I'm finally getting the steps right. All three of us are sweating. Amita reminds me of my father in her sheer relentlessness.

'Again,' she says, barely two seconds after we finish the routine. 'You're not counting properly.'

She's waspish and critical, but Palmiro encourages me with smiles and his warm, firm hands. I wish we were alone so I could practise without Amita shouting at me, but also so that I could ask him more about her and their history. She makes me feel utterly inadequate; she's so poised and beautiful.

'Maybe we need a break,' Palmiro says, and my heart leaps. 'You two stay here while I get some water.'

Amita and I glare at each other, as Palmiro runs off. She raises her eyebrows haughtily, then tosses her hair over her shoulder and finds a rock to sit on. I can't find anything suitable, so I end up sitting straight on the mossy ground.

'So,' Amita breaks the silence, 'you like Palmiro.'

It's more of an accusation than anything else.

'So do you,' I retort.

'I have known him a lot longer than you have,' she says, her eyes darkening.

'Does he like you?'

'Palmiro likes a lot of girls.'

My face falls.

'You thought you were the first one,' she states. 'He the first guy interested in you?'

I don't answer.

'Obvious.' She rolls her eyes.

'Is there something going on between you or not?' I snap.

If I'm going to take him back to Whitecroft and be pledged to him, I need to know.

She shrugs.

'I hadn't seen him for a while and I guessed he found a new friend to play with. Didn't think it would be a foreigner.'

'What does that matter?'

I know it's stupid to argue with her, but I can't let it go uncontested.

'You are too different,' she says simply. 'You don't know him and he doesn't know you.'

What can I say to that? I feel a connection with him that I've never felt with anyone else? My gut instinct is that he's a good person, and I want to be with him? He brings out the best in me? None of it sounds very original or trustworthy, but sometimes words are inadequate to express what we feel.

The silence doesn't go unnoticed by Amita.

'If you want to know Palmiro better,' she says, 'ask him about his sister.'

'I didn't know he had a sister,' I say, confused.

'She's dead,' Amita says bluntly. 'We had an outbreak of some kind of virus. She was fourteen.'

'That's terrible,' I say, wishing that I'd heard this from Palmiro instead.

'We ran out of medicine ten years ago,' Amita continues. 'I heard you have a lot stored away in Whitecroft.'

'Yes, because no one wants to go to the Infirmary,' I tell her. 'Terrible things happen in there.'

'Like what?' She forgets to be cool in her curiosity.

'They sterilise women, or inject them to bear children.'

Two things Elise revealed, and I wasn't sure if I believed them, but I realise now that I do.

'Why would they do that?'

It's my turn to shrug now.

'There are only ten families in Whitecroft. If a family was rebellious, sterilisation was one way to make their name die.'

'Why would they inject them to bear children?'

'We need more people to survive and pass down our trades.'

'It doesn't make sense to do both at the same time.'

'Well, not to the same people, no.'

Amita gathers her hair and plaits it thoughtfully.

'Sounds like you have problems in Whitecroft too. Is that why those people left?'

'Probably.'

I know that George and Joy were blanked and excluded deliberately from being cast, but I don't want to get into the detail of the casting system either. Especially as Palmiro may be about to declare his intentions towards me.

Unless I'm just one of many love interests to him, and he's not planning to commit to me.

I was so excited about the celebration tonight, but now I'm not so sure.

45

After another torturous hour, Amita leaves me with Palmiro, declaring I am better than when I started. That's not much comfort, but it's the highest praise I'm going to get from her. At least I'm used to the steps now, even if I don't execute them with any of her grace or finesse.

'Let's get cool in the river,' Palmiro says, taking my hand and leading me to the bank.

There's a small beach area with smooth stones and sand, and he removes his shoes and starts to wade into the water.

'Come on!' he beckons towards me.

'I don't want to get my clothes wet,' I say, taking my shoes off carefully.

'It's hot. They'll dry fast,' he shrugs.

I take a tentative step into the river. The water doesn't have the cold sharpness of Whitecroft, but it's cooling.

'We used to stand here and catch fish when I was a boy,' Palmiro says.

I look into the water, but I can't see anything.

'Tell me more about your childhood,' I prompt.

He looks away for a moment, towards the trees, and swallows.

'There's not much to tell,' he says. 'I ran around the island from a young age, and I was on a boat from the time I could walk. Riel has always been my best friend. He's Amita's brother.'

Oh. That makes more sense. She must have grown up with Palmiro always around her, always smiling and going on adventures, so she must have fallen in love with him years ago. He may not have noticed her, as his best friend's sister.

'I've met your father,' I say. 'Who else is there in your family?'

'I have an uncle and cousins,' he answers.

'Your mother?' I ask.

A shadow passes across his face.

'She is no longer with us.'

'I'm sorry,' I say, automatically. I don't think I will be able to ask about his sister now.

'My mother died when I was born,' I say, hoping to provoke more detail from him.

'That is sad,' Palmiro says. 'You never knew her.'

He doesn't say anymore about his own mother, though.

'You have a brother, don't you?' he asks. He's heard about Charles before.

'Yes.'

Palmiro turns away, and starts picking up some stones to skim across the water. I can't resist the opportunity.

'How about you?' I ask.

He faces the same direction as me, and then skims the stone with one swift movement. It skips over the water's surface several times before sinking.

'I lost my sister,' he says, only turning to make eye contact with me once he's finished speaking. His eyes hold pain, not immediate enough to draw tears, but tempered with a measure of anger too. There's something raw there.

'I'm sorry,' I murmur.

I wait for him to tell me more, but he doesn't. Awkwardly, I splash my way to the shore to pick up some stones of my own. I try to skim one and it sinks immediately with a plop.

'You have to turn your wrist,' Palmiro instructs, wading over to me and taking my arm. 'Like this.'

He moves my arm in the motion, then indicates for me to try again. I pick another small, smooth pebble and flick my wrist as I throw it. It doesn't skim.

'Try this one,' he says, putting another stone into my hands.

It takes about six more attempts before I manage to skim with one bounce. Palmiro's face lights up and he cheers.

This is what Palmiro does. He enjoys fixing things that are broken, teaching people how to do things. When he saw me, cowering and terrified on the boat, he wanted to rescue me. But when the opportunity arises for him to expose his wounds to me, he chooses to cover them up.

Maybe he doesn't think that I can be any good at fixing things, because I'm so broken myself.

The problem with old wounds, though, is that they don't heal. I should know.

46

'We should get back,' Palmiro says, looking at how high the sun is in the sky above us.

I know he's right, but I don't want to leave this place of stillness. The only sounds are the birds calling and the river. I'm feeling a creeping dread about the dance later, let alone anything else that might happen.

We make our way through the trees, until we meet the outskirts of the village. Palmiro gives my hand a last squeeze, and I can't tell if his eyes are longing to tell me more or if I'm just imagining it. More about what: his sister or tonight? There are a lot more questions between us now than there were before.

Viola is wearing a beautiful, purple dress when she opens the door to me, and tells me excitedly there's one for me too. Cayman sent them over so we would fit in with the other girls.

'What exactly are we celebrating?' I ask her, as we fuss over our hair and try to fix in some flowers.

'I don't know but I think it's religious,' she says, weaving some white orchids around her hairline.

'Why don't we have religion in Whitecroft?' I ask. I think I already know the answer.

She shrugs.

'It's a culture thing, probably.'

I think it's more to do with my father, but I keep quiet.

'I'd better practise my steps for tonight,' I say, leaving her to continue fixing her hair in the bedroom.

I walk into the main room of the house, and Blake sits at the table. His eyes widen and he stands up when he sees me, scraping the chair back.

'Alice,' he says, gulping. His eyes flicker and I can tell that he's trying to keep them fixed on my face. 'You look great.'

'Thanks,' I murmur.

I don't know why things have become so weird between us.

'I need to practise for the dance tonight,' I say, looking at the floor.

'I can help, if you like,' he says.

I look up in surprise.

'You don't know it, do you?'

He shrugs.

'What do I have to do, just turn you around or something?'

'It's a bit more complicated than that,' I say.

I turn my back to him and raise my fingers to my temples, trying to pretend he isn't there.

'One, two, step back, then forward. One, two, step then turn—'

He takes hold of my hand, spinning me gently, then lowering me in a dip with his other arm supporting my back. After the longest moment of my life, he tilts me upright again, and we take three steps across the floor.

'Relax your shoulders,' he says.

I breathe out, and melt a little more into his arms.

'That's better,' he says gruffly.

There's no music, just the rhythm of our steps, and my hammering heartbeat. We run through the sequence again, and this time, when he lowers me, his face is inches from mine. He's breathless too, and I can see in his eyes how much he wants me, but I'm terrified by this uncontrollable feeling that seems to wipe all sense from my mind. Think, Alice! Remember who you are, remember Palmiro…

There's a loud rapping at the door.

I pull away hurriedly, just as Viola opens the bedroom door and glimpses how we were positioned. Her eyes narrow at Blake.

'I'll get it.'

I hurry over to the door, smoothing my dress, mentally slapping myself across the face, thinking it's probably Palmiro. When I open it, my father is standing there.

'Are you ready?' he asks.

I frown slightly. I thought Palmiro was collecting me.

'Yes.'

'Good. You're sitting with us.'

'But I –' I start, then stop at his scowl.

'You will see Palmiro, if that's what you're worried about.'

Without looking back at either Blake or Viola, I call out a farewell and shut the door behind me. I follow my father, struggling to keep up with his brisk pace, and we arrive at the beach. Cayman greets us, giving me a warm smile, and gestures for us to sit in some special chairs, an arbour right overhead, decorated with beautiful flowers. There are purple ones the shade of my dress, and then also some bright yellow ones with large petals. Leon and Arnold are already there. I sit awkwardly, surveying the beach from our position of honour.

There is a large crowd of people here already, but more people are arriving continually. A group of musicians play, and my foot starts to tap to the rhythm. There's a large fire, with delicious smells from roasting food. Someone passes us a dish with sweet nuts, and I eat them as I scan the rows of people, sitting on benches, blankets and chairs. It isn't sunset yet, and the air is still hot, although the sun is lower in the sky now. The women all wear these dresses, like mine, in bright colours. The collar is large and oversized, covering the shoulders, and the skirt flares out to just below my calves. I smooth it down over my knees.

I notice George, Joy and their parents arrive, and choose to sit at the back. They don't look at my father, and I can see his jaw clench when he sees them. Thankfully, he doesn't say anything. Blake and Viola sit with a group of people around our age; I think Blake works with them. Even without looking directly at him, I feel a blush creeping over my cheeks. Why do I remember so exactly how it felt to be in his arms? The electricity of how close his face was to mine? The irresistible draw of his mouth?

Stop it, Alice. That's enough. Think about Palmiro instead. He's good-looking, sweet, with a dazzling smile. He's patiently taught me new things, and shown me the sunset. He's a good dancer. He's... not Blake. And he's not here yet, either.

Finally, when it feels like absolutely everyone is here except him, Palmiro arrives and sits right at the front of the gathering. There's a row especially reserved for him and his father, and other important leaders of Cape.

I feel so conscious of the distance between us. Our special seats are on the side, at a right angle to everyone else, and whilst I can see Palmiro, I'm not directly in his line of sight. I wish he was next to me so I could ask him more about what this celebration is and what we're supposed to be doing.

I wish he was next to me so there would be a chance I would stop thinking about Blake.

The musicians stop playing, and Cayman addresses the gathering.

'Dear friends,' he says, 'today is a day where we give thanks. It is one of our most important traditions.'

Everyone is silent, and I twist my hands nervously in my lap.

'We are the chosen ones,' he continues. 'We remember those we have lost, but instead of mourning and filling our hearts with anger that they are no longer with us, we choose to give thanks for their lives.'

I stare at Palmiro. He's looking down and I can't read his expression.

'We also take time to reflect,' Cayman says, 'upon our relationships. Are we truly grateful for the people the Creator has placed into our path? Have we allowed differences and discord to create barriers between us?'

The words create an uncomfortable niggle in my chest. Who am I grateful for? Palmiro, Blake, the Swifts… even Viola. Apart from Grandfather, there are few people in Whitecroft that I would celebrate knowing. I picture Elise on her pledging day, standing and smiling next to William. It stings less than before. But I can't be grateful for someone who caused such chaos and then left me to pick up the pieces.

'We are all one family,' Cayman says. 'If two people are fighting against each other, it hurts all of us. We cannot be the family we were created to be.'

At this point, he looks straight at my father. I feel him shift uncomfortably next to me.

'We will use our songs to express our gratitude, and to allow for reflection of our own lives. We welcome our visitors.' Here, Cayman points towards us. 'We encourage you to join us in this time as well.'

The musicians start to play again, but this time the music is more reflective and calming. The people begin to sing, knowing all the words, and I can't always make out what they're saying. But in some ways, I don't have to. As I sit and let the music wash over me, I find myself thinking of all the things I have experienced here in Cape over the past few days. I could have drowned, that stormy night in the boat, but instead, I made it to the shore. I've received friendship, and I've seen so much here that I could never have imagined. I am not usually thankful, but there are many good things that I am grateful for. And not just here. In fact, being here has reminded me of the good things in Whitecroft, too. The things I always took for granted, like the cool, fresh water, and the cosy warmth of the fire. Even the beauty of the snow.

A few rows back from Palmiro, I catch sight of Riel and Amita. They look so similar now they are side by side: they have the same striking dark hair and slightly sharp expressions. I find myself speculating about what has happened in the past with Palmiro and Amita. Has he ever loved her? Has he ever kissed her? I feel my cheeks start to burn as I remember how embarrassing my dancing was earlier today, and Amita's scornful expression. She knew I would never be as smooth and graceful as her. I'm dreading having to do it in front of all these people. It's easy for her—she's known this dance for so long, she could perform it blindfolded. I wish she had shown more understanding.

Did you show Elise understanding?

The question suddenly pops into my head. I've no idea where it came from, and I look at my father, startled. He's sighing and fidgeting, impatient with this whole ceremony.

Did I show Elise understanding? Well, that was different.

Wasn't it?

You are Amita to Elise.

There's a painful stab in my heart. I know it's true, and the sudden knowledge brings tears to my eyes. The music rises, and the voices are singing about love, and peace. Peace! How could I ever have peace with the girl who ruined my father? Who ruined my life?

'This is all shameless propaganda.'

My father's scathing tone cuts into my thoughts, and I hurriedly brush my eyes with the back of my hand. It wouldn't do for him to see me emotional.

'Don't be fooled by any of this.' Father turns to me. 'It's all lies.'

I don't reply; there's no point. But I learnt how to recognise truth a long time ago. It has to be felt in your heart. The problem is, my father has shut his heart away. I don't think even he knows how to find it.

I may have many questions about Palmiro, and there may be much I don't know about him yet, but I'm determined of this: I won't let my heart get locked away like my father's. I fold my arms in silent resolution, and just at that moment, Palmiro looks over at me. He meets my eyes and smiles.

47

The ceremony draws to a close as the sun sets over the ocean. The sky is alive with fiery pink and yellow clouds, reflected onto the rolling waves. People start to light lanterns and small fires, contained within metal baskets.

'We will eat together shortly,' Cayman announces. 'But first, it is time for our dances.'

My heart lurches, but the first dance is a group of girls, led by Amita. The music is fast and whirring with overlapping melodies, and she is breathtaking. I've never seen anyone dance like her. It's like she owns the music. The applause is wild, and I'm so distracted I fail to notice Palmiro make his way towards me.

'It is our turn next,' he says, extending his hand, and giving my father a polite nod of respect.

Before my father can say anything, I slip away, grasping Palmiro's hand tightly. Amita's group have moved away, and now other couples are taking places in the dancing area.

'Don't be so nervous,' Palmiro whispers to me.

He must be able to feel me shaking.

The music starts. I've never heard this piece before, but thankfully it's slower than Amita's dance. My shoulders are tight and rigid, but as we complete the first few steps and I haven't embarrassed myself by falling over, I begin to feel more at ease.

'You look beautiful,' Palmiro says, his lips against my ear.

I train my eyes to look only at Palmiro, and not wander to find Blake in the crowd.

As he holds me in his strong arms, and leads me around the dance area with a broad grin on his face, I forget to be worried about the steps. I'm leaning into him, enjoying the feel of his hands on my waist. I feel safe with him, trusting his friendship even if I have questions about where his heart is. Blake is a red flashing danger sign. A disaster waiting to happen.

I turn with a whip sharp movement of my head, and Palmiro lowers me and pauses, just like Blake did. I wait for that moment, that feeling that we are the centre of the universe. It doesn't come. Then he's lifting me up, my skirt flaring with the movement, spins me and catches me, moving back into the sequence.

'I'd like to come to Whitecroft with you,' he says.

'That's wonderful,' I say.

Why do I feel like I'm sinking into wet sand?

With a mischievous grin, he lifts me, higher than before, then spins around an extra time before bringing me down.

'Good,' he says. 'I knew our friendship was meant to be.'

The music finishes with a flourish, and Palmiro pulls me into a curtsey like the other dancers, then wraps his arms around me and squeezes me tightly.

'You are a brilliant dancer,' he murmurs in my ear. 'Don't let anyone tell you otherwise.'

But there's only one word on loop in my head, with red flashing warning lights all around it: *friendship*.

<h1 style="text-align:center">48</h1>

Palmiro leads me away from the dancing area closer to the caves, where I went earlier. It feels like a long time ago. The crowd thins out, and the water laps against the sand. It's quieter away from the chatter of the festivities.

'What did you think of the ceremony?'

'I loved the music,' I answer.

'What is the music like in Whitecroft?'

'A bit simpler,' I laugh. 'A pennywhistle. A fiddle. A drum. Just so we can have dancing.'

'I'd like to see your Whitecroft dances.'

'They're not as fancy as Cape ones.'

'Hey!'

A voice calling out draws our attention to a shadowy cove, not too far from where we're standing. I see George squaring up to Arnold, and Amita's standing there with an expression of disgust.

'Leave her alone,' George says.

'Is there a problem?' Palmiro strides forward, looking from George to Arnold.

Arnold glowers at us.

'You have no right to touch me,' Amita sneers at him.

Dusting her hands against her dress, as if wiping away something dirty, she stalks off. George follows her. Palmiro glares at Arnold.

'What did you do to her?'

'Nothing.'

Arnold tries to push past him, but Palmiro stops him by holding out his arm.

'She is like a sister to me.'

Arnold shakes him off angrily, and barges past us both.

'Is he like this in Whitecroft?' Palmiro asks, shaking his head in disbelief.

'Worse.'

I fill him in on Arnold's failed Pledge. Palmiro looks out to the water, where the sun no longer lights up the waves with a fiery glow. It's disappeared beyond the horizon, and the moon is visible at the top of the sky, still a pale blue.

'That would never happen here,' Palmiro comments, confidently.

'Why?' I challenge him. 'Does no one ever break a promise here? Does no one ever behave badly?'

I'm half teasing, but at the moment, I have yet to see a dark side to Cape. Maybe it is too idyllic to be true.

'I don't mean it in that way,' he says, turning to meet my gaze. 'What I mean is that nothing would ever stay hidden for that long.'

Now it's my turn to shake my head.

'I don't understand.'

'It sounds to me,' Palmiro says, finding a rock to sit on, beckoning me to join him, 'that everyone goes to their houses, closes their door, and no one knows what happens inside.'

'Well, yes,' I say, uncertainly. 'Isn't that how it is here?'

Palmiro laughs.

'Our doors are never really closed to one another,' he says, smiling. 'It is impossible to keep a secret round here. To hide anything.'

'We're alone now,' I say, with a trace of shyness. I look around to check, and we are sitting out of view.

'Alice,' he says, laying his hand over mine, 'did you never wonder why I keep taking you to isolated places on this island? I've tried all my life to find somewhere I can be alone.'

'You certainly have a talent for seeking out those places,' I reply, thinking of the fields, the boat, and the forest.

Palmiro gives a dry laugh.

'And yet,' he says, giving me a grim smile, 'the whole island is talking about us. Whenever they get a chance, people are telling me what I should and shouldn't be doing. The whole town has an opinion about you and me.'

I sit up, frowning.

'What do they say?'

Palmiro shrugs.

'Is this to do with Amita?' I press.

'Why are you jealous of her?' he asks.

'Um, because she's in love with you?'

Palmiro shakes his head.

'It's just an infatuation.'

'But did you…'

'Did I ever reciprocate her feelings?' he interrupts me, his tone reflecting his annoyance. 'She is my friend. She is my best friend's sister.'

'And I'm your *friend* too,' I say. My mouth feels so dry all of a sudden.

'Of course,' he says, looking puzzled at my tone.

'So you used to dance with Amita, and now you're dancing with me, until someone else comes along.'

'Is that what she told you?' he says, sounding annoyed. It's the first time I've heard those notes in his voice, but I'm relieved that I'm finally seeing something real.

'Well, she's not the only one who's warned me not to go head over heels for you.'

'And are you? Head over heels?' he asks, looking worried.

I look back at him, weighing my heart.

'No,' I say truthfully. 'I like you. But we haven't known each other very long.'

It isn't that, though. I think I could spend a year with Palmiro but I don't think I'd ever feel that same heat I felt from Blake. The realisation pierces my heart, because he's not mine. He's never been mine. Feeling this way is wrong and stupid, and yet again I've managed to pick the wrong boy. What is wrong with me?

'I hope you have enjoyed your time in Cape,' he says, misreading the turbulence in my expression.

'Of course!' I say, burying my thoughts. 'I can't even describe how this place has changed me.'

'Let me try,' he says. 'It's the feeling of being lost, and then being found. The feeling of being seen for who you are, not just what someone wants you to be.'

I break into a grin.

'You should write your own book,' I say. 'You're very poetic.'

He laughs, and things feel easy again between us. Friends. That word no longer seems that bad anymore.

In the quiet, the sky darkens. Stars are becoming visible, and the water looks blacker before us. The music of the celebration continues.

'Do you want to know what my name means?' Palmiro asks suddenly.

'Yes,' I say, smiling.

'It means pilgrim.'

'What's that?'

'Someone who travels somewhere. Usually to a sacred place. A place that is important for your faith.'

'Maybe that explains why you like to go all over the island on your own.'

He grins.

'It's one reason why I wasn't surprised when your father wanted me to come to Whitecroft. I knew it was my destiny.'

I give a half smile and dig my fingers in the sand. It still holds the warmth of the day.

'Tell me,' he continues, 'do you always want to stay in Whitecroft?'

I gulp.

'I hope not,' I say. 'You know how you said about people talking about you—about us—and having opinions? That's how I feel in Whitecroft. Ever since I withdrew from being pledged to Phillip, everyone has stared at me and judged me.'

'You feel trapped in Whitecroft, and I feel trapped in Cape,' he summarises, with a laugh. 'Well, I guess that means we need to find somewhere else to go.'

'Like where?' I laugh.

'If we have a boat, we can go anywhere,' he says, his eyes gleaming. 'That's what I've always wanted. To explore the rest of the world.'

I laugh at his buoyant optimism. As if we could truly go wherever we wanted.

'On this day every year I make a vow,' he says. 'I've done it ever since my sister died.'

'What kind of vow?'

I look at him closely. It feels like I'm finally seeing more of who he is.

'I vow to save someone. Because I didn't save her.'

'She was sick,' I say. 'It wasn't your fault.'

'You know the first time I've been able to keep my vow?' he continues. 'When I helped you off the boat. I knew I was saving you, but I didn't understand from what at that point. Now, I think I do.'

'What are you saving me from?' I ask, partly amused, and partly fascinated.

'Loneliness,' he says, simply. 'From your father. From yourself.'

I shift uncomfortably. It's like he's seen right through to my soul.

I watch the tapestry of stars unfold over our heads, my eyes struggling to grasp the awesome expanse of the universe, and my emotions feel like a swirling vortex. It's so messy. I want to go back to Whitecroft, to see Grandfather, even to see Elise again… But I don't know where my place is, where I fit in. I can't stay in Cape. I can't stay around Blake when I feel this way about him, it's like putting a lit match next to gunpowder. Does that mean I'm always going to be lonely? Because Palmiro's friendship is lovely, but it can't replace the kind of love I've always craved. The wholly consuming kind.

'You've got to stop worrying about everything,' Palmiro breaks into my spiralling thoughts.

'It's hard not to.'

'Have faith,' he says simply. 'If you take nothing else away from Cape, take that. Believe it in your heart.'

I nod, tears blurring my vision. Palmiro moves nearer, frowning with concern.

'Don't be upset,' he says. 'Look, I know we haven't known each other for long. My father is keen for us to be pledged together, to unify Cape with Whitecroft. Perhaps we can help each other. I can look after you, and we can go sailing together and be free from all the things that tie us down.'

'I don't know—' I falter, biting my lip. 'I always wanted to be pledged to someone I loved.'

'Love grows from friendship,' Palmiro says. 'Let me show you.'

He slowly leans closer, reaching for my face. His fingers trace over my cheek, then rest under my chin. As if we're in a dream-like trance, his thumb moves over my lips, his touch feather-light. I blink at him.

'My lips, two blushing pilgrims, ready stand/ To smooth that rough touch with a tender kiss,' he says.

'Is that from the Book?' I whisper.

He laughs.

'No, not that Book,' he says. 'We learnt it in school.'

'Oh,' I say.

'I was trying to say that I want to kiss you,' Palmiro says, after a beat, where we stay frozen with his thumb on my mouth.

'All right.'

I close my eyes and he removes his thumb, and then suddenly his lips are on mine. Warm, inviting. It's not that I feel *nothing* for him… Perhaps this could work, after all.

I just need to stop wishing that he was Blake.

49

The celebration goes on well into the night. We collect plates of food and Palmiro looks around for his friends.

'There's Amita.'

I point her out. She's talking animatedly to Riel, shaking her head vigorously. George is standing a short way off, not in the conversation, but watching them. I'm about to say that perhaps we should leave them alone, but Palmiro strides off in their direction. Amita notices him coming and smiles, stepping back from her brother.

'Hello stranger,' she says. 'Are you going to sit with us now?'

'Sure.'

Palmiro beckons to me to sit next to him.

'Riel, why don't you get us some drinks?' Amita asks, in a sharp tone.

He stares at her determined expression, and sighs.

'I meant what I said,' he says, before heading off to the food table.

'Everything okay?' Palmiro asks her.

'It is now I don't have to be a dance instructor,' she says, then grins at me. 'You did well.'

'Thanks.'

I blush. This is high praise indeed.

Riel soon returns and the conversation meanders around, avoiding any controversial topics. Families and different groups have spread around the beach, the fires burning strong, and the musicians have changed over. Under the arbour where I was sitting before, Cayman has taken my seat and is talking with my father. The Crests have gone.

'I need to speak to your father,' Palmiro says, following the direction of my gaze.

Amita, who had been joking about something, falls quiet.

'About what?' she asks.

'Amita,' Riel warns.

'So it's true then,' she says, leaning back with a sigh of defeat. 'You're going to Whitecroft.'

How do they know? I look questioningly at Palmiro.

'We don't have secrets round here,' he tells me, by way of explanation.

'It was bad enough when *you* were going,' Amita says, giving Riel's shoulder a shove.

'I still think I should go,' Riel says.

Amita stares at him open-mouthed, and Palmiro frowns.

'You don't need to. I will go.'

'I don't like the idea of you being alone over there,' Riel says.

I want to say that he won't be alone, that I will make sure that no harm comes to him, but I understand what Riel means. Alone and separated from his own people.

'And what am I supposed to do?' Amita asks, angrily. 'Sit around and wait for you to come back? What if you never come back?'

'Let me speak to my father and the General,' Palmiro says, standing.

'I'm coming with you.'

I scramble to my feet and take his hand. I can feel Amita and Riel watching as we walk towards the arbour. Cayman sees us coming and stands up to welcome us. My father stands, too. His lip curls in distaste when he sees our joined hands.

'Father,' Palmiro says, 'and General, I would like to ask your permission to go with you to Whitecroft. I will teach people to sail, if you will allow me to have your daughter. I will take the vows and the Pledge and do whatever your customs require.'

Cayman beams at us. I look nervously at my father.

'Certainly,' he says, and I nearly faint with shock. 'Whatever will secure my daughter's happiness.'

'Wonderful!' Palmiro shakes his hand, and then throws his arms around his father.

I stand there, staring at my father. He has never cared about my happiness before. This is not good. From the outside, he looks like a benevolent parent, but I can see the cold steel in his eyes.

Palmiro draws me away, chattering excitedly about all the people he needs to introduce me to, and it feels like we talk to everyone on the whole island until the break of dawn. I smile and nod, but I'm feeling a growing panic that things are moving so quickly. I told him that I wasn't really in love with him, but he seems determined that we can develop stronger feelings for each other with time. And physical affection. Being kissed by him wasn't an unpleasant experience. But if he's the only person I ever get to kiss in my whole life... Then I think I'd be disappointed.

Am I just a terrible person for thinking that?

I'm so tired I could fall asleep standing up, and I finally bid farewell to Palmiro and his extended family and walk back to Viola's house. The sky is starting to lighten with the dawn, but everything's murky. A few gulls appear, streaks of white against the dark ocean.

Alone on the beach, near the coves, I can see my father talking with someone. My eyes are blurry and I rub them. Perhaps I'm not seeing clearly. It looks like he's talking to Riel.

That can't be right. I need to sleep.

As I approach the house, I can hear Viola's voice.

'When did this dream turn into a nightmare?' she says. It sounds like she's crying.

I hear a low murmur—Blake's voice. Then Viola's voice with its crystal clarity:

'No, I'm done. I've had enough of you and this island. I don't care what you do, but if there's a boat going back to Whitecroft, I'm getting on it.'

Great, it looks as though I'll be stepping into a warzone.

I hesitate just outside the front door, but I hear a door inside slam and assume that Viola's gone into the bedroom. I open the door and walk into the main room.

Blake's sitting with his head in his hands. When he looks up at me, his eyes are red.

'Why is nothing I do or say ever good enough for her?' he asks.

My heart goes out to him, looking so forlorn and miserable, and against my better judgement, I cross the room to lay my hand on his shoulder. He leans his head against me, and I wrap my arms around his head and shoulders, holding him tightly.

After a minute, Blake pulls back and stands, achingly close but not touching me.

'When you go back to Whitecroft, will you take her?' he asks.

'Of course,' I say.

He nods, satisfied.

'I heard you're going to be pledged to Palmiro,' he says, searching my face for my reaction.

'It seems to be what everyone wants,' I say.

'What about what you want?'

'I've never had any real say about that,' I tell him.

He looks into my eyes, silently telling me not to do it. His proximity is making my heart beat faster, treacherously, and I think of Viola, probably sat on her bed sobbing.

'I need to go to bed,' I say, taking a step back.

Perhaps everything will seem clearer in the morning.

50

'Alice! Alice, wake up!'

I open my eyes and Viola is standing over my bed. Memories flash through my head: the celebration, fires on the beach, dancing with Palmiro, the kiss, Blake and Viola's argument…

'Alice, you need to get up now.'

Viola starts pacing back and forth, wringing her hands.

'What's the matter?' I ask, rubbing my eyes. 'What time is it?'

'It's the afternoon,' she snaps. 'Everyone's coming here for an emergency meeting.'

She sweeps out of the room, and I throw off my counterpane. I can hear voices just outside the front door. What's going on? Why is Viola so serious?

'You asked him to go!'

It sounds like Amita, and she sounds like she's half-crying, half-shouting.

'I didn't think he would do this.'

Palmiro. I take two steps towards the door, but then someone lays their hand on my arm.

'Slow down, Princess.' Blake hands me a drink. 'Why don't you sit here?'

I take it gratefully and sink down into a chair, just as George, Palmiro and Amita burst through the door. Her beautiful face is blotchy with tears. When she sees me, her face contorts.

'This is all your fault,' she spits. 'I wish you had never come here!'

Palmiro holds her back.

'Amita, this is not Alice's fault,' he says.

She shakes him off angrily and walks over to the window, her back to us. Viola emerges from the bedroom. I look at her, then at Palmiro in confusion.

'What's going on?'

Palmiro looks at me with pain in his eyes, but says nothing.

'They've gone,' Blake says, standing behind me and laying a hand on my shoulder.

I look back to Palmiro for confirmation.

'They took a boat and left while it was quiet, early this morning,' Blake continues.

'Who?'

My voice is barely audible.

'Your father, the Crests—'

'And Riel!' Amita cuts in. 'My brother!'

'But, I don't understand,' I say, my thoughts reeling to calibrate round this information. 'I thought he wanted Palmiro to—'

'Of course he did!' Amita says bitterly. 'My brother, thinking he's doing some sort of noble sacrifice, has agreed to take him to Whitecroft. The General expects Palmiro to come after him, and then he'll have two valuable sailors from Cape, instead of one. And one will be the leader's son.'

'Maybe my father thought Palmiro and I would follow in a different boat,' I say. 'After all, there are two boats from Whitecroft held on the meeting point island.'

'Not any more,' Viola says. 'A radio message came through from Cressida. She said that your brother and William left in a canoe to collect George's boat a week ago.'

'So if my father arrives at the meeting point, there will only be one boat there,' I say.

'They will be there by now,' Blake says.

'How could my father know about Charles?' I point out.

'You don't think he has any radio communication with Whitecroft?' Blake asks skeptically.

I vaguely remembered my father telling Xander that he would ask the Steads to make him some kind of radio. I never knew if they did.

'So he's abandoning me?'

Silence. After my father's behaviour on the boat trip over here, it's not surprising—but it still stings. I'm too numb to cry. Blake squeezes my shoulder more tightly.

'It's a move in the game he's playing,' he says. 'But the game isn't over yet.'

I drop my head into my hands.

'You seem to like it here in Cape,' Viola says, a slight scathing note in her tone. 'Don't you want to stay here and live happily ever after?'

'Not if Riel is walking into a trap,' I retort.

'Hah!' Amita responds.

'We should go to get him back,' Palmiro says.

'Then *you* walk right into the trap,' Amita says.

'What alternative is there?' he asks, raising his voice. 'Surely you don't want me to leave him?'

'I don't want to lose both of you,' she says, her voice cracking.

They stare at each other for a moment.

'There was more in Cressida's message,' Viola says.

She steps closer to me, and there's more sympathy in her expression now.

'Your grandfather is sick.'

She takes a deep breath.

'Cressida does not think he will make it through the Freeze.'

It feels like a cold stone has dropped in my stomach.

'Is Elise with him? Is she looking after him?'

Viola hesitates.

'Elise is sick too,' she says. 'Cressida doesn't know if it's a virus or… if she's carrying.'

I cover my face with my hands. *In nine months, we all know where you'll be.*' Those were some of my last words to Elise before I left Whitecroft. There's a stabbing sensation in my chest. Guilt. When Ada was carrying, she was so sick she couldn't get out of bed. Elise stayed with her and nursed her. Who will look after Elise and Grandfather if William is sailing?

'Is Cressida there to help them?' I ask Viola.

She shakes her head.

'Her family want her to stay with them for the Freeze. She's worried that if she goes back, she might catch whatever virus your grandfather has. And the first snow has already come.'

I imagine Grandfather's tiny cottage, snow up to its small windows. It would be freezing inside if the fire wasn't kept going. The closest people would be Blake's family, but would they be likely to go there? They wouldn't think anything was wrong.

'Cressida said that before the snow, there was a storm. William and Charles may have been caught in it on their way to the meeting point, or delayed there because of it.'

I remember how terrifying the boat trip was, being tossed by the waves, and that was in a decent sized vessel. I can't imagine my brother in a flimsy canoe. *Let him be okay. Let him live.*

'Cressida asked if there was any way you could come back,' Viola finishes, looking straight at me.

I look straight to Palmiro.

'When can we leave?'

51

'It's not that simple,' Palmiro says. 'Look out of the window.'

Amita is still standing by one of them, so I move to look out of the one on the other side of the room. Sheets of rain are falling, creating huge puddles in the dirt outside the yard. The sky is grey for the first time. I've never seen it rain here before.

'It's a tropical rainstorm,' Amita says. 'If you think this is bad, it will be far worse out there.'

She means the sea. My stomach churns.

'Do you have a map or charts for navigation?' I ask Palmiro.

'Yes,' he says slowly.

'We don't need to go to the meeting point,' I say. 'If we could chart a course that goes direct to Whitecroft, we might be able to get there before my father, and go straight to my grandfather and Elise.'

Palmiro looks at George.

'It's possible,' he says. 'The meeting point was used so that we could sail there and back without arousing suspicion in Whitecroft. It's not the quickest direct route.'

'And we don't need to use the Whitecroft boats,' I add quickly.

'You want to just use a Cape boat and go straight to Whitecroft?' Palmiro says, sounding unsure. 'That's a long way and there's only two of us.'

'I can come,' Amita says immediately.

I stare at her in shock.

'No one will know,' she says, 'so I can help Riel. Maybe help him to sail back.'

'The navigation is not straightforward,' George says. 'There are some areas of very dangerous waters. You need someone experienced.'

'Will you do it, George?' Amita looks at him, her eyes pleading.

I'm about to cut in to say that George couldn't possibly want to go back to Whitecroft, when he says, turning to face her,

'I will, Amita. I'll do it for you.'

Now I'm really shocked. They lock stares for a moment and then Amita throws her arms around his neck and kisses his cheek.

'Thank you, George!'

Next to me, Blake clears his throat.

'Viola and I will come too,' he says. 'We can see our families again. Plus, I'm not missing out on a big adventure.'

We all look at one another, in growing excitement.

'Are we really going to do this, together?' I say.

'Everyone, place your hands in the middle,' Viola says, placing her palm face down in the centre of the table.

One by one, we all place our hands one on top of the other, different skin tones and calluses overlapping.

'This is a big thing to do,' Viola continues. 'We have to trust one another. Back in Whitecroft, some of us were in a Pact. I think we should do the same.'

Her eyes fall on me for a moment. Perhaps she's worried that I might betray them all to my father.

'What are we promising?' Amita questions.

'Loyalty to one another,' Blake says, looking from person to person. 'We all make sure that everyone is safe. We do nothing to jeopardise the safety of the group.'

'We need a leader.' I find my voice. 'Someone who can make the final decision if we are undecided. It needs to be someone experienced.'

I look directly at George.

'George?' Amita says, smiling at him.

'If you want me to,' he nods.

'That's settled then,' Blake says.

We withdraw our hands, and Palmiro says,

'I need to go and see my father.'

'Let's pack provisions and meet at the dock in an hour,' Blake says.

I'm going back to Whitecroft. I just hope I'm not too late.

192

52

It's still raining when we set off, but I'm much better prepared than last time. We're all wearing orange *lifejackets* (Palmiro explained what they were), and our boat is called a *galley* with oars as well as sails, so we're able to have more power and not just be helpless to the direction of the wind. George commands us, with Blake steering the ship and the rest of us rowing. It makes such a difference to be in this group where everyone is going to look out for each other. It gives me confidence as I pull on the oar, on the same side as Amita while Palmiro operates on the other side of the boat with Viola. Amita is just as determined as I am to get to Whitecroft as quickly as possible.

Whilst it's wet and the sky is overcast, we're avoiding the worst part of the storm. Looking across the water, we can see where the rain is heavier, in blurry mist between the clouds and the water. George has set our course and we will completely avoid the meeting point. With visibility so poor anyway, it would be unlikely for anyone to see us.

I can't stop thinking about Grandfather and Elise, willing them to hold on until I get there. It's strange: when I left Whitecroft, I would have said I'd be happy to never see Elise again. I feel so differently now.

Maybe it was Cayman's words at the ceremony that *we are all one family*. Maybe it was the songs about peace. Either way, I feel a sudden urgency that I can't leave things the way they are with Elise. I can't leave our relationship broken if it's in my power to fix it.

After a stint of rowing, where my hands are numb and locked onto the oar, George tells us to take a break. We're on course and catching the wind now. Amita and I sit on the deck and pass a bottle of water between us, and some nuts. My arms are aching, but I don't feel nauseous like I did before. I wipe my face and squeeze out the worst of the drips from my hair. Amita is staring out into the distance.

'I think Riel's going to go after Arnold,' she says.

'Because of… what happened?' I ask. She nods. 'What did he do?'

She sighs.

'He wanted to dance,' she says. 'He was moving away from the group, out to the cove, and I didn't really notice. Then he pushed me against the rock wall, in the shadows, and tried to kiss me. Lucky George was there.'

'I'm so sorry,' I say.

'It wasn't your fault,' she says, then flushes slightly as she remembers what she said to me earlier. 'And it wasn't your fault that Riel went, either. No one forced him. I was just angry when I found out.'

'I understand that,' I gulp. 'Please tell me, though… Is there anything between you and Palmiro? I want to know.'

She takes another sip from the bottle and looks away for a moment. Across the deck, Palmiro laughs with Blake, flashing his white teeth.

'The thing with Palmiro,' she begins, 'is that he makes you feel like you're the most important person in the world, when you're with him.'

I can agree with that.

'It's not that he's being deceitful, or insincere—it's just his way,' she sighs. 'Maybe I thought he cared for me more than he really does.'

I've been there. All those times I succeeded in making William smile, I took as a personal victory. Then I saw how his whole body lit up around Elise, and realised the victory was hollow.

I can't help but question whether I'm in the same position as Amita, though. Palmiro's been very interested in me—but then, I'm new around here. I'm a novelty. When he was asking me how

I felt about him, he didn't reveal much about his own feelings. Yes, he kissed me. But was it more of an *experiment* than a real kiss? A sort of look-what-we-could-be? Maybe he was testing it for himself as well as to prove a point to me. Maybe he gives a false impression.

If Amita could be fooled by him, then I certainly could too.

Standing a short distance from Blake and Palmiro, George holds onto a taut rope and stares at Amita. When he notices me looking, he looks away.

'I think someone else cares about you,' I say, nodding my head towards George.

She looks over in surprise, her eyes widening.

'George? I never thought of him in that way.'

As we go back to row, her eyes move towards him, drawn irresistibly.

George is certainly impressive. He is at least twenty years old than us, but he has a quiet, calm confidence in the way he commands the ship. He listens carefully to everyone and shows no favouritism. He doesn't seem to judge me, even though I discovered the group as they were leaving Whitecroft. He makes people feel safe. Having him and Palmiro has transformed the way I view sailing. Although it's soaking wet, windy and not without danger, I'm enjoying the feeling of working together with everyone to reach Whitecroft. It makes me feel I'm doing something positive.

If I can get back to Whitecroft safely, it gives me a second chance.

The hours pass. Palmiro swaps with Blake to steer, and George joins Blake in rowing for a stint. We have the wind on our side, thankfully, so with the added oar power, we are making good progress. But the closer we get to Whitecroft, the more the temperature drops. We're drenched anyway, but my teeth start chattering with cold, and my knuckles are white when I grip the oar.

'We need to build a fire,' George shouts. 'We need light and heat.'

He calls Palmiro and me over to help him. There's a metal fire pit fixed onto a platform on the deck. The rain is finally easing, but it's going to be hard to light anything with the wind and wet atmosphere. We fill the fire pit with fuel and then Palmiro and I help to create a shield, so that George can ignite it. It's a frustrating process but eventually we get the smoulder to catch into flame.

'We need to keep someone by the fire at all times, to sustain it and also check that it doesn't spread,' George says.

'I'll do it,' I volunteer.

'We're on course,' Palmiro tells him. 'Why don't we suggest that everyone catches up on sleep for a few hours?'

George and I are left sitting by the fire alone. The darkness is closing in swiftly—it was never a very bright day anyway—and it's funny to think that yesterday, I was dancing on the beach with the sun setting, and now I'm on my way home.

'I didn't think I'd be making this journey so soon,' George says, poking the fire.

'I'm sorry that you've been drawn into this,' I say.

'Like Blake says, can't miss an adventure,' he grins.

'You never came this way?' I ask.

He shakes his head.

'I used to do trips with your aunt Loretta, but not down this way.'

Loretta was Elise's mother. Well, she was the one who carried her.

'Tell me about them.'

GEORGE

Loretta, the Sea and Me

53

When we were young, before we entered the Casting, Loretta was always staying over at our house. She loved being at home with her father in the Farmlands, but she also came alive when she was on the water.

The summer before she was due to enter the Casting, Loretta would work all day in the fields, then walk to our house. We'd take the boat out in the evening, and just sit, watching the stars come out, letting it drift in the middle of the ocean. We weren't trying to get anywhere in particular—it was just being away from Whitecroft, from all the gossip and rules and, for Loretta, the constriction of what they wanted her life to become.

Each day we'd notice the stars a little earlier, as the darkness drew in more quickly, and the air temperature dropped like a gasping intake of breath in the moment your body hits the seawater.

'My time's running out,' she told me.

I looked at her sadly. I loved the smell of summer that still fragranced the air: the cut grass and sweetness of overripe berries. I was happy with my lot, fishing for Whitecroft. Most other girls seemed excited to be cast and then build their own homes. Loretta just saw a ticking clock.

'I wonder sometimes how long I'll last, once I'm carrying.'

It was true that her mother died in childbirth, and in that first generation, the mortality rate was high. I couldn't believe that someone as strong and full of life as Loretta could succumb to it.

'You're not weak in your constitution,' I laughed. 'There's no reason why you won't outlive us all.'

She was like Cressida: physically strong, used to hard labour. I didn't see why childbearing would be any different.

'It isn't just the physical carrying,' she told me. 'It's the lack of freedom. They want me to be tied down, in and out of the Infirmary, for the next ten years of my life. After that, I'll have so many responsibilities with children and the Farmlands that I'll never have time to sail. I'm not supposed to, as it is.'

'You never seem to care much about the rules,' I said.

'It's choice I care about,' she said. 'And they're going to take it away from me.'

She was lying in our boat, her hair like black velvet around her head, and her hands were crossed over her flat stomach. I sat as close to her as I dared, and fought the urge to place my hand over hers, or stroke her hair.

'You know, if you were cast with me, you'd be allowed to sail. It would be your trade.'

'If I was carrying, they wouldn't let me. I'd be punished.'

She twisted her body to look up at me.

'Anyway, you're three years' younger than me,' she pointed out. 'Although I can't see myself being cast this year. There's no way John Crest will choose me. If he does, you'll have to smuggle me away where no one can find me.'

I clenched my fist. The thought of John Crest running his hands all over her made me murderous.

'I won't let them do that to you,' I told her.

'Are you going to take on the General?' she teased, raising her eyebrows. 'He seems quite proud of his little system he's set up.'

It was just as well we were out at sea when she said things like this. She could have got into real trouble if anyone in Whitecroft heard her. But Loretta usually spoke first and thought about it later. Head over feet.

'That's why I think you need to *play* the system.'

I meant: that's why I think you should choose me. But she didn't hear it like that. Instead, she went quiet. When she next spoke, it was obvious she had a totally different train of thought to me.

'It would be great to beat him at his own game.'

'What are you talking about?'

'You know, use the system he's put in place in order to strengthen the parts of Whitecroft he's trying to weaken.'

'Why would he want Whitecroft to be weak?'

She looked at me, almost with pity.

'George, you're such a good person you just don't understand how power-grabbing, ruthless people work. He only wants Whitecroft to be strong when he can take credit for it, and keep the town under his control. My family and your family are not willing to follow him blindly, and he knows it. So there's no way he would let us be cast together. I need to think of a way to outsmart him.'

I wondered if she was actually considering being cast with me, then. Perhaps for the first time. I was too excited to think more carefully, and I blurted out my heart.

'I love you, Loretta.'

She immediately sat up and stared at me in shock.

'What?'

'I love you.'

There was only a small distance between us. The waves lapped quietly and the stars watched silently, as if time was frozen, as Loretta looked at me with her bright eyes.

'George.' She spoke finally, and I knew that I had made a mistake in telling her. 'You're so young. You can't love me. It's no good. Nothing good can come of it.'

She didn't seem to feel anything for me; perhaps, because she wouldn't let herself feel anything. She was more guarded after that moment, that stupid moment where I couldn't stop myself from being honest and truthful with her.

She was wrong, though, when she said that nothing good could come of my love for her. When she was in trouble, later on, she came to me. When she died, she knew I would always look out for Elise, in case anything happened to her father. Through loving her, I came to understand why she did what she did.

She wanted to beat the General at his own game, and she did.

ALICE

54

'There's still so much I don't understand about what happened,' I say, tears gathering in my eyes. 'My mother being cast with my father, my aunt being blanked but then carrying Elise… Both of them dying in the Infirmary. My father never spoke of it. It's his rule, not speaking about the past.'

'People do speak about the past in Whitecroft,' George says, adding more logs onto the fire. 'Think about it: every time we tell a story, we share about something that happened yesterday or a month ago.'

'I wish I'd heard more stories like yours,' I tell him.

The truth is, this is the most I've ever spoken to George in my whole life. I've not spent much time around the Swifts.

I look up at the beautiful velvet sky, decorated with so many bright stars. There are some days when the sky seems to judge me and hang over me like a curse; but not tonight. Tonight, the universe seems warm and safe somehow. Perhaps it's due to being on this boat, drifting quietly through the calm waters, with this unlikely group of people. My own Pact.

It's crazy, because I'm so far from home… from anywhere… but I finally feel like I belong.

'I'm sorry about what happened, with you and my aunt.'

George shrugs, looking out into the darkness.

'Sometimes people don't make the choices we want them to. We still love them anyway.'

He examines my face for a moment.

'You understand,' he says. 'You love your father, but you disagree with him.'

My cheeks burn, although he probably won't notice. It's the

shame of being disloyal that I just can't shake.

'You won't always agree with Palmiro either,' he continues. 'Although it might not seem that way now.'

Being reminded of my future, being pledged to Palmiro, gives me the sensation of drowning, trying to scream underwater. I try to shake it off.

'Everyone says that we're too different.'

By everyone, I mean Viola and Amita. I wrap a blanket around my legs for extra warmth, wondering if George will chime in with similar thoughts. I suddenly really want to hear his opinion. He doesn't say much, but I feel like he sees and notices a lot.

'Too different?' he echoes. 'Because he comes from Cape and you come from Whitecroft?' George shakes his head emphatically. 'Listen, whoever you love, you're going to be different to them. You won't always agree. The point of love is that you both choose to keep going and find ways to overcome your differences.'

'What if we can't, though?' I ask, voicing my deepest fear. 'What if I bring him all the way over to Whitecroft, and things don't work out between us?'

'You have to choose to make things work,' George says. 'Both of you. That's what my parents taught me, anyway.'

It sounds like something my grandfather would say. Thinking about him gives me a stab of pain. How is he? How long does he have left? Will I make it in time?

'Alice,' George says, 'are you sure that being pledged to Palmiro is really what you want?'

I lift my eyes to meet his. There doesn't seem to be any point lying to him.

'I don't feel like I have a choice,' I whisper.

I drop my head onto my knees, hugging them to my chest, and feel a few tears escape.

'I meant what I said, about choosing to make things work,' he says. 'But you have to *want* it. That's why I knew I had to let Loretta go. I couldn't force her to love me, or to change our relationship from friendship into something more.'

'Before I came to Cape, I didn't really have friends,' I confess. 'So I'm finding it hard to tell the difference.'

George gives me a wry smile.

'If you're pledged to someone, you must want to be with them in the good times and the bad. To stay by their side even when things get tough. The only way you know that is by experience. Relationships are easy to start. When they get tested, if they still last… Then you know that what you have is real.'

Unconsciously, I turn my head towards Blake's direction. It looks like things between him and Viola are not going well. It might even be over between them. But that doesn't mean anything, I tell myself. It still doesn't mean that I'm free from Palmiro. And even if Blake was available, would I just be a new novelty for him, then, instead of Palmiro?

'I want something real,' I murmur, my voice cracking.

'Don't accept anything less, then,' George says, smiling kindly. 'You deserve love, Alice.'

He sits there quietly as I sob.

'Sorry,' I say, wiping my eyes.

'For what—being human?' George raises an eyebrow. 'It's all right to cry. You don't have to be perfect all the time.'

'That's funny, Blake said—'

I stop, remembering my first conversation with Blake on the island. He told me I didn't have to be little Miss Perfect all the time. He *saw* me. And the more I think about this, the more I realise that Palmiro, for all his kindness and interest, hasn't really seen me in the same way. He's noticed me, but it's not quite the same, somehow.

I break down into sobs again.

'You like him,' George says.

I nod miserably, sniffing and wiping my face with the blanket.

'Does he know?'

I shake my head. Maybe this is why I've never had friends. I'm a terrible friend to Viola, who's made space for me in her home and waited in a cave with me for hours. I don't know what

Palmiro would think of me if he knew how I felt. He'd probably feel betrayed. So I hope Blake has no idea how I feel, because if he did…

Well, things are already complicated enough.

'That's why you're upset.'

I sniff again.

'Quite the predicament,' George says, poking the fire and adding another log.

'What would you do, if you were me?' I ask.

George looks at me with his steady gaze.

'I'd wait,' he says, 'until things became clearer. Until something changed, or until I was sure of what was right.'

I look down at my hands, twisted in the blanket.

'I'm not very patient.'

He chuckles.

'No one is.'

His expression turns sober again.

'In matters of the heart, it's easy to be impulsive. You have to resist that when other people's feelings are involved.'

He doesn't say it, but I know he's thinking of Viola.

'Can you tell me what you think of Palmiro?' I ask, keen to change the subject and hear what he thinks, given he's seen Palmiro much more than I have.

George pauses for a moment.

'I first met him a few years ago,' he says. 'He started sailing to the meeting point island with Cayman. He's a brilliant sailor. I've watched him at the dock. But you know that. You're asking me about his character, aren't you?'

I nod, hugging my knees more tightly. The air is colder now, with a growing sharpness. I'm grateful for the fire.

'He's someone who takes his responsibilities seriously,' he says. 'He goes all over Cape, seeing everybody, checking if anyone needs help. He smiles at everyone, and he follows through when he says he'll do something.'

'That's good,' I say, nodding eagerly.

'The only thing is, when someone is sociable and helpful, it can sometimes mask what they're really thinking and feeling underneath,' George continues. 'Even though he loves people, and he's always talking and laughing, I don't think Palmiro shows his true self to many.'

His true self. It only underlines to me that there are invisible barriers between us. He doesn't see me, and I don't really see him either.

'What do you think of Cape?' George asks, breaking into my increasingly morose thoughts.

I perk up immediately.

'It's so different to Whitecroft. So much warmer.' I pull the blanket closer, and remember dancing on the beach, the sand soft and comforting. 'The people there are so welcoming. There's always music, and the way they sing… They're always so joyful, even though I think their lives are harder than ours in Whitecroft in some ways.'

'The land is not so easy to farm,' George says, nodding agreement.

'I enjoyed the ceremony,' I say, with some shyness. It's so alien to our ways in Whitecroft. 'Although my father said it was all lies and propaganda.'

'He just criticises what he doesn't understand,' George says. 'I think Whitecroft could use a little more faith, love, gratitude and forgiveness, don't you?'

I nod and smile. George is just so accepting. Wherever he is, I think he would fit in and get along fine with everyone. In Whitecroft, I'm like a spiky thistle, stinging anyone who gets too close. I don't want to be like that anymore.

But I'm worried that going back, that's exactly what's going to happen. That even though I think I've changed, and I feel like someone new, returning to Whitecroft will mean that the old Alice comes back. These friendships, fragile and brittle, will break. I'll be left alone again.

I have to make sure that doesn't happen.

55

The voyage continues, the night slowly passing and edging into dawn. George and I are allowed to rest once Palmiro awakens to take charge, and I sleep fitfully, snatches of noise disturbing my dreams. It's hard to keep warm, and Cressida's counterpane has certainly seen more miles in the past few weeks than ever before, but I hold on to the thought of going home to Whitecroft and Grandfather... and Elise.

As much as I love Cape, it isn't home. Is Viola right, that I would feel more like her if I was there longer? She seems anxious and ill at ease, perhaps nervous about the reception that awaits her. Her mother was so devastated when she left.

The sun is high in the sky when I wake up, and I join the rowing. Palmiro looks bright and eager as he tells me that we're on course with a good wind behind us.

'Do you have any idea how much longer it will take?' I ask.

He gestures to the open water and shrugs.

'It's hard as there are no landmarks. Just keep going, that's what we always do. We'll get there.'

He's in his element. He's not fazed at all, and I think back to just before he kissed me, when he said *we can go sailing together and be free from all the things that tie us down...*

Perhaps he wants to be pledged to me because he sees it as a ticket to travelling the world, without his father's reproach.

Amita rows in front of me, her arms strong and unrelenting. She hasn't lost her determination. I can tell she's worried about Riel, but she says nothing. Viola looks as though she's physically struggling. She's pale and tired, and possibly a little queasy.

'Why don't you take a break?' I suggest. 'Get some food.'

Viola manages to make a sort of porridge for us all, and we

brought fruit as well. Palmiro's right: there's nothing on the horizon. The endless water merges with the sky. At least the cloud is clearing. The sun is visible, even though it's weak, and there are still large areas of the sky obscured.

'It feels like we're at the end of the world,' I say.

'This is the best place,' Palmiro says, with a grin. 'This is where there are no rules.'

He was always happy and smiling on Cape, but on a boat, it's like he truly comes alive. It reminds me of my aunt Loretta, from what George told me. I can relate, to some extent, to the feeling of freedom here. Out on the water, there's no one to judge you.

Amita rolls her eyes.

'Come on,' she says. 'Let's get back to it.'

We resume our positions, Amita muttering angrily under her breath. Not long after we've started rowing again, she calls over her shoulder,

'You know why he likes the water? Because he's free from his obligations, that's why. Amount of times his father needed him and it was "oh, where is Palmiro?" Always gone, that's where. On the water, on the mountain… He just wants to hide and pretend he's like everyone else. But he isn't.'

I focus on rowing, unsure how to respond.

'Ever wondered why Palmiro gave you the most detailed tour of Cape, going to the places nobody goes?' she continues. 'Any excuse to escape. And that's what this is all about to him.'

I take a long pull on the oar.

'He wants to help Riel because he feels like it's his fault that Riel left,' I point out.

'It *is* his fault!' Amita says sharply. 'And if he hadn't been dancing all night with you, he might have noticed.'

'You were dancing too,' I say.

'My brother puts loyalty first, above everything,' she says fiercely. 'That's how Palmiro should be.'

'Everyone's different.'

'You think it won't happen to you? His father, his best friend, me… Palmiro has broken faith with all of us. What makes you think that it will be any different for you?'

Her words sting me right in the chest, even though they vocalise my own fears. Maybe *because* they vocalise my fears.

'He told me about his sister,' I say. 'And what you said about him escaping through showing me around—he told me that himself.'

'He is our leader's son,' Amita says emphatically. 'You must understand this, because you are a leader's daughter. His life is not his own, and the sooner he realises that, the better. Our people need him.'

I have no answer to this. I keep rowing, but my heart is racing with panicked thoughts. If Blake stays with Viola, and Palmiro rejects me, then I'll be alone again with no prospect of being pledged. Ever.

'I suppose you think he should be with you,' I say bitterly.

She shrugs.

'I am not talking about romance,' she says. 'I'm talking about duty.'

Why must they always be in opposition?

Palmiro catches my eye from the other side of the boat and smiles. I grimace back. My arms are burning, but so is my heart. And every time I look at Blake, it only gets worse.

56

The hours drag on. Still there's no sign of land. George looks at the sky, worried. There had been patches of sky visible, but now there is a thick block of dark cloud approaching quickly. We move up and down on the waves, sea spray in the air.

'I think that's going to hit us soon,' George says.

'Is there any way to avoid it?' Viola asks, sounding panicked.

'We need to stay on course,' Blake says.

'Not if it means we drown,' Viola snaps.

'No one is going to drown,' Palmiro says.

'You've never sailed this way before. Have you?' Viola asks, unnecessarily. We all know no one has sailed this way before.

'We don't have far to go,' George says. 'Anyway, we don't have enough supplies to take any detours.'

I look over to where we kept the fire going last night. The log supply is severely diminished and though we're being careful with what we drink and eat, we aren't prepared for any long-term voyages.

'I have to get to my grandfather,' I remind everyone. 'Even just an hour could make a difference.'

'Well, we need to row faster,' George says.

I'm not used to all this physical work and I already feel like Amita is rowing twice as fast as me, so my heart sinks. I've got that faint sick feeling of being tired and part of me just longs to lie down in a soft bed, pull the covers up to my chin and shiver myself into some state of warmth. Out on the boat, we're always battered by the wind and even when it's not raining, I still feel permanently damp.

This is not about me. I remind myself. This is about Grandfather and Elise.

With renewed effort and vigour, we cut through the increasingly choppy water. We can barely speak, we're all rowing so hard, and George is steering. There's a heaviness that's settled upon us—part grim determination, to keep going no matter what, and part of it is deep misgiving that we're heading into treacherous conditions. It's a huge effort, but the boat is moving closer to our destination. But every time I look at the sky, the cloud has moved too, thickening above our heads.

The air is icy, and my fingers went numb long ago, but at least my body is warmed by the exertion of rowing. Cold, wet sleet starts to fall, splashing down my face. It's so irritating that my hands aren't free to wipe it away. The sleet creates a hazy mist and it's hard to see much beyond the boat.

'I thought I saw land!' George shouts. 'But I can't be sure.'

Hope flares within my heart, but part of me also wonders if George is hallucinating. We're all so desperate. The wind picks up, and the movement of the boat becomes more extreme. I swallow down my nausea and keep rowing.

The storm brings its own darkness, but it must be nearing twilight now anyway. We have no fire; we're depending on arriving by nightfall.

Help is my only thought.

Somehow, we keep going. The waves grow taller, and larger amounts of water spray onto the deck. The sleet rains down on us, and George has to shout over the wind. Just at the point where I don't think I can physically go on, George yells,

'Land ahoy!'

It feels like we're fighting the wind, and the boat is going in circles, though we must be making some progress. I'm panting and out of breath, and when I look up to the horizon, I see land ahead, but it still looks so out of reach.

'There are rocks here. We need to get around them,' George calls.

His face is fixed in concentration as he navigates, when the tide pulls us off course and the wind battles against us. Every stroke is like pulling the heaviest object in the world through thick molasses, like you're trying to move the entire ocean.

'The sail needs adjusting!' Amita springs up and runs, unbalanced with the tossing ship, to the mast.

Amita struggles against the fierce wind, George hollering instructions at her, and we stop rowing because without her we will just go in circles. Palmiro and Blake both stand and step towards the sail, but then suddenly the boat judders and I feel the vibrations of impact. Amita loses her balance and falls, but as she's holding the ropes, she doesn't make impact with the deck. Her arms are badly twisted at an awkward angle, and she cries out in pain. Palmiro lifts her down and Blake finishes trimming the sail. Viola and I exchange a panicked look.

'What happened to the boat?' I shout to George. 'Shall I go and look?'

George shakes his head emphatically.

'Too risky!' he yells. 'You could get swept overboard.'

Amita is curled up with a blanket, holding her arm. I can see Palmiro talking to Blake.

'Viola, go and look after Amita,' Blake says, managing to walk over to her without stumbling. 'I'll take your place here.'

We rearrange our positions, and as Viola leaves, he gives me a smile that cuts straight to my heart.

'Come on, Princess, let's get you home.'

Stupid as it is, his words give me a surge of adrenalin, and we start to row with vigour. My hands are chafed and raw, and I keep thinking about potential holes in the side of the vessel, but I also think about land. I watch Blake's arms pulling on the oar, the movement of his shoulders, and I feel carried by his strength. Each stroke is a step closer.

At some point the storm blows over—or maybe we just row out of it—but I notice that the sleet has ceased. The sea's blackness is spreading with the darkening sky. The mist clears and we don't hit any more rocks.

I can just about make out the shape of the land now. I never thought I'd be so happy to see Whitecroft again.

57

Predictably, it isn't straightforward to arrive on dry land. It's dark, and impossible to light anything, because everything was drenched by the sleet or spray of the ocean. George asks Viola to test the depth of the water with a long cane, but she can't find the sea bed. We keep rowing closer, but the thought of another night on board this cold, wet ship is unbearable.

'I don't know how we're going to do it without waiting for dawn to break,' George says, shaking his head.

I want to cry with frustration—to be this close to Grandfather, but held back. What if I'm too late?

'Look!' Blake says, pointing.

A small light blinks from the shore. Hope burns in my chest immediately.

As we are all straining our eyes to focus upon it, another one appears nearby.

'Do you think there's someone there?' I ask.

George pulls out a metal whistle, tied around his neck and gives a loud signal. We hold our breath and watch as the light moves backwards and forwards in response.

'There is!' Viola says. She looks ready to sob with relief.

George gives another blast on the whistle.

'Right, final push everyone,' he says.

With renewed energy, we pull towards the shore. Amita sends Viola back to help George, who gives her the cane to check for rocks and depth. Some kind of inner fire helps me to move my exhausted arms and fight for each stretch of closing distance. George starts to call out, and we hear a response, muffled by the wind. It sounds like a woman's voice.

'I think it's my mother,' Viola says, looking as though she might faint. I can't see her all that clearly, but she's swaying unsteadily.

'Are you all right?' I ask, panting between pulling on the oar.

'Mum!' she cries, waving frantically.

The light moves again.

In a dream-like blur of time and movement, we row closer to the sparks of light until we're able to make out the shape of the dock, lit by several lanterns. Amie Taylor stands, her face illuminated with the lantern in her hand, and tears are streaming from her eyes. George and Palmiro together expertly jump onto the dock and secure the boat, then help Viola out first. She runs into her mother's arms, the lantern dropped, and then righted by George, and it pierces my heart to hear their sobs as they are reunited.

In the darkness of the boat, I hear Blake make a small groan in his throat. Aching and stiff, I extract myself from rowing and reach into the shadows to find him. I pat his back and rest my hand on his shoulder. He's still sitting, frozen in position, but he immediately places his hand over mine.

'I thought I was doing the right thing, bringing her to Cape,' he says. 'But I was wrong.'

I squeeze his shoulder. Palmiro and George are helping Amita, carefully, to climb down onto the dock, so we stay where we are.

'Maybe none of us realise how deep Whitecroft is lodged in our hearts,' I say, thinking of my own emotions as we approached the shore.

'Or certain people.'

He stands up, but instead of letting my hand fall, he keeps hold of it. My heart races as he faces me, our bodies close in the darkness.

'I don't want to be pledged to Palmiro,' I blurt out.

'Why not?' he asks softly, moving even closer towards me.

'I think you know why,' I whisper, and I tremble—I actually tremble.

His other hand, the one not holding mine, reaches up to cup my face.

'I'm a terrible friend,' I say, on the edge of tears again.

'Alice!' Palmiro calls me. 'Are you coming?'

I pull away from Blake, grabbing my bundle with my counterpane. I need to remember why I came back. Grandfather, Elise… Maybe I can give the counterpane to Grandfather for extra warmth. Palmiro takes my hand to assist me off the boat, while Blake stands directly behind me. Ignoring the situational irony, stepping onto the dock feels euphoric. We actually made it.

We all stand awkwardly on the dock while Amie and Viola are still hugging and crying.

'I hoped you would come!' Amie says, through her tears.

'I'm sorry,' Viola repeats, over and over.

'Why don't we go into my cottage?' George says, indicating to Palmiro.

We make our way along the dock, onto the shingle, and follow George with one of the lanterns.

'Amie, has the boat with William and Charles arrived back yet?' George asks.

'No,' she replies. 'That's why we've been putting the dock lights on. We thought they would have been back days ago.'

'There may be another ship as well,' George says. 'We'll leave the boat for now but we'll need to move it in the morning.'

I notice Palmiro is shivering. It's funny, I've shivered my way through the voyage, but I've been so happy to step onto dry land again, I hadn't noticed the cold.

'We'll build a fire straight away,' George says, hanging the lantern up by the cottage door and ushering us inside. He gathers wood from his store and follows us in.

I've never been inside the Swifts' cottage before. George lights a match and then a few candles give some illumination to the dark space. Blake helps him to build a fire, and George sends me to the larder to bring out some food. I find a jar of nuts and some apples.

'Can you look at Amita's injury?' George asks Amie.

She wipes her face and Viola holds a candle so that she can look at Amita's arm.

'What happened?' she asks.

Amita explains, and demonstrates her limited movement.

'Can you try to reach your hand like this?'

Amie puts one hand over her head. She guides Amita's hand, and Amita cries out, but then something clicks back into place.

'Does that feel better?' Amie asks. Amita tries out some movement and nods. 'I think it was dislocated. We still ought to check it over at the Infirmary.'

'I can take her,' George says immediately. 'You should take Viola home.'

'Yes,' Amie says, avoiding looking at Blake.

Blake says nothing, but his jaw twitches.

'I need to go to my grandfather,' I say.

'Snow's deep out there,' Amie says.

I turn to George.

'Can I borrow your sledge?'

58

Packing up the sledge with lanterns, fuel and some (rather limited) food supplies, I set off with Palmiro and Blake on the path to the Farmlands. The carpet of white snow brings a brightness of sorts into the darkness of the trees on either side.

'You don't have to come,' I tell Blake.

'I'm not hanging around on my own waiting for Whitecroft to come and lash me for running away,' he says. Then he adds, under his breath, 'And there's no way I'm leaving you.'

Blake's family live out in the Farmlands too, so he knows the path well. I can see he's bothered about Viola but I don't want to antagonise him by asking about it.

Palmiro is uncharacteristically quiet. He helps to prepare the sledge, and then pushes it along with us, but he looks shivery and pale.

'Are you all right?' I ask.

He nods, but says nothing. It feels like there's suddenly distance between us, even though we've been on the boat the whole time together.

I focus my energy on driving the sledge forwards. This initial section of path will be uphill, but then hopefully there will be a long stretch of going downhill where we won't need to push so hard. We manage to take a side path, avoiding the centre of Whitecroft, and hopefully Amie, Viola and Amita will get to the Infirmary without raising too much notice. Most people would be inside their homes by this time, but you never know.

Blake's words renew my sense of anxiety; will I be punished for leaving Cape? But then, I could argue that my father hadn't expressly forbidden me. He just… left without me. It's too complicated to deal with those emotions, so I swallow them down and focus on our journey. The path looks endless in the daylight; even more so in the consuming darkness. I try to rally myself by considering how much closer I am to Grandfather and Elise now than I was two days' ago, but staring into the black void ahead, it isn't much comfort.

I have no idea what I'm going to find when I arrive.

All three of us are silent, heavily weighed down by our thoughts, and despite our physical exhaustion from the sea voyage, we're grimly determined to push through this final stretch. Pushing a sledge with the strength of three people isn't anywhere near as difficult as the rowing. When we reach the peak of the path, and then start the descent, the sledge quickly gains momentum and we end up running.

'Jump on, Alice,' Blake tells me, helping me up from behind.

Clumsily, I fall onto the sledge and hold on tightly to a rope, tethering a lantern, while the boys pick up speed together. Our visibility is very immediate, so part of me worries that we might crash into something now that we're going faster, but I also know that the path is just a plain dirt track. There's something exhilarating about this. The cloud seems to have cleared and the stars are mapping out the smooth velvet sky. I've never loved Whitecroft like I do in this moment, flying across the snow with the scent of pine in the air. It feels magic.

Perhaps it's the contrast from being on the boat, tossed by the waves with the greatness of nothingness all around us. Here, we're hemmed in, but in a reassuring way, by the solid earth beneath us and the trees fencing us in from the wind.

We reach the end of the downhill stretch, and the sledge slows.

'I'll jump off and help you,' I say, swinging my legs down and crunching into the snow.

I grab onto Palmiro to help to right myself, but he falls down with me. Blake carries on pushing the sledge forwards, and I laugh, scrambling up and dusting snow off my skirt and cloak.

'Sorry, I didn't mean to take you down with me,' I say.

Palmiro is still on the ground.

'Palmiro?'

I crouch down and turn his shoulders so I can see his face. He's shivering violently and his eyes are unfocused.

'Blake!' I shout.

I quickly undo my cloak and wrap it around him. His clothes are thin, and they're not made from the thick wool that mine are. Blake runs up and assesses the situation.

'We've got to get him on the sledge,' he says.

'I'll get blankets.'

Blake hoists him up over his shoulder, and I hurry to prepare a space on the sledge and unpack some dry blankets we found at the cottage. We lay Palmiro down, and rearrange the ropes so that he's secure and can't fall off.

'You ready, Princess?' Blake asks me, dryly.

I lean over and shove my full weight against the sledge. He joins me, and we drive the sledge forwards. There's less exhilaration now, and pure desperation. It feels like everyone I care about is at risk.

I try to calculate how long we've been travelling already, what kind of distance we've covered, but it's impossible to know. One foot in front of the other. That's the only thing I can focus on.

Time is a strange vortex, expanding and compressing in the most inexplicable way. We could have been running for hours;

perhaps it was only minutes. When the clearing for Grandfather's cottage becomes visible, I cry out with relief. We push the sledge right up outside the door, and Blake steps back, straightening his spine and wiping his brow.

'You know, I find it easier to be the bad guy than the hero,' he says.

I fling my arms around him, startling him, and sob onto his shoulder.

'Thank you,' I say, my voice muffled.

He hugs me back, then, with unexpected warmth.

'We're in this together,' he says, pulling back and meeting my eyes.

I'm so relieved he came with me. I don't know how I would have done this without him. Now that I'm finally here, I struggle to think clearly. I need to get inside, but I need to help Palmiro.

I step towards him, while he still shivers on the sledge, but Blake holds out his arm to stop me.

'Wait,' he says. 'You don't know what you're going to find in there.'

He gestures towards the cottage. It's ominously dark.

'Let's go inside first, before we bring Palmiro in.'

I nod, sudden fear gripping me. Reading it in my eyes, Blake takes my hand.

'It's okay,' he says. 'Whatever happens… We'll deal with it.'

We turn and climb the steps to the door.

ELISE

59

At first, I think I'm dreaming.

The tiredness is like cement in my veins and eyelids. I don't feel I could move if I tried. But I'm hearing noises: voices, feet on the steps. I can't grasp who it is, because it feels like so long since I saw anyone except Grandfather.

The thought of him drives me to move. I have to get up—how long has it been since I last checked on him? Time is blurring and whenever I'm not staggering around, I'm asleep. My throat is dry and I raise my body slightly, stretching out my hand for the cup beside my bed. It's so hard to lift my head, but I manage to take a few sips. I put the cup down and lie flat for a few seconds to recoup my (pitiful) strength.

'Hello?'

I didn't imagine it. The voice is female, with an edge of familiarity, but I can't place it. I open my mouth but I struggle to make a coherent sound.

'Here,' I croak.

I slowly move my legs down so that my feet graze the floor, and push myself up with my elbows until I'm sitting up. I sit there, waiting for the dizziness and nausea to subside.

'Elise.'

Alice stands in my doorway, staring at me with a stricken expression. I must look terrible with my musty nightclothes and unwashed hair.

'Grandfather.'

I manage to choke out the word, pointing towards the door.

'I will go to him now,' Alice says, looking about to leave.

'Take me.'

I hold out my hand, needing her to help me up. For a split second the past hangs between us like an icicle about to drop and smash into a hundred pieces. Then she takes my hand, and comes beside me to support me as I stand.

We've never been as close as this to each other before.

She smells of the sea.

We shuffle awkwardly forwards, squeezing through the doorway, and then move through the next door into Grandfather's room. The air is cold and the fire went out in the main cabin long ago. It feels like death.

'There's a chair.'

It's Blake's gruff voice, and I feel his strong arms lift me away from Alice and lower me onto the chair next to Grandfather's bed. The three of us listen to our own breathing in the gloom, with a lantern I don't recognise on the floor in the corner. Grandfather is white. His chest moves occasionally, but I'm taking three breaths for each time he breathes.

Alice kneels down on the floor next to my chair, takes his hand into hers, and weeps.

Tears start into my eyes, but less from the nearness of death. The reality of that hasn't sunken in yet. I'm crying because I'm seeing Alice's heart in a way that I've never done before, and out of sheer relief that she's here and I'm not alone to face this anymore.

Blake takes a step backwards.

'I'll get Palmiro.'

I remember Palmiro from sailing to the meeting point, months ago now. A lifetime ago. Is he really here? I look at Alice, her travelling cloak still on, covered in snow. How long did it take them to get here?

'I'll light the fire,' I say. I should never have let it die.

'I can do it,' Alice says, sniffing.

'No,' I say gently, pushing myself up from the chair to stand. 'You stay with him.'

I hobble into the main room just as Blake walks in, Palmiro over his shoulder.

'Lay him on the rug,' I instruct.

He's shaking, and I gather up some blankets from the chairs to cover him.

'Can you hear me, Palmiro?' I ask. 'It's Elise.'

He nods. His eyes are fearful, so I rub my hands on his arms to try to warm them, through the blankets, and tuck them in tightly around him. Blake starts building the fire with layers of fuel, and then lights it.

'Is Will with you?' I ask, knowing what the answer will be.

Blake shakes his head.

'There were bad storms,' he says. 'We came straight here, without stopping off at the smaller island. We think he's there, waiting for calmer conditions to set off. They may have left by now.'

'You came back.'

He meets my eyes, then looks away.

'Things change. Viola wanted to see her family.'

'But you didn't?'

He shrugs.

'Now that I'm here, I'll go over and see them in the morning. No use going now. Not when everything's… like it is.'

He looks at me with sympathy. Between us, Palmiro shivers on the rug, and through my grandfather's open door, it sounds like Alice is crying again.

'You must be hungry,' I say, ignoring the rolling nausea in my stomach.

'Don't play the hostess.' He reaches over and touches my sleeve, to stop me. 'Go back to bed.'

'How can I?' I ask. 'Have any of you slept?'

He doesn't answer, so I know they didn't. They must be exhausted.

'Listen, if you could take the mattresses from my bed and Alice's, and put them in Grandfather's room, then we can rest while keeping watch on him. You could sleep on the chair in here with Palmiro, and keep the fire going.'

'All right,' he agrees. 'But first, I need a drink. Have you got anything stronger than water?'

60

Although I feel tired and wrung out inside, I lie awake on my mattress and listen to the laboured breathing of Grandfather, and Alice's soft sighs as she finally sleeps. I imagine our mothers, camping out with him when they were young, and there's something beautiful in the symmetry.

Yesterday, I could never have pictured this scene now.

Yet I'm unmistakably glad that Alice came. I've never been pleased to see her before. She seems… different, somehow. Less guarded, perhaps. I can't doubt her sincerity.

My heart aches that Will is still out there somewhere, but the fact that they arrived safely gives me hope that he will, too. He could come back tomorrow.

The rest of the house is quiet, so I expect Palmiro and Blake are sleeping too. Blake made sure the fire was burning strongly. It's such a relief that it's not all down to me anymore.

Maybe tomorrow we can make some broth and bread. Maybe tomorrow, I'll finally start feeling better too.

I wake to a gentle pressure on my shoulder.

'Grandfather's awake,' Alice whispers.

I open my eyes, though the sluggishness of sleep is hard to shake off. Dim light comes from the gap between the curtain and the window. It's morning, not long after dawn.

My empty stomach churning with nausea, I carefully roll onto my side, then sit up. After waiting a moment, I push myself up to stand and sway, unbalanced, until I grab onto Grandfather's bed.

Alice is on one side, holding his hand, so I go to the other. His skin feels cool to touch, fragile as paper.

'Elise,' he says.

When he speaks, it's like a murmur as he breathes out. His eyes flutter open but close again quickly, like he hasn't got the strength to see anymore. He turns his head to the other side.

'Alice,' he says.

'Yes, Grandfather,' Alice says. Her voice squeaks, and I can hear the tears in it. 'I'm here.'

'You girls,' he speaks slowly, painfully, 'must look after each other.'

Alice lets out a sob. He turns his head back towards me.

'Elise,' he says. 'Promise me.'

I look at Alice, crying as she holds onto his hand, and gulp back the lump in my throat.

'I promise,' I say.

I can feel a tear escape and run down my cheek. His fingers press lightly against my hand, and then his hand falls limp. With his head rolling back against the pillow, Grandfather takes a breath. And then he doesn't take another.

I watch as his chest remains still, the sight hypnotic, while in my head a thousand memories are swirling like autumn leaves in the wind. Walking together in the woods, working together in the fields. Making bread. Eating broth by the fire.

I often thought my life was too simple, too boring. How many times I wanted something different. But now, as I look back over the life my grandfather gave me, I see how beautiful and perfect it really was.

The grief collapses inside me. I lower my head to kiss his hand, and I sob.

ALICE

61

When Elise starts to cry, I quietly leave the room, thinking she must want to be alone. Brushing my tears aside, I'm startled by Blake, who must have been standing outside the door. He looks at me for a moment in an unspoken question, then seeing the answer in my face, pulls me against his chest in a crushing hug.

'I'm sorry,' he says.

I hear the words vibrating through his chest; my sobs drown out everything else.

Once I've pulled back and tried to control my emotion, I notice Palmiro, standing over by the door.

'How are you?' I ask, striding towards him.

When I reach him, holding out my hands, he clasps them, but holds me at a distance instead of drawing me in closer.

'I am sorry about your grandfather,' he says, in a more stilted manner than usual. 'I am sorry that I was a burden to you in getting here, rather than help.'

'It's not your fault,' I say, shaking my head.

'I'm going to see my family,' Blake says, picking his cloak off the hook by the door. 'Palmiro's going to come with me.'

Palmiro nods and drops my hands. His posture is wooden and gives me a sharp sense of foreboding.

'Come back soon?' I say, my tone laced with desperation.

He gives a nod and then steps backwards. Blake gives me a last, lingering look, as though he wishes he could stay, but he feels like he has to go. My mouth moves but no sound comes out. The door closes softly and I take a deep breath, fighting off another surge of emotion. It's no good getting upset. Elise is still unwell and there's barely anything to eat here.

I check the fire is going well, then I start measuring out flour to make some bread. Once I've left the dough to rise, I start making porridge. I'm surprised and alarmed at how low the supplies are. Usually, Grandfather would have large sacks of flour and oats to use through the Freeze. There don't seem to be any here.

Everything's quiet in Grandfather's room. I gently push the door open. My eyes are drawn to check him first, but there's no movement in his chest. His eyes are closed as if he's sleeping peacefully. Lying on her mattress, Elise has fallen asleep. I was going to ask if she wanted some porridge. I don't know when she last ate anything substantial. She's got a haunted, shadowy look about her face.

I leave her to sleep, and eat alone, every chink of the bowl and spoon echoing around the cabin. I've managed to keep the fire going, and I feel safe enough to doze in the chair, hoping I will wake up to replenish the logs. I'm glad that George gave us some firewood. I fall asleep wondering how Viola, Amita and George are doing, and whether Palmiro and Blake will come back soon.

When I wake, I stoke up the fire. I step outside for some fresh air, and the biting cold revives me. The oxygen here feels purer somehow. Judging from the position of the sun, it's early afternoon. Birds call, but the woods are otherwise silent. There's no one in Cressida's house, and Blake's family are further along the copse.

Feeling the ache of grief and loneliness, I find myself drawn towards the path. I can't explain the deep sensation of dread within me, and with each step, I'm more determined to find Palmiro and check that he's fully recovered. He must have gone into shock, but he looked like he blamed himself.

The forest has an oddly restorative effect on me, considering I've never spent much time walking among the trees. The scent of the pines is soothing, and the path feels soft under my feet. I'm alive, and I'm back in Whitecroft. I said goodbye to Grandfather. I can still help Elise.

Thomas Hughes' cabin becomes visible. Blake's mother died when the twins, Alexis and Sophia, were born. They're only a few years younger than me. As I approach, I check the windows for a glimpse of Palmiro, but everything is quiet. The sense of foreboding returns.

I knock the door, and hear some movement inside that gives me some relief. Alexis appears at the window, and then hurries to open the door.

'Alice,' she says, her expression sympathetic. 'I'm so sorry to hear about your grandfather.'

Tears start in my eyes, and I nod, unable to speak.

'Come in and have a drink with us,' she says, standing back to usher me through.

I step inside uncertainly, as I've never been here before, and Sophia greets me and points to a chair. There's no one else inside the cabin.

'Where are Blake and Palmiro?'

The twins exchange a glance. Alexis hurries over to the kitchen to pour me a drink.

'Sit down, Alice,' she says.

I obey, feeling as though I haven't got the energy to stand anymore. She hands me a cup with a warm spiced drink. I gulp it down gratefully.

'Father was worried that if the Council caught him, Blake would be punished for leaving Whitecroft,' Sophia says. 'He's gone to Whitecroft now to see what's happening.'

'Blake?' I ask, confused.

'No, Father,' Alexis says.

'So where's Blake?' There's a moment of silence. 'And Palmiro? I need to see he's all right.'

'Palmiro was fine,' Sophia says. 'But Alice, they're both in danger. Father told them they had to leave and that he would find them when it's safe for them to return.'

'Leave?' I repeat. 'Where have they gone?'

Alexis shrugs.

'Probably the woods. Blake's done lots of hunting trips out there with Father.'

'What am I supposed to do?' I ask, angry and in disbelief that they've just abandoned me. 'My grandfather is dead, Elise is sick, and there's not enough food.'

'We made some extra food for you,' Sophia says, gesturing towards a small bundle on the table. 'We were going to bring it over, but now you're here.'

'Thank you,' I say quietly.

I take the food and stumble back to Grandfather's house, numb with the thought that Palmiro and Blake left me, and faced with the cold reality: I'm on my own.

62

The first thing I do once I've placed my bundle on the table is to revive the fire. I need to bake the bread, and Blake's sisters have given me a few rolls, cheese and more of their spiced drink in a flagon. I'm grateful, because it seems that food is scarcer than usual.

I return to Grandfather's room and gently nudge Elise's shoulder.

'Elise, I think you should drink something. Have some bread.'

She stirs but groans a little. She shakes her head in a slight movement on the pillow.

'I can't,' she says, her eyes still closed. 'I feel too sick.'

'Remember when Ada was ill?' I say. 'She said that eating something helped the nausea go away.'

Elise's eyes snap open.

'Ada?' she says. 'Ada was carrying.'

I don't have to say anything. The realisation drops like a stone into a river.

'You think—' she falters. 'But I—'

Her eyes close again, this time with her forehead furrowed in painful comprehension.

'How did you know?' she asks, reopening her eyes. 'I suppose you did predict it.'

Her tone is bitter. I wince inwardly.

'It's not rocket science,' I reply, but then I look over at Grandfather and remember his charge for us to look after each other. I sigh. 'Cressida sent us a message and suggested that you might be…'

Neither of us can say it.

'I thought I was just ill,' she says. 'I expected to be better after a week. What am I going to do? I can't stay out here alone through the Freeze. Ada was ill for *months*. Where is Will?'

Her voice cracks, and tears glisten in her eyes. She's already dehydrated enough.

'Look, if we made it over the sea, then I'm sure William and Charles will arrive anytime now. Along with my father and Riel.'

'Who's Riel?'

I tell her about what happened in Cape, how they left suddenly, and how Amita is with George waiting to rescue her brother.

'We have to go to Whitecroft,' Elise says. 'I want to be there when Will's boat comes in. And I want to see George.'

'What about Grandfather?'

'We'll have to leave him,' she says. 'We can't bury him on our own, or send his body out to sea either. Unless we ask Blake and Palmiro to help, but I don't want to delay getting to Whitecroft.'

'I don't know where Blake and Palmiro have gone,' I tell her. 'I think Thomas Hughes told them to hide.'

'We have to go, then,' Elise says. 'Can you help me up?'

The urgency of going to Whitecroft gives her a brief burst of energy, but once we're outside and snow falls lightly around us, I can see her take one final look at the cabin and hesitate.

'You can sit on the sledge if you get tired,' I say. 'It isn't that far, really.'

I'm being optimistic, for once. Part of me hopes that William and Charles have already arrived, and will appear on the path before our eyes.

They don't.

I realise how much illness has weakened Elise when she falters against a gust of wind. I'm pulling the sledge and she staggers up the slight incline beside me. We both wear our travelling cloaks, and warm hats I found in Grandfather's cabin. It still hasn't sunk in that he's gone. I press the grief into a tight compartment inside my heart, and focus upon the path ahead.

It's afternoon, but the thick snow clouds block out the weak sunlight. I've walked to Whitecroft and it's only taken me an hour, but that was without snow crunching beneath my feet, and no sledge. Or someone who looks like the next blast of wind might blow them away. I stamp on my misgivings, because what is the alternative? If we stayed at the cabin, we could probably keep the fire going for a little longer, but what would we eat? What would we do with Grandfather's body?

I also feel increasingly nervous about George, Viola and Amita. What happened to them? What if they were seen? If Blake has taken Palmiro into hiding, perhaps Thomas knew there would be punishment for him, and a suspicious reception for any foreigner. What will happen when my father returns, with Riel on board? I hate the thought of being trapped in the cabin, out in the Farmlands, when I feel I need to be at the shore to make sure nothing goes wrong.

The thought of Charles and my father, both at sea on different boats, is hard to grasp. I won't feel at peace until they're safely back, and then, I'll need to ask my father why he left without me.

I wonder what he'll say.

'Alice.'

Elise's voice is faint. I turn to see that she's stopped a few paces behind me, swaying like she's about to collapse. I drop the rope and hold her up by the elbows.

'Come onto the sledge,' I pant, dragging her over.

She crawls onto it, shivering. I try pulling the rope but the sledge barely moves. I walk round to the back, put both my hands on the wood, and push with my whole body weight.

Best not to think about how long this is going to take.

63

After a much shorter stint than I hoped for, I have to stop and gasp in some air. It feels like the snowfall is heavier now, with thicker flakes sticking onto my eyelashes. There's no sign of William or Charles, despite constantly wishing they would appear. I've even thought hopefully about whether Blake might be taking Palmiro back to Whitecroft, and I might see them in the distance and call out for their help.

There's an eerie stillness all around, like the snow absorbs the sound of the landscape. I can hear Elise breathing in sharply, shuddering with cold. I remember the strength I found to row through long hours on the boat, and muster it up again to push the sledge.

I need to be better.

Coming here with the sledge was a challenge, given how exhausted we all were after the voyage, but I'm realising now how much easier it was. There were some downhill stretches, and I had Blake to share the load when Palmiro got so ill we were pushing the sledge with him on it. It seems that Blake definitely bore the brunt of the load, when I feel the weight of Elise against my puny muscle.

I don't think I can do this.

'Are you all right, Elise?' I call, straining to look over at her.

'Y—yes,' she says faintly, nodding her head. Or perhaps she's just physically convulsing.

I remember Palmiro, his lips and face blue, and blink the mental image away. My heart twists when I think about him, and the horrible emptiness of not knowing exactly where he, or Blake, are.

Ahead, the path stretches out, a small incline and then nothing more visible from the brow of the slope. I take a deep breath.

If you are there, if you can hear me, please give me strength.

I bend over and start to push the sledge. After a few minutes, my legs are burning and my chest is tight. Come on. I have to do this. I try to keep my pace going, and I can't think about anything else beyond the heavy weight of the sledge, the pounding of my heart, and my ragged panting. Every step is a step closer. Don't stop. Don't stop.

As we level out and then begin to tip downwards, the pain eases and I feel the momentum start to carry the sledge forwards. I keep running, building up speed, and then even when the ground is flattening out again, I can maintain a good pace. Feeling increasingly hopeful, I run on, fuelled with a spark of excitement that I'm doing this; I'm going to reach Whitecroft, and William and Charles will come back, and I'll find George and Amita and I will no longer bear the burden of caring for Elise alone.

But the daylight is fading. Snow falls from increasingly darkened clouds, from the ominous deep shade of grey to the angry violet bruising, towering from the horizon and multiplying as the wind picks up. After Cape's lazy sunsets, this feels like a very different, hostile sky. I remember Palmiro telling me how beautiful the Creator's colours were, and I try to see the beauty in the shadowy cloudscape above me. All the same, it's the type of beauty I'd rather appreciate from the safety of being indoors.

My boots churn through crisp snow on the ground, the hem of my dress and cloak dampened. I picture George inside his cottage with a roaring fire. Even if no boats have returned, we can wait for them. Amita must be desperate to see Riel.

With some surprise, I realise how much I care about them. Sailing together has bonded us, even though we hardly knew each other before the voyage. Here I am, pulling Elise on a sledge through deep snow. I can barely recognise myself.

This is a good thing. I never liked myself before.

Just as when we travelled on this path from Whitecroft, there are few landmarks to spot on this endless road. It's impossible to tell how far we've come, and how much further there is to go.

But I manage to find a rhythm, my breathing settling, and my body forces the sledge forwards, my arms locked out in front of me.

Palmiro said the Creator made us for a purpose. What if I was made for this moment? To be here right now, pushing Elise away from our dead grandfather and towards fire, shelter and life?

After a long stretch of flat path, where I've maintained some speed, we reach an uphill slope. I grit my teeth and pound towards it, waiting for the resistance to increase. The sledge feels heavier, a leaden weight, and I growl against the protesting pain in my arms and legs and push harder. With a triumphant shout, I reach the top, and allow myself to stretch tall, punching my hands in the air. Against the stormy sky, a flock of starlings ripple in a murmuration, a perfect synchronisation of movement.

'Look, Elise!' I call, laughing and pointing as the birds swarm, swoop and move off towards the horizon.

As my heart swells with gratitude, I hear these words:

You are worth more.

ELISE

64

I heave myself off the sledge, determined to stand. Alice is grinning with delirious happiness, and I don't understand why. Why is she suddenly so set on helping me?

'You've changed,' I comment, shaking snow out of my skirt.

'I know,' she replies, still smiling. 'Are you sure you're well enough to walk?'

'I want to try again,' I say, thinking of Will. Just one minute faster would be worth it, to see his face more quickly.

'Do you know how close we are now?' she asks.

I look around. There's no visible difference in the trees or the path, but the air smells faintly of the sea.

'I think we're nearly there now.'

I don't know how she's managed to do this, to push me this far, but with the end in sight, I feel a burst of energy.

'Let's go,' I say.

The path is level for this section, and I totter along, drawing in deep breaths of salty air. I hope I feel well again soon. I hope my strength returns.

The light is fading fast, but we take a shortcut, a rough path through a field, which means that we avoid going into Whitecroft. The moment when we look down to see George's cottage, with smoke coming from the chimney, is a sweet relief. I lean my weight against a tree, gazing at the sea—stupidly hopeful of catching a glimpse of William. The horizon is clear. The murky grey water merges with the heavy cloud. It's still snowing here, but only lightly. Still, it means visibility is poor. Perhaps it's raining out on the water, and the spray forms a misty obscurity that the gulls swoop in and out from.

'No sign of my father or Charles' boat,' Alice says, straining to look out ahead. 'We're not too late.'

Someone whistles from within the trees, behind me. I twist, the movement making me nauseous, and grip the tree harder. Alice jumps, then runs into the trees.

'Wait!' I croak. 'You don't know who—'

'Blake!' I hear her shout.

I peer into the thicket to see Alice throw her arms around him, nearly knocking him over in her enthusiasm. After a moment of hesitation, he encloses his arms around her.

'Hello Princess,' I hear him murmur.

I blink in surprise. When did Alice get so close to Blake? What happened to Viola? I rack my blurry memory. I think Blake said that she wanted to see her family, which is why she didn't come out to the Farmlands with them. Maybe there was more going on than he revealed.

'You're still standing,' Blake jokes, walking towards me and nodding at my tree support.

'Nice of you to say goodbye,' I comment caustically. Alice might be giving him a hero's welcome, but I'm not impressed.

'My father told me to hide,' he says, his eyes narrowing defensively. 'We came here so we could keep watch on the shore.'

'Where's the other guy?' I catch Alice's eye as I look back into the forest. She blushes slightly.

'Palmiro's gone to mark the dock with lanterns,' Blake says, avoiding looking at Alice. 'He was worried that visibility will be poor again tonight. They may well arrive.'

My heart flips with a sudden rush of hope. Finally, finally, I'll see Will again.

'You had better hide that sledge in the forest,' Blake suggests. 'Easier to get down to the cottage on foot. Watch the path—it's slippery, and it's getting dark.'

'Don't you want to come with us?' Alice asks.

'Can't leave my post.'

They stare at each other for a long moment. I clear my throat.

'Right, we ought to leave.'

'I'll hide the sledge.'

With seemingly boundless energy, Alice darts off. I stare at Blake, who shifts uncomfortably.

'I'm sorry we left suddenly,' he says. 'I genuinely thought it would be better that way. You wouldn't have to feed us, and you were grieving your grandfather. I didn't want to be a burden to you.'

'The only reason I'm alive now is because of Alice,' I reply. 'And I don't even know if I can trust her.'

Blake frowns.

'You saw her eyes when your grandfather died. How can you doubt her sincerity?'

'I don't doubt her love for him. I just don't know if this sudden transformation of her entire character is genuine, and how she feels towards me.'

Blake shakes his head.

'There's bad blood between you, and that's down to the General. He did his best to drive a wedge between you, because he knew that together, you'd be unstoppable. Don't let him win.'

A short distance away, Alice drags the sledge through the trees and then starts to push it underneath a bush.

'Look, if you really need convincing, know this: she came back for you.'

My eyes widen.

'I mean it,' he says. 'She didn't know if she would be in time for your grandfather. She knew he didn't have long left. But when Cressida said that you were ill… I think she wanted to save you.'

For some reason, it brings tears to my eyes. Stupid, irrational emotion.

'I don't know why,' I say, brushing them with the back of my hand.

'Because you're family,' he says. 'Messy, yes. What was it that old Francis Derby used to say? *Unity is worth fighting for.* That's why we're all here.'

'Ready to go?' Alice asks, walking back towards us.

Trust her, Blake's eyes say.

'Ready,' I reply.

65

The path down the cliff is steep, with loose stones bouncing, scuffing up dust, and then falling over the edge. I already feel like I need to lie down again. My head is heavy and my balance is off. I step tentatively, like an old woman, while Alice goes ahead of me and patiently waits for me to catch up.

'Watch out for that rock,' she says, just as I miss my footing and stumble forwards.

She grabs my hand and steadies me.

'Let me just help you down this section,' she says.

She doesn't let go.

I'm too tired to argue, and I need her help more than I want to admit to myself, so I allow Alice to lead me down the perilous way. The gulls are calling in their last foray before nightfall. Here the snow is nowhere near as thick or as deep as in the Farmlands, melted in the salty air. My knees are shaking and my shoulders shiver with the cold, blasting wind from the sea. Alice's hand is warm.

What's happened to her? Why has she changed? Did something happen on the island?

My questioning thoughts churn inside me, like my unsettled stomach, until finally we reach the end of the descent.

'I don't know why you're helping me,' I say bluntly, letting go of her hand once we're on level ground.

She looks at me for a moment, searching my eyes with her brow furrowed.

'I wanted to put things right,' she says. 'What I did before… with George's boat, and threatening you… It was wrong, and I'm sorry. I shouldn't have tried to stop you from being pledged to

William. That wouldn't have solved my problems in the way I wanted it to. I was fooling myself.'

I stare at her suspiciously, but Blake seems to be right. She is genuine. Now I feel wrong-footed, and unsure how to respond. Does she expect an apology from me? She's not going to get one.

I just want to lie down.

'Come on, we're nearly there,' Alice says, positioning herself at my side and supporting me with her arm around my waist.

We stagger across the shingle, and it's now the darker side of twilight. A row of lanterns has been lit, along the edge of the dock. There's light inside George's cottage. Behind us, the black ocean churns expectantly.

My eyes are so heavy, they start to close involuntarily. I jerk them open again. Just a few more steps.

By the time we reach the cottage door, I'm slumping and I would be on the floor if it wasn't for Alice holding me up. She manages to throw it open, and we stumble inside.

'George!' Alice cries. 'We need to lay her down.'

Strong arms support the other side of me and they lift together, carrying me through the familiar cottage. Shells on the walls. Joy's room.

As they lower me gently onto the bed, I feel the ugly, familiar heaving in my throat.

'Here.'

Somehow Alice understands, and grabs a chamber pot just in time. I managed a few hours; that's something at least. There's not much left to throw up, and at least I'm in the right place now. Once I've emptied my stomach, I fall back on the pillows, exhausted.

Will is coming. Will is coming.

ALICE

66

'How long has she been like this?' George asks me, in the narrow corridor just outside the bedroom.

I've made sure Elise is covered with a blanket and has a drink by her bedside, and I've left the door ajar so I'll hear if she needs me.

'It's as Cressida said,' I confirm, and watch his face set in concern.

'And your grandfather?' he asks, even though he knows the answer.

'We lost him,' I say, with a nod.

George lays his hand on my arm.

'I'm sorry. He was a good man.'

'This Freeze is brutal.' I shake my head. 'Your parents are better off on Cape.'

'I certainly don't want them to come back here.'

I follow him back to the main room of the cottage, where the fire is blazing. Amita stands, her arm tied in a sling, and offers me her chair and blanket.

'You look like you've had an adventure or two,' she comments dryly. 'As if the voyage over here wasn't enough. Sit down and tell us what happened.'

I sink gratefully into the chair, pulling the blanket over my knees, and George hands me a warm drink. It tastes like pure nectar.

'There's not much to tell,' I say, between sips. 'Blake, Palmiro and I took the sledge to the Farmlands. Palmiro became ill, shivering with a fever. Perhaps he was too cold. When we got to my grandfather's cabin, he and Elise were alive, but there was no fire and barely any food. Blake looked after Palmiro, I helped

Elise, and then we both stayed with Grandfather until…'

I swallow back tears, and drink more.

'You saw him before he died,' George says, gently.

I nod, feeling a sob in my throat.

'What happened to Palmiro?' Amita asks, her eyes urgent. 'Is he all right?'

'I haven't seen him,' I say, my voice cracking. It stings, stings that he left me. 'Blake took him to his father's house, but then by the time I got there, they had both gone into hiding. We just saw Blake at the vantage point at the top of the cliff. I thought you would have seen him, because he came down here to light the dock.'

'Has he?'

George strides over the window and looks out.

'He didn't come here,' Amita says, disappointed. She must be filled with nervous energy, waiting for her brother.

'How is your arm?' I ask.

'It'll heal.' She shrugs. 'Amie smuggled us into that huge monstrosity—the Infirmary, you call it?'

'It was our airship,' George says. 'You must have one too, surely?'

'Ours is nothing like *that*,' she says emphatically. 'You have more medicine in one of those poky store cupboards in there than we have on our entire island.'

'It was meant to service all the people, not just Whitecroft,' George explains.

'But Whitecroft didn't want to share,' Amita says acidly.

George nods, conceding the point.

'Did anyone see you?' I ask.

'Only Eden Taylor,' George says.

'That turned out to be an awkward moment,' Amita says, with a dry laugh. 'We were just about to leave, and this old lady turns up, ignores me and George, and takes one look at Viola and says she's "carrying", whatever that means. Then Viola bursts into tears, Amie starts crying too, and wailing, so we just quietly left them to it.'

'Viola's carrying?' I look sharply at George, and feel a twist of something in my gut. Guilt. Jealousy.

'There may be more than one reason that Blake's gone into hiding,' he says.

'Do you mean she's carrying a child?' Amita asks. 'That makes more sense. What's so bad about that? Why is everyone crying about it?'

George looks at me to explain.

'Viola and Blake left without going through our usual customs of being pledged,' I tell her. 'Plus, they were breaking the rules by running away. Added to that, a lot of women struggle with childbearing here. My mother died; Blake's mother died. Many of us grew up without our mothers.'

'Why do they die?' Amita asks, shocked. 'I mean, we have none of your technology or your medicine, and we don't lose mothers in childbirth.'

I shrug. It's one of Whitecroft's mysteries that no one has ever unravelled. The rule against talking about the past doesn't help.

It's selfish, but I just feel a sinking disappointment. Blake can't be mine. He'll have to be pledged to Viola.

'You still haven't told us about how you came back here,' George points out.

I lean back in the chair, exhausted just thinking about it.

'We used the sledge. I had to push Elise some of the way, as she wasn't strong enough. She's desperate to see William. Blake seems to think they'll be arriving tonight.'

'It makes sense that they wouldn't be far behind us,' George says. 'You must be worn out. Have some food and then rest. I'll keep a look out.'

'Come on, Riel,' Amita says, staring out of the window.

If she's anything like me, she's probably repeating his name in her head, along with Palmiro's. The past two days are a soupy mass of complicated emotions. Grandfather, Elise, Palmiro... and Blake. I don't know why the news about Viola surprised me so much. I knew they were living together; I was with them. As much as I try to put him out of my mind, his face is the last one I see before I fall asleep.

250

67

'Alice.'

George's voice awakens me. My eyes snap open.

'There's some light on the water. It might be one or two boats coming in.'

I throw the blankets off and sit up, my feet touching the ground. This is it.

I jump up nervously, and George places a finger to his lips.

'Elise is still sleeping,' he says.

We look at each other for a moment. Should we wake her? But if our experience the other night is anything to go by, it could take a while to moor the boats. Plus, I'm still not sure what to expect when they come in. I'm sure William and Charles will be their usual selves. What about Riel, the Crests and my father? What will he say when he sees me? I'm supposed to be back on Cape where he left me.

'Don't wake her,' I say.

I tiptoe behind George into the main room. He's kept the fire going. Amita's chair is empty.

'Where's Amita?' I ask immediately.

George fetches my cloak and holds it out to me.

'She must have gone out while I was walking outside the cottage,' he says.

'Gone where?' I ask.

He shrugs helplessly.

'She may be injured, but she's used to stealth. I think she's gone to find Palmiro, so they're together when Riel lands.'

At the sound of his name, a pain stabs my chest.

'Why? Don't they trust us?'

'Whitecroft doesn't have a great track record,' he points out.

'What are they planning to do—grab Riel and sail straight back to Cape without us?'

I say it half-joking, but it might be true. I never expected much loyalty from Amita and I barely exchanged two words with Riel, but Palmiro? Was he pretending all this time? What about the promises he made me, that he was going to be pledged to me?

'I have no idea, but I think they will feel safer together,' George says.

I fasten the clasp of my cloak and pull on my woollen hat. George strikes a match and lights a lantern, closing the glass case and setting it on the floor. Then he lays his hand on the door handle, ready to open it.

'Alice,' he says, turning back to face me. 'This situation is a bit like a tinder box. One loose match, and everything will go up in flames. Do you understand me?'

'You mean that my father wants war.' I swallow.

'He lost a lot of power when I went to Cape,' George says. 'He's desperate to regain it, somehow.'

'I know,' I sigh. 'You don't have to tell me what he's like, George. Don't forget he left me behind. I'm not on his side anymore.'

'I believe you,' George says, holding my gaze. 'But I think he won't hesitate to manipulate the natural bond you have for him as your father. Be prepared.'

He opens the door into the cold night, and we step outside. It's no longer snowing, or raining, and the mizzly mist has cleared. In the frosty air, we look out onto the dark carpet of pebbles and the indeterminate blackness of the water. The lanterns are burning, warm and inviting glows along the dock. There are no stars; the sky must still be heavy with cloud.

'Look over there.'

George points, and I follow his direction and notice the faint lights, bobbing in the distance on the water.

'You see it too.'

I start at the unexpected sound of Blake's voice, and then laugh and reach out to find him in the dark. I clasp at his arm and pull him next to me.

'I can barely see a thing out here.'

'Your eyes will adjust,' he says, flashing his white teeth. 'How long will it take them to come in, George?'

'Hard to say. Why don't you two stay here and I'll see if I can get a closer look? You're not intending to make your presence known, are you?'

'Not unless I have to,' Blake replies.

George nods, his face illuminated by the lantern, and then walks further down the beach.

Blake and I stand in the dark, listening to each other breathe. Our hands find each other and his grip is warm. It's like when we were on the boat, when everyone was climbing onto the dock. But that was before I knew about Viola… And I should pull away…

'I've been thinking about you,' he says.

His voice is raspy, like he hasn't done much talking for a while. I stay frozen in place, unable to break away.

'When I saw you on top of the cliff earlier on, you looked so happy you could fly.'

I give a nervous laugh.

'I've never been so glad to see George's cottage.'

'I had no idea you were going to come all the way back here,' he says. 'If I had, I would never have left you. As it was, I was just trying—'

He stops abruptly.

'Yes?' I question, turning my face towards his, even though I can't see much in this darkness.

'It doesn't matter,' he says. 'I deserved a slap in the face, and you threw your arms around me like I was the person you most wanted to see in the world. I've been thinking about that all afternoon, and hoping I can get you to do it again somehow.'

'Blake,' I say, giving his hand a warning squeeze. 'I heard Viola's carrying.'

A low noise comes from his throat.

'You knew, right?'

'I guessed,' he says, anger rising in his tone. 'I knew she wanted to come back, but this must have been the final straw for her.'

'Amie knows now,' I tell him. 'She'll look after her.'

'Yes, that's what I'm afraid of.'

His hand breaks away from mine, and he gestures in the dark.

'Ever since we left Whitecroft, she's been miserable. You know, before, when we were meeting in secret, it was exciting and fun. She said she was attracted to me because I was different. Now I'm beginning to think that she imagined I was someone else, or that she was someone else. Either way, when she realised that being in Cape wasn't going to change who we were, she started to wish she'd listened to her mother.'

'You did take her away from her family,' I remind him. 'Amie was devastated.'

'It was her choice!' he raises his voice. 'I thought I was going to make her happy. I failed.'

'I'm sure that's not true,' I say, even though I don't really know Viola well enough to claim it. She has undoubtedly been miserable most of the time, and I've witnessed more arguments between them than anything else.

'You know, I've never been good enough for her,' he says. 'Here in Whitecroft, the Taylors are like royalty. They're at the top of the pecking order, along with you, Charles and your father. I was always just a boy from the Farmlands. I thought that going out to Cape would change all that. No sooner are we within reach of Whitecroft, then she's crying for her mother and abandoning me, like she wished she could just erase everything that's happened between us.'

I wince at the pain in his voice. I can't see his face, and maybe that's why he's being so brutally honest with me, and with himself.

'You don't know that,' I say. 'She's just scared because she's carrying and she wants her family close by. That doesn't mean she's rejecting you.'

'She was pretty clear before we left Cape that she wanted to come back and forget that we'd ever been together,' he says, his frustration evident. 'Her father's going to kill me.'

'You can put things right. Take a Pledge to her.'

I say it, but it feels like cement in my throat.

'Is that what you want me to do?' he asks, raw desperation in his voice.

'Why are you asking me that?' I say quietly.

'Because I know you understand!' he cries out. 'You withdrew from being pledged to Phillip.'

'Yes, but I'm beginning to think I can't pull back from Palmiro now,' I say. 'Not when so much is at stake.'

'Even after he left you?'

The words hang in the air between us.

'Well, he was with you—'

'He wasn't.'

I stare at where I think Blake's face is. My eyes have adjusted enough to see his outline; the shape of his hair, and his shoulders.

'What do you mean?'

'I mean that when we left to see my family, he stopped long enough to pick up some supplies. When I was chopping wood for the girls, he slipped out. I knew then, that he was going to come back here to be here when Riel arrived. I settled at my watch station, and I saw him a few times, but only from a distance. He wasn't aware of where I was.'

'You made me think that he was here with you!'

'You had just pushed Elise on a sledge all the way from the Farmlands. You were on cloud nine. I couldn't tell you the truth. I didn't want anything to wipe out your smile,' he says, his voice tender.

'Stop it!' I say crossly. 'Whatever you say, it doesn't change that Viola—'

'Doesn't want me, and actually never wanted me,' he interrupts me. 'She used me, Alice. She used me to get out of Whitecroft, and then was annoyed to discover that Cape wasn't the paradise she hoped it would be. Now she blames me for that, and for all of her problems.'

'I'm sure you can work things out, when both of you are less angry.'

'Alice, you're not listening to me.'

'And you're not listening to me, either!'

I take a shaky breath in, then exhale.

'I don't know what Palmiro is doing, but it may not be any kind of betrayal at all. He may have made a plan with Amita, and decided that it was best to not include any of us.'

'And let me guess: if your daddy comes back, and decides that it might be politically useful to pledge you together because it makes it look like he cares about peace and unity, you'll go along with it.'

'What choice do I have?' I ask, my own anger rising. 'Do you have any idea what it's been like for me since you left for Cape? I've been reduced to staying with Charles for months on end, because I'm not welcome in my own house anymore, and I'm not pledged. I went to stay with Grandfather, and Father summoned me to go on the boat. I didn't really want to go. As it happened, I'm glad that I did. I wished I'd had more time with Grandfather, but going to Cape changed me. Palmiro changed me; he *wanted* to be around me.'

My throat chokes up and I cover my face with my hands. Everything is so messed up and I can't even begin to unravel it.

'Alice.'

Blake wraps his arms around me, tight as a vice, and holds me as I sob.

'Listen to me,' he says, reaching for my hands and pulling them down from my face. His eyes are shining in the darkness. 'You are beautiful. And until you realise that, you're going to think that every Palmiro is a knight in shining armour who can do no wrong. You don't need rescuing, Alice. Never, ever forget that.'

Suddenly his mouth is on mine, and I taste the salt of tears and the warmth of his lips, and it's nothing like when Palmiro kissed me; it's messy and rough and desperate as though our lives depend on it. He is my oxygen and I gasp and gulp him in. If he wasn't holding me up, I would collapse.

'Blake!' I cry out, hoarsely.

'You're perfect,' he murmurs, trailing kisses up to my ear.

'I should give you that slap you said you deserved,' I say, but my panting breath betrays me.

'You don't mean that,' he says. 'Tell me you feel the same.'

'I followed my feelings before,' I say, 'and it didn't end well.'

'This could be different, if you allow it to be.'

'Blake.' I place my hands on his chest and push him back gently. 'It's easy to do this in the dark where no one can see us. I've done too many things in my life in secret. Let's get through tonight, and see what tomorrow brings.'

He breathes in raggedly.

'Okay, Princess.' He kisses the tips of my fingers.

'I already feel sick enough, thank you.'

I jump at the sound of Elise's voice, cutting dryly through the darkness.

'Elise! How long have you been there?'

My cheeks are on fire. I was trying to get her to trust me, and now she's going to see me as a sneak again.

'Long enough,' she says. 'What's going on?'

'It's complicated—' Blake begins.

'Not with you two.' Elise cuts him off. 'I mean with the boats.'

We point out the lights, and the moving light of George's lantern as he walks further down the beach. I can't tell if they're any closer, and I can't really focus on anything apart from Blake kissing me.

Blake *kissed* me.

What is Palmiro going to say?

ELISE

68

'So what's the plan?' I ask, trying to ignore Alice's raging embarrassment, and my own lurching stomach.

'Looks like George is going to help the boats in,' Blake says. 'I think I should stay in the shadows unless I'm needed.'

'Does the General know that you're here? Any of you?' I sift my memory for what Alice told me.

'No,' she answers. 'He left suddenly, with the Crests, and with Riel. We left after that, and we took a different route to beat him here.'

'We have the element of surprise then,' I muse. 'Where are the others?'

Alice looks at Blake for a moment before replying.

'They've… gone into hiding. We think.'

I turn to face her with a questioning frown.

'Palmiro left Blake, and Amita left—presumably to join him,' Alice explains. 'They're probably here somewhere, watching and waiting to see what happens.'

'They don't trust the General. Sensible,' I comment. 'Who else was on the boat with you? Viola?'

Blake is stoney-faced and silent. Touchy subject.

'Is she likely to make an appearance tonight?' I press.

'No,' Alice says, after a quick glance at Blake.

Hence why they decided to seize the moment for a passionate embrace. I refrain from verbalising my thoughts, though.

'I think we need to be very selective about what we reveal to the General,' I say. 'Something like you, Alice, persuaded George to take you home to Whitecroft, when you realised you'd been left behind.'

'Is he really going to believe that just Alice and George sailed here, alone?' Blake says, skeptically.

'You said yourself that you weren't going to make your presence known,' I point out. 'Viola isn't here. Nor are the two islanders.'

'Do you think there are two boats coming in together?' Alice says, straining her eyes to see through the darkness.

'It does look like two separate lights,' Blake says.

I can see the dock, lit up, and the distant lights on the water. It has to be Will and Charles. If they don't return tonight with the others, I don't know what I'll do.

'If it's William and Charles, they have been away for a long time. They'll be exhausted,' Alice says. 'I can't imagine my father is going to be on top form either. I know they had Riel, but he and the Swifts struggled on our way over to Cape.'

'Why is Riel coming?' I ask.

'Supposedly to train others in sailing, because George left,' Blake says. 'But it's already proved a successful ploy in luring Palmiro and Amita here, too.'

'Do you think that's what he wanted?' Alice asks, looking worried. 'You never said that before.'

'I only mean that if Riel's visit went on a bit too long, it would attract another boatload of islanders,' Blake says, shrugging. 'If the General wants to give Whitecroft a reason to start a war, I'm sure he'll manipulate the situation accordingly.'

'He's not in charge anymore,' I tell Blake.

'That's not how he acted out there.'

'Is that true?' I ask Alice.

She nods.

'I don't understand how he has the audacity—' I fume.

'Well, we didn't know much about what's happened in Whitecroft since we left,' Blake says. 'Viola kept sending messages to Amie, but you could never send much in one go.'

'I don't understand what Palmiro and Amita are going to do, on their own, in a strange country,' Alice says. 'They'll freeze to death if they're not careful.'

'Let's get the boats in, send everyone home, and then see if we can find them,' I suggest. 'Where is Riel going to stay?'

No one answers. Already George's cottage is full, if Alice and I stay with him there. And hopefully, Will too.

'How about we send him home with Charles?' Alice says. 'We know he'll be safe there.'

'What about you?' I ask Blake. 'Not planning on camping out in this, are you?'

'He can sleep in George's cottage too,' Alice says, blushing as I raise an eyebrow. 'As long as he stays out of sight when the boats come in.'

I've waited so long for this moment, but I hadn't realised how long it would take the boats to draw closer to the shore. When we waved them off, it seemed like minutes and they were gone. Since I came outside, the lights are nearer, but it's impossible to see anything clearly. I still have no certainty that it's Will, although I can't consider the alternative.

Alice and I are both shivering in the cold night air, so Blake sends us back inside the cottage to prepare some food and build up the fire. I pace back and forth restlessly, fighting the nausea, and rehearsing what I'm going to say to Will.

How soon should I tell him I'm carrying?

After my tenth lap of the room, I notice that Alice sits quietly at the table, her hands clasped in her lap.

'Why did he leave without you?' I ask her suddenly.

'Who: my father or Palmiro?' Alice asks, a touch of the old sarcasm present. It poorly masks a raw sadness.

'The General,' I clarify. I'm reluctant to endow him with titles he doesn't deserve, like *father*.

'Perhaps he saw it as his chance to finally be rid of me,' she says. 'I served my purpose, forming an alliance with the islanders—which he no doubt has no intention of honouring. And it seemed there was someone willing to be pledged to me— unlike here.'

'You were going to be pledged to Palmiro?' I ask.

She nods, and then her face crumples. She covers it with her hands.

'I think I was just fooling myself,' she sniffs. 'It was too good to be true.'

'What about Blake?'

I sit down next to her, and watch her wipe away tears.

'He just... kissed me—out of nowhere.' She's crying and rubbing her face furiously. 'And Viola's carrying and it's such a mess.'

'Viola's carrying?' I echo. Looks like Blake may have bitten off more than he could chew.

'Do you... think less of me now?' she asks, looking up at me with tear-stained cheeks and red eyes. Alice seems to actually care what I think.

'It's none of my business,' I say, holding up my hands.

She nods and looks down at the table, sniffing quietly.

'I mean, for what it's worth,' I continue, 'I worked with Blake for years in the fields. I know him well. He's impulsive. He would never intentionally hurt anyone, but he doesn't always think about the consequences for his actions.'

'I told him to be pledged to Viola,' Alice says, glumly. 'I know that's the right thing to do.'

'If they were going to be pledged, I don't know why they didn't just stay in Whitecroft,' I point out. 'I thought they wanted to run away.'

'I think Viola found it to be very different to what she expected.'

'Things always are,' I say, exhaling my other lives and possibilities. What if I hadn't been pledged to Will? What if I'd gone on the boat with George?

We sit in silence, and the minutes roll by. The only sound is the fire crackling.

Then we hear a shout.

69

Rushing outside, we see instantly that the lights are closer, and with the slightly varying movement, it does look like two boats. Will! Down at the dock, George is shouting and waving his lantern. It sounds like there is a response from one, maybe both boats.

'Let's go,' Alice says, dashing forwards. Then she remembers how frustratingly slow I am at the moment, and takes my arm.

'Come on,' she says. 'You can lean on me.'

We make our way down to the dock, over the uneven shingle, and it's slow progress without a lantern.

'Don't worry,' Alice reassures me. 'They won't be in yet.'

The back-and-forth exchange continues, and I'm sure I can hear Will's voice. A thrill of excitement sizzles through me.

'I hope they're all right,' I mutter, mainly to myself.

'I'm sure they're fine,' Alice says, squeezing my hand.

It's odd seeing her so... empathetic. With real human emotions, when for so long, all I saw was the mask.

'Maybe everyone should go to Cape,' I say, not really considering that I'm speaking out loud.

'Why?' Alice asks, innocently.

'You've come back a different person,' I tell her.

Although part of me wonders if she was always like this, but I never saw it. I never gave her the benefit of the doubt.

'I learnt a lot out there,' Alice says, nimbly forging a path across the pebbles, and taking me with her. 'You should go if you get the chance.'

She can't see my expression, but she guesses that she's put her foot in it again. After all, she spent several months scheming to get me off Whitecroft on George's boat.

'I mean,' she says hastily, 'it helps to understand how the islanders live. There are ways which we can help each other. Amita said we have far more medicine than they do. But she also said that barely any mothers die in childbirth.'

I place my hand protectively over my stomach. She doesn't mean to, but she's done it again.

'Sorry,' she says, flustered.

'Maybe I could go over there to have the baby,' I joke, not sure how to handle Alice's apologies.

'It's possible,' she says.

Although we both know that Will is unlikely to agree to it.

Finally, we reach the wooden dock, just as George is grabbing a rope from…

'Will!' I shout, and dash forwards, leaving Alice behind.

In the glow of the lights along the dock, I can see the boat, drawing alongside and with Will and Charles working together to manoeuvre it. Will looks directly at me, his face lighting up in surprise.

'Elise!' he calls, waving his hand over his head.

'You're alive!' I say, feeling tears start in my eyes and a sob in my throat. It's like I've been holding my breath ever since he left, and now I can finally breathe again.

It's a blur, as George shouts instructions, and then Will is climbing over and onto the dock… And then suddenly I'm in his arms, collapsing against him with grief and joy, sobbing uncontrollably.

'I'm home,' he says, his grip iron-tight around me.

ALICE

70

My heart rises to see my brother, as he climbs out of the boat, and I greet him.

'Hello, Charles.'

He sweeps me off my feet in a crushing hug that I don't expect.

'Alice, I'm so glad to see you,' he says, sounding genuine. 'George!'

He turns to George and wraps his arms around him, clapping him on the back.

'I was not expecting to see you here, but we couldn't have brought her in without you.'

He looks at Elise and Will, still in each other's arms and lost to everything else. Edward Turner, looking less hardy and robust than usual, clambers down and shakes George's hand gratefully.

'Rather a longer voyage than we anticipated,' he says. 'I've never been so glad to see Whitecroft.'

'I know how that feels,' I murmur.

'We've got to help Father's boat in now,' Charles says. 'We ended up travelling back together.'

'I'm glad you missed the worst of the storm,' George says. 'Though that meeting point island isn't exactly designed for long stays.'

'I never want to eat another apple again,' Charles jokes. 'That was all the food we had, by the end.'

George has moved the boats so that our boat and Charles' are neatly positioned together, leaving room for Father's boat to come in. I look up to where he's standing on the deck, and his expression as he sees me is murderous.

My heart falls. Perhaps part of me hoped that this had all been a misunderstanding; he hadn't meant to leave me behind, really. But as the Crests run around and Riel calls out to George, all I see is the coldness in my father's eyes. If he could slide a knife under my ribs right now and get away with it, he would.

I stumble back, as if I've been hit.

'Are you all right?' Charles asks me.

I blink at him. I haven't been *all right* for years, not really, although it feels like some kind of healing has begun since my time at Cape. My father's abuse—I can't think of a better word of what to call it—has dripped poisonous venom into my veins, and it's only now that I'm waking up to it. I knew, when I saw his reaction to my withdrawal from being pledged with Phillip Stead, that I couldn't live with him anymore. Looking at my brother, Elise and innocent parties like Riel, I'm determined that he can't continue to wield his toxic influence over their lives too.

'Alice?' Charles repeats, looking concerned.

I take a step closer to him and lay my hand on his arm.

'He left me in Cape,' I say, with an odd calmness. 'He left without me. George brought me home. Please don't let him do anything to George.'

Charles stares at me, shocked, and then looks over at George, who is helping Riel onto the dock first. Once Riel's feet touch the floor, George leans over and speaks urgently into his ear. Riel's eyes flit back to my father's boat, and he nods.

'Please keep Riel safe too,' I add. 'Let him stay at your house.'

'I—' Charles falters. 'Yes, yes I will.'

'I'm staying at George's cottage,' I tell him. 'Go home to Ada, then come and find us in the morning.'

Charles nods, speechless.

'Go now, before he can stop you,' I urge. 'Riel, my brother is happy to host you for your stay in Whitecroft. He will take you to his home to rest from your journey.'

Riel checks with George, who nods his approval, and Charles shakes himself into action.

'Let's walk up,' he says, gesturing to Riel to follow him. 'Edward, come with us. Will, are you two coming?'

'Yes,' William answers, his arms around Elise's shoulders and turning her towards the distant light of George's cottage.

They start walking, just as Arnold Crest jumps down from the boat and glares at me, then George.

'Something bothering you, Arnold?' I mock lightly.

'Alice, join the others,' George says.

'Will you be all right?' I ask him.

He nods.

'I mean, I'm sure they're all grateful, because there's no way they would have been able to dock without you lighting the way for them,' I add. 'In fact, why don't you leave them to it?'

'I'm just securing the boats,' he says, wrapping rope around a post. 'It's easy to get it wrong, you know, and we can't afford any expensive mistakes.'

Leon Crest jumps down, looking pale and unsteady.

'Back in Whitecroft at last!' he gasps.

Finally, my father climbs neatly onto the dock, looking unscathed from whatever journey he's endured.

For a moment, we stare at one another.

'Come on, George,' I say, taking his arm. 'Let's go.'

71

'I never saw that boat before,' George says, as we follow the others up to his cottage.

'It was hidden in the Infirmary,' I explain. 'My father always has a Plan B.'

'He didn't look too happy when he saw us,' George says, looking at me to gauge my reaction.

'Does he ever look happy?' I say, trying to conceal how much his hatred sent ice daggers into my heart.

The truth is, I feel shocked to the core. I don't know if I was expecting him to suddenly transform into a loving parent, but I wasn't expecting such a venomous reception. I keep looking back over my shoulder.

'They'll need to secure the boat,' George says. 'They won't be right behind us.'

It doesn't stop me constantly looking out of the window once we're inside the warm cottage, squashing around the table, and sharing out food. Elise leans sleepily against William, watching him eat, and Charles enjoys some too before leaving with Riel. Edward went straight up to Whitecroft, desperate to get home. Riel says little, but takes food gratefully and seems happy to stay with Charles. None of us mention Palmiro and Amita; it feels awkward to say that we don't quite know where they are, and we don't want Riel to disappear into the night when he's only just arrived. There will need to be conversations tomorrow about what we should do.

As Charles and Riel wave goodbye and melt into the night, I wonder if Palmiro and Amita are following them. But what then? Will they knock on Charles' door? Where will they sleep? It all seems so strange, and I'm too tired to think about it. Ultimately, they know where we are, if they need us.

Elise and Will head off to sleep in George's parents' room, and George bids me good night. I take a candle with me to Joy's room, and close the door behind me. I unfasten the clasp of my cloak, and hang it up. It's seen some adventures now. I slip out of my boots, and pad over to the bed. I reach out for the covers, and then freeze.

There's someone in the bed.

I grab the candle and lift it to illuminate the lumpy body, which shifts suddenly, and groans. By the time I light up his face, I know it's him.

'Blake!' I hiss.

His dark hair flopping over his eyes, I see his fist clench the blankets more tightly, and then he turns away from the light.

'Blake!' I try again, terrified someone will hear me.

'Hmm?' he says, no doubt with his eyes still closed.

'You are sleeping in my bed!' I whisper. More than anything else, I'm cross because I'm exhausted and what am I supposed to do now?

'Calm down, Princess,' he drawls, stretching an arm out over the pillow. 'There's plenty of room.'

I stand, rooted to the spot in shock. I shouldn't even be in the same room as him. This is so inappropriate.

Then, outside, I hear a noise that could be an owl or a human. Although he must have walked back to Whitecroft by now, I irrationally picture my father. He knows where I am. What if he's waiting until everyone is asleep, and then he's coming to find me?

Placing the candle quickly back onto the bedside table, I lift the covers back and climb into the bed. At least Blake is wearing clothes. He turns onto his side, facing the same way as me, and rubs his hand up and down my arm.

'You're shaking,' he says, tightening his grip. 'What's wrong?'

He's more alert now—finally—and I can feel his head raised off the pillow, his mouth close to my ear.

'I saw my father,' I whisper. 'I think he's going to kill me.'

There is a pause. Silence is thick in the cottage, the hum of the ocean in the background. Blake resumes rubbing my arm, warming it and calming my shivers.

'I won't let him near you,' he says, practically growling.

I believe him. Absolutely.

'Now close your eyes and get some sleep.'

I know I should leave and sleep in the main room, on the floor or in a chair perhaps, but I voyaged and travelled through snow, and my grandfather's dead, and I pulled Elise on a sledge, and Blake kissed me, and I just saw my father, and I haven't got any strength left to resist. It's mad and stupid but I feel safe here in Blake's arms, and there's no way I'm going to sleep all alone by the front door where anyone could come in and find me. When I say anyone, I mean my father.

It makes no sense, but I feel like I'm home.

'Goodnight, Blake,' I murmur.

'Goodnight, Princess.'

ELISE

72

Finally, we're alone. I've clung to Will's side since he got off the boat, and his arms have constantly been around me, and yet— still, there's distance. As he closes the door behind us in Chandler and Aurelia's old room, his face only partially lit by the weak candle flame, I take a deep breath. The walls dance with shadows, and the weight of everything I have to tell him.

'Do I get a kiss?' he asks, playfully.

My heart physically aches. He's probably spent all this time at sea imagining a passionate reunion, when at the moment, I just want to lie down and close my eyes and hope the nausea passes without actually vomiting.

Hesitantly, I put my arms around his neck and press my lips to his. Inside, I feel nothing. I lay my head on his shoulder instead, and we stand in the ringing silence.

'I feel tired,' I whisper.

Reluctantly he pulls back, looking more closely at my face.

'What's wrong?' he asks.

Avoiding answering for just a little longer, I remove my boots and my cloak, then my outer garments. I sit on the bed, resisting the urge to lay down my head.

'Grandfather died this morning.'

He didn't expect that. He had just been taking off his boots, and now he lowers himself next to me and puts his arm around me.

'What happened?'

'He was sick. I've been sick too.' I look up to meet his eyes, knowing the magnitude of the news I'm about to tell him. 'I'm carrying.'

His eyes widen, and he squeezes my arm.

'Really? How are you feeling? Is everything all right?'

I sigh.

'I feel sick and exhausted all the time,' I tell him. 'I didn't do a very good job of caring for Grandfather. It was only when Alice arrived—'

'How did she get back?'

'George brought her.' I decide to stick to the story we agreed. This situation is complicated enough already. 'They bypassed the meeting point island and arrived here a few days ago. Cressida sent a message.'

'And she helped?' Will asks. Alice's track record has not been great with us.

'She did,' I say, remembering how she held Grandfather's hand and sobbed. 'She helped me, too. I couldn't have come here without her. She pushed me on the sledge.'

'Did she tell you what happened on Cape?' he asks.

'No, not really.'

I wasn't exactly in a position to interrogate her, given I could barely talk.

'Riel said he was coming to Whitecroft to train up more sailors,' Will says. 'Without him, I don't think we would ever have got off the meeting point. It was really tricky, with the weather being so unpredictable.'

I still feel angry that he didn't take me with him.

'Did you bring the canoe back with you?'

'It's in the boat.' He nods. 'When we were paddling out to the island, the waves were so big. It was terrifying. I was so glad you weren't there.'

It stings too much not to retaliate.

'No, I was just lying, unable to move in a freezing cold cabin, while my grandfather slowly slipped away before my eyes.'

'I'm sorry—I had no idea—'

'Exactly!' I snap. 'Nor did I! I had no idea where you were, why you were taking so long—'

A sob bubbles up, and I swallow it down.

'These past few weeks have been a nightmare.'

'Well, they weren't exactly a dream come true for me either,' he says. 'Stuck on an island with a storm raging, barely any food—'

'You know the answer, then?' I interrupt, seething. 'Next time, let someone else go.'

'Charles volunteered. You didn't want me to leave your brother—'

'Charles is old enough to make his own decisions. You should have thought more about me.'

'I was doing my duty to you, and to Whitecroft,' Will says, his jaw setting. 'I'm sorry about your grandfather, and about you being ill and alone. I couldn't control the weather. I wasn't deliberately staying away from you.'

I throw myself down onto the pillow, in a mixture of rage and exhaustion. Tears brim in my eyes, and drop onto the pillow when I blink.

'Let's sleep, and we can talk more in the morning,' Will says, with a sigh of defeat.

I close my eyes, willing the swirling in my head and stomach to calm, and hear him remove his clothes and blow out the candle. He climbs into the bed, and curves his body around mine, kissing the back of my head.

'I'm sorry,' he whispers. 'I love you.'

I cry as quietly as I can, my head pounding with the weight of unpent emotion, and all I can think is: *Sorry is not enough.*

ALICE

73

I open my eyes and the amount of light from the edging of the curtain surprises me. I must have slept heavily to recover from the last two days. Something shifts beside me, and I remember. Blake.

My heart beats faster. What am I going to do? If anyone finds out about this… My chances of finding a pledge will be destroyed forever. I was already panicked enough that Palmiro would find out about the kiss.

I slip out from under the covers, feeling the stinging cold of the morning air. Lacing my boots, I pick up my cloak and allow myself a lingering look at Blake's innocent expression as he sleeps. He will ruin me.

Opening the door just wide enough to slip through it, I close it carefully, then walk into the main room of the house. George looks up from the fireplace, stirring porridge. I feel myself turning red already; does he know that Blake's here?

'Did you sleep all right?' George asks.

Hiding my face by walking over to the window, I nod, not trusting my voice.

'It's been quite a few days,' he says. 'I'm sorry to hear that Avery's gone. He was a good man.'

Outside, the sky is cloudy, but with a few streaks of pale blue sky visible. The sun feels brighter, like it's managing to break through the cloud in places. I can see the empty beach, and the white foam of the waves.

'Yes,' I whisper.

The gravity that pulls the tide of my life in has suddenly up-ended. The fixed points have shifted. Grandfather, my father… Even more reason to cling tightly to Charles and Elise.

'Would you like some breakfast?'

George hands me a warm bowl, and I sit in a chair by the fire.

'You must have been exhausted too,' I say. 'You didn't want to stay in bed?'

'Old habits die hard,' he remarks, licking his spoon. 'I've always had to be up early. Got used to it.'

There's no sign of Will and Elise, so I presume they're sleeping, like Blake.

'What do we do now?' I ask George.

I don't really expect him to have an answer. I'm beginning to feel responsible for this whole situation. I was the one who insisted we should leave Cape. I brought everyone back to Whitecroft, and now what? What's going to happen to George, Blake and Viola? Where are Palmiro and Amita?

'I was thinking I could offer to help Riel train more sailors,' George says. 'I want to go back to Cape, but I may not have to run away if I make some arrangement with the Council.'

'What about the others?' I ask, thinking of Palmiro and Amita.

'I think Viola will want to stay,' George says, giving me an appraising look. 'I'm not sure about Blake.'

I blush and look away. When did I become so hopeless at keeping secrets?

'I meant the islanders.'

'Why don't you ask them yourself?'

He nods towards the door. There's a short knock, and then it opens and all three of them step inside.

Seeing them together, without their usual friendliness, makes me raise my hand to my mouth to cover my surprise. I never got on that well with Riel or Amita, but my eyes rest on Palmiro. He looks at me with emotion in his eyes, but I can't read it clearly.

'We were just wondering about you,' George says, keeping his tone nonchalant. 'Why don't you sit down and have some food?'

Amita looks at Palmiro, and he nods.

'Thank you, George,' he says, rather formally, as the three of them take seats around the table.

'Does Charles know you're here?' George asks Riel, serving

him some porridge.

'He wasn't awake when I left, but I told Ada.'

George nods.

'Where did you go?' I blurt out, my eyes on Palmiro.

'I wanted to explore Whitecroft,' he says, coolly, as if he didn't just vanish. 'Amita found me yesterday and we investigated a few things.'

'Why didn't you tell us, instead of disappearing?' I ask angrily. 'I wouldn't have done that to you, in Cape.'

'We are here in Whitecroft under quite different circumstances to you being in Cape,' Palmiro says, in a measured tone that only serves to increase my anger.

'Where did you even sleep?' I continue. 'We were worried about you with the temperature.'

'You don't need to worry about us,' Amita says, scathingly. 'We can look after ourselves.'

'You're still injured,' I point out.

Her eyes flash but before she can reply, Palmiro speaks again.

'We didn't want to burden you,' he says.

'You said that before,' I comment bitterly.

'Well, it's true,' he says. 'This is a small cottage. You had two boats arriving last night—'

'So you were watching, in the shadows?'

'Of course we were watching,' Amita snaps. 'The whole reason we're here is to look after my brother.'

'I didn't ask you to come,' Riel speaks up.

'I would not leave you alone with these people,' she mutters.

There's the sound of footsteps along the corridor. I jump, thinking it's Blake, but it's only William.

'I thought I heard voices,' he says, running a hand through his hair and assessing the scene. 'Palmiro! It's been a long time since we met. You didn't say that others came on the boat with you and George.'

He directs this last sentence at me, and suddenly everyone's eyes are on me.

'Didn't want people knowing about us, did you?' Amita asks,

her eyes narrowed.

'I was trying to protect you!'

'Did you tell him about Blake?'

The way she asks this makes me feel exposed, like she's seen everything that's happened between us, although I don't think that's possible.

'Blake's here too?' William asks.

'He's over at the Farmlands,' George says.

'Actually,' I say, taking a deep breath. 'He's here now.'

On cue, Blake appears in the corridor, his shirt crumpled and his hair in a mess over his forehead.

'I didn't know there was a meeting,' he says sleepily. 'What have I missed?'

There's a heavy silence while Will looks from my ruby cheeks to Blake, helping himself to porridge and slouching into a chair. Palmiro's eyes narrow.

'How many of you stayed here last night?' he asks.

'Can we focus on the issue, please?' George cuts in, more sharpness in his tone than usual. 'We did you a favour by concealing your presence yesterday. If you blow your cover, you'll lose your advantage over the General.'

'What do you suggest?' Amita asks, a challenge in her tone.

'Stay here with me, and come out fishing. Come back at nightfall each day, and no one will come out here and see you.'

'Do you have enough space for us?' Palmiro asks pointedly.

I can't meet his gaze.

'I'm taking Elise home today,' William says. 'I'll probably use a horse.'

'I need to get back to the Farmlands,' I say. 'We need to sort out everything with Grandfather.'

'I'll walk back with you,' Blake says.

Palmiro looks daggers at him. He continues spooning porridge into his mouth.

'They don't know you're here, either,' Amita says.

'And I want it to stay that way,' Blake says.

'Maybe it would be easier for us to hide in the Farmlands,'

Palmiro says to Amita.

She makes a face.

'How can we look after Riel if we are all the way out there? I say we follow George's plan.'

Palmiro nods. Now he's avoiding my gaze. I don't know why, but all the promises he made just seemed to evaporate once he got here and he got ill. Maybe it shook him up, made him realise this isn't a game. Maybe it's starting to sink in that they might be here for a considerable amount of time. They can't sleep rough and vanish for months on end.

'That's settled then.'

Blake picks up a bread roll, breaks it in half, and offers it to me. Feeling the sting of Palmiro's coldness, I take it.

74

Whitecroft is eerily quiet. The Town Square is a white, empty space for snow to drift and gather. Where is everyone?

It's true that in the Freeze, people like to stay indoors. The Council have fewer meetings, and most trades go into hibernation, while everyone focuses on surviving.

Blake walks beside me, ready to hide if there's any sign of life, but the place is deserted. We call first on Charles, breaking the news of Grandfather's death. He decides to make arrangements for a coffin so that his body can be transported to the shore, for our customary sea burial. We were never allowed to bury our loved ones or have memorials. All part of letting go of the past.

Once I've told Ada about Elise, she starts packing up some provisions for her. That reminds me, the larder is nearly empty. I stop by the storehouse to collect flour, oil and preserves.

'We should find Cressida and tell her the news,' I say. Cressida is Blake's grandmother, but she's staying with her daughter, who's married to a Taylor.

Blake winces but agrees.

We find the house, situated close to the Infirmary, and I'm glad when we are welcomed inside to leave the cold shadow of that looming grey building. Cressida knows as soon as she sees me. She bundles me into her arms for a warm hug, which she has never done before.

'I'm sorry,' she says.

'Thank you for sending the message,' I say. 'Otherwise I wouldn't have come back in time.'

'I heard you may not have come back at all,' she says. 'And you—'

She pulls Blake in for a hug next.

'You've been getting in trouble again, I see.'

'Have you seen Viola?' he asks.

It sends a physical pain through me when he says her name. They have history together I can't erase.

'Yes,' Cressida says, in a tone that suggests she doesn't want to be placed in the middle.

'How is she?' he asks.

Cressida pauses, examining him.

'Happy to be home,' she says finally. 'She's been through a lot.'

Blake looks about to speak, but she holds up her hand.

'Why don't you sit down, and I'll get you something to eat?'

We sit at the table, and Cressida offers us fresh bread and drinks.

'I suppose I'm the bad guy now,' Blake says.

'I didn't say that.' Cressida frowns at him.

'You said Viola's been through a lot. What about me?'

'You're not carrying.'

At least he keeps his mouth shut at that.

'Is Viola at home?' I ask. 'Do people in Whitecroft know that she's back?'

'I don't think it's common knowledge.' Cressida sighs. 'But people will know, sooner or later.'

'We need to be getting back,' Blake says.

'Do you want to try to see her first?' I say, gulping down my drink.

'You can't leave yet,' Cressida says firmly. 'I want to hear all about Cape.'

I start, describing the heat of the sun, the long stretch of beach and the jungle forest. The songs and smiles of the people. It all feels like a distant dream now, but it brings warmth to my heart just talking about it. Blake joins in, telling her about the exploring he did, the way he worked with people on the beach and in the forest. He often went fishing too.

'They don't have rules out there that you can only have one trade,' he says. 'And you can go anywhere you want. When you get a boat, you could sail and chase the horizon. There were no limits.'

'Maybe you just didn't *see* the limits,' Cressida comments. 'It does sound like a wonderful place. I'm so glad you were able to go.'

'You make it sound like a nice little vacation,' Blake says bitterly. 'When we left, we weren't supposed to be coming back.'

'That's life,' Cressida says with a shrug. 'Some things are nothing like what you expect them to be.'

'Some *people* are nothing like what you expect them to be,' Blake mutters.

'True,' she says. 'Go and see Viola.'

75

At first, I think Amie is going to close the door on us. She shuts it over so there's just a narrow gap left, with half of her face and body visible. Then she sighs.

'You'd better come in.'

We step into the hallway and down to the main area of the house. The Taylors have bigger houses than most people in Whitecroft. They are known for having the most children.

The fire is burning, crackling with logs, and Viola is sitting in a chair next to it, covered with a blanket. Her eyes widen when she sees us, and she looks about to stand, but then thinks better of it.

'Where have you been?' she asks Blake, ignoring me.

His face tightens in annoyance.

'I've been to the Farmlands to see my family. Last night I was at George's, because the General's boat arrived, along with Charles'.'

I feel myself blush, and look down.

'You could have sent a note, or something.'

'I didn't get the impression you wanted to see me.'

I risk a glance at Amie, wondering if we should leave them alone, but she clasps her hands together in front of her chest and her cheeks flush pink with barely restrained anger.

'She's been recovering from that terrible voyage,' she says. 'In her condition—'

'Why didn't you tell me?' Blake snaps, ignoring Amie and staring at Viola. She looks pale and weak—not unlike Elise. No wonder it was easy for Eden to make an instant diagnosis.

'I didn't want to believe it.' Viola's face crumples, and she buries it in her hands.

'Don't cry,' Amie says, clucking her tongue and walking over to Viola, laying a hand on her shoulder. 'I'll send him away if he's upsetting you.'

'I have a name!' Blake steps forward, and I can't help it: I stretch out my hand to pull him back. 'You can't pretend I don't exist!'

'Carrying without a Pledge. The shame of it,' Amie mutters, shaking her head.

'But you don't want her to be pledged to me, do you?' Blake says.

'I want her to be with someone who will look after her,' Amie says. 'Not carry her off to a strange place and then abandon her.'

'I haven't abandoned her,' Blake says, through clenched teeth. 'I'm here.'

Viola is still sobbing. I wish I had already left, but I'm frozen to the spot.

'You're upsetting her!' Amie accuses.

'Why aren't you questioning yourself more?' Blake says. 'If anyone was abandoned, it was you. Viola wanted to leave; did you ever ask yourself why?'

'She thought she was in love,' Amie says, scathingly.

'No, she just thought that I could get her out of Whitecroft,' Blake returns.

Viola sobs some more. I wonder if she can even hear this conversation.

'Blake,' I say, trying to rein him in.

He looks at me, then sighs.

'Viola,' he says, this time in a gentler tone. 'Come with me, and I'll look after you as best as I can. If you stay here, I can't do that. It's up to you and I don't want to force you. It's your choice.'

'Of course she doesn't want to go with you,' Amie scoffs. 'She made her choice as soon as she stepped off that boat.'

'Viola?' Blake asks again. I can't bear to look.

There's the sound of sniffing. I stare at the floor for several long moments. Then I look up to see Viola shaking her head. Blake gives a grim nod.

'I'll be out at the Farmlands. Send word if you need me.'

He gives Amie a final glare, then strides towards the door. I stammer an apology, then hurry after him.

76

It takes until we've passed the first gate on the path to the Farmlands before Blake explodes.

'Did you see the way she spoke to me? As if I was nobody.'

He stamps through the snow, leaving angry footprints.

'Viola just… sits there,' he continues. 'Like she didn't plan the whole thing. Playing the innocent victim.'

'I think she was just upset—'

'Upset!' he exclaims. 'Why does no one care if *I'm* upset? It's my child she's carrying!'

I flinch. His eyes are wet with tears.

'I care,' I whisper. I wish I didn't care, to be honest. It would be easier that way.

'You saw the way she rejected me.'

'She might change her mind,' I point out. 'She's just upset.'

'What am I supposed to do?'

I can't help tears starting in my own eyes. We've stopped walking and now we're facing each other, the cloudy sky above us, and thick snow covering the hedges, trees and path before us.

'Keep walking,' I tell him. 'Keep putting one foot in front of the other. Do what's right; it's up to her what she chooses.'

'And what about you, Alice?' he says. 'What do you choose?'

I turn back towards the Farmlands; it's too hard to hold his gaze.

'I'm going home.'

It's funny, but the miserable house where I lived with my father for so many years hasn't been home to me for some time, if at all. Cape was wonderful, but that wasn't home either. On this path to my grandfather's cabin, even though he's gone, I fix my desire to live there and make it my own.

Blake falls into step beside me, silently. I link my arm through his and squeeze it reassuringly.

'Don't worry,' I say. 'It will all work out in the end.'

'I don't know where your optimism comes from,' he says, but he's matching my pace.

The birds flutter in and out of the hedges, and the further we get from Whitecroft, the more I can breathe.

'I wonder how long Amita and Palmiro will be able to hide,' I say.

'Not long, if they keep checking on Riel.'

In the quiet, our boots crunch the snow. No fresh snowfall today.

'Do you wish it was him walking with you now, instead of me?'

I can feel Blake's eyes on my face. My cheeks start to turn pink.

'How am I supposed to answer that?'

'Be honest,' he urges.

'No,' I tell him. 'I wanted you to walk with me. Just like I wanted you with me last night, or I would have gone back to sleep in the lounge.'

'I guess I should apologise for stealing your bed,' he says, with a sly grin. 'But I made a very deliberate choice. I knew you'd be in Joy's room.'

'Everyone else would have turfed you out,' I say. 'And to think I was worried about you, being out in the cold.'

'The tough guy persona is just an act, I'm afraid.'

We walk on, but this time the peace has settled between us. I realise that George's sled is still hidden away at the vantage point, but we don't need it now.

'Do you think Palmiro knew, about the bedroom?' Blake asks.

I blush just at the thought of it.

'I think so.'

Blake gives a mischievous grin.

'Good.'

'It's not a joke,' I say, frowning.

'He needs to realise that he can't disappear and expect a beautiful girl like you to wait around for him.'

'I don't need you to misbehave in order to teach him a lesson.'

'That wasn't my primary motive,' he says, his grin expanding. 'But I think it also had some effect.'

'He still chose to stay with Amita,' I point out.

Blake says nothing, but his grip tightens on my arm.

We hold onto each other all the way to the cottage.

77

When we arrive, the knowledge that my grandfather's body is cold and waiting for me inside makes me falter. For a moment, Blake and I stand and stare at the house, remembering how we arrived just a few nights ago, and everything that has passed since then. Without consideration, I lean more heavily onto his arm, sinking slightly against him.

'It's all right, Princess,' he says, bringing his other hand across to squeeze my arm. 'We'll go in and make the fire. Remember, Charles is coming. You don't have to do anything until he arrives.'

I nod, not trusting my voice. With my heart pounding, we make our way up the steps and enter the cabin together.

The scene is untouched from when I left with Elise. Somehow that feels like a lifetime ago. The air is chilled, although not as musty as when we first arrived. Blake starts building the fire, and I unpack the supplies. I measure out flour into a bowl and start making dough for bread. The door to Grandfather's room is shut.

As I make my way around the kitchen, I move a vase onto the sill. The possibilities of this being my home now, of making this space my own, bring a line of light, breaking dawn on the horizon of my grief. It's a plain, simple cottage, but if it's mine, it will be beautiful.

'There,' Blake says, warming his hands on the fire. 'It's going nicely now. I need to chop you some more firewood.'

'Thank you,' I say. 'Before you do that, would you mind helping me to move the mattresses back to the beds?'

They are both in Grandfather's room. Blake swallows then nods.

I lead the way, laying my hand on the doorknob and boldly opening it. There he is, lying in his bed where we left him. He's got the odd, waxen stillness of death, but it's still him.

With tears in my eyes, I step around the mattresses and mess of blankets on the floor, and drop a kiss onto his forehead. I touch his cold, stiff hand. Then I turn to Blake and point to the mattress closest to my feet.

'Let's start with that one.'

We move the two mattresses back, to Elise's room and to mine, and I gather up all the blankets too. I close the door to Grandfather's room behind me.

Blake goes outside to chop wood, and I make up the beds. I also change my clothes and find a damp face cloth to wash my face. There's a small mirror on my bedroom wall. The girl looking back at me is not the same person who was here a few weeks ago. It's as if the pinched, hard lines of my face have softened with love and sorrow.

I hear voices outside and hurry to the door. Charles has arrived.

'I left my horse at Pembridge,' he says. 'The coffin won't be ready until tomorrow. I thought I'd come and see him now.'

Blake gives me a nod and stays outside, chopping more wood. I take Charles to the bedside.

He sits in the chair next to the bed, clasping at Grandfather's hand, and tears run down his cheeks. He stretches out his other hand to me, beckoning me closer. I step forward and he takes my hand.

'I'm sorry I wasn't here,' he says.

I let out a small, strangled sound at the back of my throat. Charles springs up out of the chair and wraps his arms around me. I collapse in sobs against him. I'm crying for my grandfather, but I'm also crying for everything else too: the burden of carrying things alone, the pain of my childhood, and the wounds of my father.

'You don't have to stay here,' Charles says, trying to soothe me. 'I can make other arrangements for Riel, and you can come back to us.'

'No.' I pull back slightly, and wipe tears from my cheeks. 'You're very kind, Charles, but I want to stay here. I want to make this my home now. My own place. And it's very important that Riel stays with you, and not Father.'

I try to explain what happened in Cape, and my suspicions that Father will use Riel to cause some conflict with the other nation.

'I don't suppose he mentioned that he left me behind, when you were on the island?' I say.

'He said that you wanted to stay with Palmiro,' Charles replies. 'When you told me that he left you, I didn't know what to think.'

'I was supposed to be pledged to Palmiro,' I say, fresh tears starting in my eyes. 'But everything's changed now.'

'I don't like any of this,' Charles says, frowning. 'Once Riel's given some training, I think we should take him straight back to Cape.'

'Riel's not here alone.'

I tell Charles about Palmiro and Amita.

'That would explain why he suddenly disappeared, then.'

'If you befriend him, he might come to trust you,' I say. 'If we work together with them, then we can prevent Father from starting a war.'

'War?' Charles repeats. 'Why would he want a war?'

I shrug.

'More land? More people? It's power, isn't it?'

'I always thought he was happy with Whitecroft. It was everything he ever wanted.'

'I don't think he's ever been *happy*.'

Footsteps tramp into the house, and we hear the sound of logs being set down on the floor.

'I should bake the bread,' I say. 'Why don't you have a few moments in here alone?'

Charles nods, and gives me another squeeze.

Blake's kneeling by the fire, building a neat pile of logs. Then he stokes the fire up using the poker, and lays it down, standing when he sees me.

'You all right, Princess?'

I give a half-sob, half-laugh, and throw my arms around him.

'Thank you,' I murmur.

'I would love to say it was selfless heroism, but that would be untrue.'

His eyes fall to my mouth, and I stare at his hungry expression. I could stay here forever soaking up the way he looks at me. I place a finger over his lips.

'Charles,' I whisper.

He kisses the finger, then catches it in his hand and draws it down to his side. There's a long, agonising moment where our faces are close enough for our breath to mingle, but not touching. I close my eyes and then his lips meet mine, gentle and soft.

'Alice.'

The way he says my name makes my heart beat faster. I feel drunk on this heady emotion, enough to sway on my feet, but then suddenly, I hear the sound of horses' hooves. My eyes widen and I step back.

I was here, in this very room, with Elise on that fateful day when my father arrived to haul me off to Cape. I have an instant conviction that it's him, that he's arrived to take me back with him to Whitecroft.

'Hide in the bedroom,' I instruct Blake. 'Don't come out unless… you have to.'

He's barely disappeared when there are footsteps outside, and the door opens.

My father walks into the room, and gives me a menacing smile.

78

'Alice,' he says, hissing my name like a curse.

'Most people knock the door,' I say, coldly.

'Family don't need to stand upon ceremony,' he says, gesturing with open palms.

'Family don't leave each other behind.'

'I thought you wanted to be with Palmiro. It wouldn't matter to you where—'

'It wasn't what we agreed,' I interrupt him.

His eyes glitter. He draws himself up and clenches his fists at his side.

'So you thought you'd find your own way back,' he says, stepping closer with a sneer. 'Well, daughter, it's time you stopped interfering and learned your place.'

'My place is here,' I say firmly. 'You need to go now.'

He gives a cold, empty laugh.

'I heard Avery is dead.'

I flinch slightly. It's enough to confirm it.

'We've played enough games, Alice,' he says. 'Here's what you're going to do. Ride back with me, and the Crests, to Whitecroft. Tell Charles you need to stay with him. Then Riel can move into my house, which is what I planned from the start.'

'No.'

His eyes narrow.

'Perhaps I'm not making myself clear—'

He reaches out to grab my arm, and in a flash I slip out of his grip and grab the poker, holding it out in front of me. He steps backwards, a rare flash of fear in his eyes.

'You wouldn't,' he growls.

'Try me.'

'Alice?'

Charles emerges from Grandfather's room, staring in surprise at the scene before him. I don't lower the poker.

'Get out of my house,' I say. 'I refuse to be used by you anymore.'

Father looks from me to Charles.

'She's out of her mind,' he says. 'I've come to take her back to Whitecroft; perhaps Ada can look after her—'

'No!' I say, brandishing the poker for emphasis and moving forward, forcing him to back towards the door.

'Alice is happy here,' Charles says, coolly. 'You need to leave her alone.'

Father is now visibly shocked at this open rebellion.

'I am ashamed of you both,' he says. 'Treating your own father in this way?'

'Get out!' I shout, striding towards the door, still wielding the poker.

He turns and runs outside. I follow and see him jump up onto his horse, indicating to Leon and Arnold to go. They stare at me, amazed.

'If any of you dare to come inside my house without an invitation, you'll regret it.'

I stand, pointing the poker out at them like a sword, while Charles stands beside me. Father sets off at a gallop into the forest, and the Crests follow in his wake. I drop the poker with a clatter.

'He's going to kill me,' I say, turning to look at Charles. 'Literally.'

'Surely—' Charles begins, but I cut him off.

'No, Charles, you have to listen to me. You can't pretend anymore that everything's fine. I can't pretend anymore.'

'You don't have to pretend anything.'

Blake stands in the doorway, looking at me with fresh admiration.

'You showed him that you can stand up to him,' Blake says, his eyes glittering with love and pride.

Wait—*love?*

'I am one hundred per cent behind you,' Charles says. 'But I don't like the idea of you out here, on your own. What if he comes back, with more people next time, and we aren't here?'

'I won't be alone,' I say. 'Blake's going to stay with me.'

Charles looks at Blake in surprise, as he moves closer to put his arms around my waist.

'But you're not pledged!' Charles says.

'I promise you, I will protect your sister's honour,' Blake says. 'I made that mistake once before, and I'm not going to do it again.'

'No one knows he's back from the island,' I point out. 'No one needs to know he's here.'

'I think I'll send Will over here to check on you every day,' Charles says, looking at Blake suspiciously.

'Excellent,' Blake says.

'Do you really think Father is going to do something with Riel?' Charles asks me.

'You saw how much he wants Riel to be staying with him.'

'I'll talk to Riel tonight,' Charles says. 'I'll try to find out more about what Father is planning, too. Look after her.'

He nods to Blake, then waves goodbye, walking off into the trees in the direction of Pembridge. Blake turns me to face him.

'You were magnificent,' he says.

'I should have done that a long time ago.'

'Perhaps,' he nods. 'But you've done it now.'

'Do you think Charles believes me?'

'I think he's definitely much more aware of what's going on than he was a few months ago.'

He stands there, looking down tenderly at me.

'Did you mean it, when you said you wanted me to stay?'

I nod.

'I meant what I said to Charles,' he says.

'Thank you,' I say. 'Blake, I don't know what's going to happen with Palmiro and Viola, and I can't make you any promises. But right now, I feel like we need each other to get through this.'

'Let's just take it one day at a time.'

He bends down to press his lips to mine. It's a bittersweet blend of something pure and something raw, something powerful and protective, and something dangerous.

'Let's go inside,' I whisper.

He leads the way, and on the threshold I pause, hearing the sound of twigs snapping, as if under someone's weight. The trees rustle in the breeze. I can't see anything in the shadowy forest.

'Are you coming?' he asks.

I turn back to the cottage, following him inside. Was it someone watching? I think of Palmiro with a sickly ache in my stomach. Then I close the door and bar it.

ACKNOWLEDGEMENTS

I've loved writing this book. It surprised me. I loved inhabiting Alice's character, thinking about how she works, and taking her on an epic journey of transformation. I also loved bringing the very non-religious culture of Whitecroft face to face with a faith-filled culture. To me, faith brings hope, love and joy, and the story of the Son being rejected so we could be chosen is well documented, but if you're not familiar with it, try reading the gospel of Mark.

Even though Elise is technically the orphan in this series, I wanted to show how Alice, in many ways, is the true orphan. She's the one who's had to deal with parental coldness and rejection, which has led to a scarcity mindset: the fear that there will never be enough, the belief that it is necessary to do whatever it takes to look after yourself, because no one else will. This mindset is ultimately destructive and isolates us from meaningful community. I wanted to show Alice's journey in realising that in love, faith and true friendship, there is a better way to live.

I want to thank my Mum, for being my super fan, and for Andy, Megan and Josh, for being so patient as I lug my laptop into all terrains and situations to 'just finish this chapter.' Thanks to Lindsay for her encouragement and early reading, and to my amazing ARC team. I massively appreciate each and every one of you.

Finally, I want to thank my Father God, who has adopted me as a daughter in His kingdom. I know I'm never alone.

About the Author

Sophie Toovey loves reading and writing romance. She's an English teacher who drinks too much tea, and a total Jane Austen geek. She lives in Wales, in the UK, and enjoys smart romcoms where there's a bit of grit and realism. She writes clean, closed door romance with kisses only. Sign up for her newsletter at sophietoovey.com and receive a free ebook of *I Want You Back*, a contemporary retelling of *Persuasion*.

Connect with Sophie
Listen to audio chapters for free on Youtube
Instagram @Sophie_Toovey
Twitter @SophieToovey
Tiktok @sophietoovey

The Bay of Knives

Release date 8th February 2025

1

I'm afraid to move, in case I spoil the moment.

Alice sits next to me, her head resting on my shoulder, dark hair spilling over my collarbone. I realise I've stopped breathing, and try to take some deep breaths to restart my oxygen intake. The tips of my fingers brush strands of her hair, rivers of silk. She's perfect, and that's why I can't move or speak.

I am good at ruining things. Lately, I've even ruined a person's life. Probably more. If I really stopped to think about the consequences of my actions, I would have to chart the ripple effect from Viola to her parents, her family, and our unborn child. Child. The thought makes me dizzy and I push it away.

Here in this cabin, Alice and I are at the edge of civilisation. But the unchartered territory capturing my attention is her heart. Outside, the forest could burn like an inferno, and I wouldn't stir if I knew we could be safely cocooned in here.

Rather than flames, each tree is heavy with snow. The world is white around us, with either a pale sun to shimmer over it with a golden glow, or a sharp silver moon, sliced like an apple in the sky. An army of stars flicker, the same stars that watched us struggle through the black ocean to return to this lonely place. I always wanted to leave Whitecroft, but I could stay in this cabin forever, frozen in time.

I know that the spell will have to break. I will have to face Viola again. Alice might be reunited with Palmiro, the first one to notice her. She may go through with her Pledge to him. But right now, she needs me. So I'm content to stay here, for one more moment.

Just one more.

2

How can I describe Whitecroft?

It's a slow, quiet town, surrounded by sea on one side, and trees on the other. In the heart of the Freeze, the snow remains deep: knee-deep on the path, piled high against cabin windows and doors out in the Farmlands. The days are short and dark. Even in the Town Square, it will be deserted once the moon is up. The wooden frames of fences and posts stand like silent observers, as fires burn inside the log cabins and families sew blankets together. If you listened, you could hear the noise and hubbub from nearby homes. Out here in the forest, all we hear is the howling of the wolves.

I first heard them the other night. It was part of the reason why I didn't want to sleep outdoors, opting instead to claim a bed in our friend George's cottage. It's right by the sea, and the sound of the crashing waves sent me to sleep. Alice didn't realise I was there, and was shocked when she found me. When I moved over to make room for her, she slipped under the covers. The usual rules of modesty and decorum don't apply when it's freezing cold, and you're worried your own father might kill you.

Her father is the General. He used to be in charge here… in some ways, perhaps he still is. I sailed with George on his boat to get away from the strict regime. I took Viola. We thought we were in love.

When we reached Cape, everything was warm and homely. They had a beach too, but it was full of white sand and fishing boats. Viola and I were given a hut, and it was like a new beginning. I worked in the jungle, in the fishing boats, or on the shore. It's funny, I've worked in fields, and a forge, and now on Cape. All very different places. But work is work, isn't it? You find your rhythm through repetitive tasks. You look forward to mealtimes, and freedom.

Cape was the freest place I'd ever been in. There were no restrictions on where I could go, and if I'd wanted, I could take a boat and sail off and no one would object. Except Viola. It was strange: when we were in Whitecroft, and we talked about what we would do when we got to Cape, she sounded keen and enthusiastic. She wanted to explore, too. But as soon as we arrived, I could see her disappointment. Used to the technology of Whitecroft's Infirmary, her eyes bounced from the thin huts to the fruit-based food and to the floor. They were poorer than we realised.

Or maybe, we were richer than we realised.

Either way, the tears started pretty soon. I encouraged her to go and join the girls on the beach, working with the fish, but she shrank back from doing what she viewed as dirty work. I'll admit, her crying started to annoy me. Her self-pity stemmed from her own self-importance, and I found it frustrating. She would try to hide it from me when she was upset, but the red eyes always give it away, don't they?

And then Alice arrived.

We were all shocked when they came: the General, two of the Crests, and Alice. Palmiro met them on the meeting point island and brought them the rest of the way. He told me afterwards that they had a terrible voyage through a storm and almost drowned. We weren't sure why they had come, and it seemed clear that the General had a hidden agenda, but Palmiro asked if Alice could stay with us. I wasn't enthusiastic. I thought she would probably spy on us, report back to her father, and maybe find some way of forcing us back to Whitecroft. Part of the motive for the journey seemed to be to either recover George, who was Whitecroft's most experienced sailor and had been responsible for fishing, or to find a replacement for him. Palmiro's friend Riel ended up volunteering to come back to Whitecroft to train up more sailors.

Alice surprised me, though. She threw herself into life in Cape, and was up early each morning, ready to go out and explore. Palmiro took her everywhere. There was a light in her eyes I'd never seen before. As Viola sulked in our hut and refused to make friends, Alice was learning the dances and songs and laughing with none of her usual poised self-consciousness. The night of the festival, Cayman gave me two dresses to give to Alice and Viola. I came into the house and they were stood next to each other, in these identical clothes, but where Viola looked awkward and reluctant, Alice looked radiant. I think I began to realise, then, what was happening in my heart.

I'm not justifying what I've done. I took Viola away from her family. Now that she's carrying, that's my responsibility too. But since we got back to Whitecroft, she's been in her parents' house, and shown no interest in being with me anymore.

To be honest, I'm glad.

I helped Alice through the snow to her grandfather's cabin, when Palmiro was shaking with cold and unable to help anyone. I saw her tenderly care for Elise, when they used to be enemies. I saw her holding her grandfather's hand right before he died. If Viola expected me to run after her, she was disappointed.

When Palmiro suddenly lost his warm interest in Alice, I felt the danger. I couldn't bear to watch him break her heart. I took him away, leaving abruptly, and he left me soon afterwards. I tramped off into the forest, determined to lie low and find out what Palmiro was doing. When Alice pushed Elise all the way to Whitecroft in a sledge, and found me watching the shore from the clifftop, she was deliriously happy to see me. She threw her arms around me, and I knew resistance was futile. I couldn't stand on the sidelines anymore. She'd suffered too much.

I can't imagine the impact of growing up with her cold father. All Palmiro had to do was take her hand, and teach her to dance, and she was prepared for her father to join them in a token gesture union, which would supposedly symbolise peace. In reality, the General abandoned her. He left her on Cape, and she only returned because she was determined to see her grandfather before he died. Palmiro and Amita came, because they were worried about Riel. They're staying with George, out of sight of the main town.

There are so many unknowns now. So many 'what next?' questions. But I'm here for Alice. I gently lift her head so that I can press my lips to hers, like blades of grass brushing sunlight and turning to gold. This moment is everything, where the emptiness is made whole.

3

'When I was young, I came here every summer.'

I break the silence to tell Blake something he already knows. But there's power in speaking, and someone agreeing with you, affirming that your truth is real.

'I've never been here before in the Freeze,' I continue, feeling his hand stroke my hair. 'I used to wonder what it would be like. Looking out of the window now, at the snow on the trees, and the birds disturbing it, hopping along branches, causing clumps to fall away onto the ground when they fly off... It's all how I imagined. Still, quiet and peaceful.'

'It is,' Blake agrees. I hear his voice vibrate through his chest, my ear on his collarbone. 'You can go for days without seeing anyone.'

We sit, and perhaps we're both thinking about the people who've come here in the past two days. Firstly, my father tried to persuade me to go back to the main town, and pretend to be too upset to stay out here on my own so that my brother Charles would invite me to stay with him again. Only unknown to him, Charles was actually inside at the time, and heard everything he said. The Crests were waiting outside—he obviously didn't expect me to refuse his request—and their surprise was great when I forced him outside, threatening him with a poker as a makeshift weapon.

It's a difficult relationship.

I knew Father was only asking me to do this in order to get Riel out of Charles' house, and staying with him instead. There was no concern for my welfare, although he'd left me behind, I'd just crossed the ocean, and seen my grandfather die. I've put up with a lot from him in the past, and I'm old enough now to make my own choices. I don't want to be his puppet anymore.

Since that encounter, I've been afraid of him returning, but so far, only Charles has come with a few men to collect Grandfather's body. Now it's just me and Blake here, and tomorrow I'll need to head back to the shore for the sea burial. I'm trying not to consider how empty this house is now. There are three bedrooms: mine, Elise's and Grandfather's. Blake stayed with me last night because I didn't want to be alone. It's something I desire and dread simultaneously.

In Whitecroft, very few people live alone. They're usually pledged or living with family. After things got so unbearable with Father, I lived with Charles for a while, and I had been preparing to stay with Grandfather for the Freeze before Father decided to take me to Cape. I don't have to stay here, but I long for a place I can call my own. I don't want to have to wait to be pledged for that.

'Will you go and see your family tomorrow?' I ask, thinking of his two sisters and father, living a short walk away.

'Yes,' he says. 'You're going in William's carriage to Whitecroft, aren't you?'

I nod. I'm grateful for the transport, as I've walked the distance several times in the past week, but I'm also worried that Elise will revert to her usual hostility towards me. When I arrived at the cabin, I had to nurse her alongside Grandfather, and taking her to Whitecroft, I finally felt like some of the barriers between us were broken. But it's a fragile truce, and a few days of distance between us may break it.

Maybe she blames me for Grandfather's death. She had been too ill herself to care for him; perhaps if I had been there, as I had originally planned, I could have looked after him and he would never have deteriorated so quickly.

I try to focus on the hypnotic flames of the fire, and not on the wave of guilt that churns like nausea in my stomach.

I knew he was old, and weak, and that he couldn't live forever—but part of me can't believe that he's dead. I just always wanted him to be there, for endless summer stays, and apple-picking and baking bread. We never talked much. I wish I had asked him more about my mother; she died when I was born. Of course, I knew the rule that we should never speak about the past. In the Farmlands, it felt easier to break it.

'I take it my grandmother is going to meet you there,' Blake says.

Cressida was one of my grandfather's closest friends, apart from the Swifts, who all left to go to Cape. She usually lives right next to our cabin, but she's been staying in Whitecroft with her family this Freeze.

'She wasn't very pleased with you last time we spoke to her,' I say, remembering her questions about Viola.

'I gave up trying to please her long ago.' Blake shrugs.

'She only tells you the truth because she loves you,' I point out.

'Maybe she should love me a little less, then.'

It's a joke, but given that I've lost both my grandparents now, it falls on the ground like a knife slipping off a kitchen surface. Unintentionally deadly.

'Sorry,' he says, automatically. 'I shouldn't have said that.'

It's some progress for him to admit it. He wouldn't have done, before.

Before he went to Cape.

Before he got to know me.

Before he kissed me.

'Is that how you feel about Viola?'

I throw a knife of my own down. Blake's hand freezes, and then drops from my hair.

'I told you before, I don't think she ever loved me,' he says, with hardness in his voice. 'She used me to escape Whitecroft. Now she's decided that she's back, and loves being here, she has no room for me in her life anymore.'

'What about the baby?' I ask, and I feel him wince. I've drawn blood with this question.

'I'm not planning to shirk my responsibilities,' he says defensively. 'The question is, will she let me in?'

I sit up, turning to face him, and meeting his eyes full on.

'I'm not asking you questions to be difficult,' I tell him. 'I just don't want to be selfish anymore. I've spent too much of my life like that.'

'You are not selfish,' he says, taking my chin.

'I am,' I return, 'and here's the proof.'

I press my lips to his and feel the relief of being lost in this emotion, which effectively drowns out my grief. But at the back of my mind, I can see Viola's tear-stained face.